Ambientes

AMBIENTES

New Queer Latino Writing

Edited by

LÁZARO LIMA

and

FELICE PICANO

The University of Wisconsin Press

The University of Wisconsin Press
1930 Monroe Street, 3rd Floor
Madison, Wisconsin 53711-2059
uwpress.wisc.edu

3 Henrietta Street
London WCE 8LU, England
eurospanbookstore.com

1   3   5   4   2

Printed in the United States of America

A version of "Magnetic Island Sueño Crónica" by Susana Chávez-Silverman first appeared as "Currawong Crónica" in *Chroma: A Queer Literary and Arts Journal* 6 (Spring 2007), reprinted by permission of the author; "Haunting José" by Rigoberto González first appeared in *Men without Bliss* (Norman: University of Oklahoma Press, 2008), reprinted by permission of the publisher; a version of "Shorty" by Daisy Hernández was first published in *Sinister Wisdom* 74: Latina Lesbians (2008), reprinted by permission of the author; "Arturo, Who Likes to Shave His Legs in the Snow" by Lucy Marrero first appeared in *Alchemist Review* 30 (April 2007), reprinted by permission of the author; "Kimberle" by Achy Obejas first appeared in *Another Chicago Magazine* 50 (July 1, 2010), reprinted by permission of the author; "I Leave Tomorrow, I Come Back Yesterday" by Uriel Quesada first appeared as "Salgo mañana, llego ayer" in *Lejos, tan lejos* (San José: Editorial Costa Rica, 2004), translated into English by Amy McNichols and Kristen Warfield, reprinted by permission of the publisher; "La Fiesta de Los Linares" by Janet Arelis Quezada first appeared in *Women Writers* (Winter 2001), www.women writers.net, reprinted by permission of the author; "Porcupine Love" by tatiana de la tierra first appeared as "Amor de puercoespín" in *Dos orillas: Voces en la narrativa lésbica* (Barcelona: Egales Editorial, 2008), edited by Minerva Salado, and in English in *Two Shores: Voices in Lesbian Narrative* (Barcelona: Grup E.L.L.Es, 2008), edited by Minerva Salado, reprinted by permission of the author; "Dear Rodney" by Emanuel Xavier first appeared in *If Jesus Were Gay and Other Poems* (Bar Harbor, ME: Queer Mojo/Rebel Satori Press, 2010), reprinted by permission of the publisher.

Library of Congress Cataloging-in-Publication Data

Ambientes: new queer Latino writing / edited by Lazaro Lima and Felice Picano.
p.   cm.
ISBN 978-0-299-28224-0 (pbk.: alk. paper)
ISBN 978-0-299-28223-3 (e-book)
1. Hispanic American gays—Fiction.
2. American fiction—Hispanic American authors.
3. Homosexuality in literature.   4. Gays' writings, American.
I. Lima, Lázaro.   II. Picano, Felice, 1944–
PS647.G39A46   2011
813'.6080868073—dc22
2010041228

Contents

CONTENTS

Editors' Note
The Name of las Cosas

Ambientes: New Queer Latino Writing seeks to provide a timely and representative archive of queer Latino literary and cultural memory in order to enact a more inclusive "American" literary canon that can apprehend the present and the future of queer Latino literary practice. We have assembled a diverse and representative sample of contemporary queer Latino writing in order to provide a source of pleasure for readers as well as a resource for instructors and students who have too often been deprived of this crucial though underanalyzed component of national literary culture.

Consistent with our belief that Spanish is not a foreign language in the United States, we have not italicized words in Spanish. Those words that do appear in the anthology in italics, whether in Spanish or not, have been italicized by the authors and usually connote emphasis but not a different linguistic register or the notion that Spanish is a foreign language in this country. In keeping with standard Spanish grammatical usage, the singular "Latino" or plural "Latinos" in the preface and the introduction refer to both sexes and allow us to avoid the graphically more sluggish "Latina/o," Latina/os," or "Latin@s." In doing so we also suggest the obvious: to believe that graphic characters can reform inequality, linguistic or otherwise, is a fatuous proposition if structural inequalities are not concomitantly addressed. Further, taking Spanish seriously in the United States requires understanding its structures, its speakers, the colonial legacies that haunt both, and why Spanish continues to be classed as "inferior." When we consider that the United States is the third-largest Spanish-speaking country in the world (out of twenty-one countries whose official language is Spanish plus the U.S. territory of Puerto Rico), then we must confront the language issue with urgency and creativity.

In both the preface and the introduction we refer to Latinos as persons of Latin American ancestry living in the United States. Certainly, Spanish is not the only language in Latin America, but regrettably majority culture still incorrectly racializes and classes many Latinos as "foreign," and, too often, as just Spanish speaking (read: "Mexican"). When we consider that, aside from Mexican and Central American migration and immigration to the United States, Brazilians constitute the third-largest migrant or immigrant group, then it becomes expedient to include Brazilians—who often have to learn Spanish and, eventually, English to enter local economies—under the admittedly less than precise but necessary rubric "Latino."

We received many fine submissions for this anthology in both English and Spanish. The best of both were included in *Ambientes*. Those submitted in Spanish have been translated into English in order to entice a broader readership into seeking out the Spanish originals, perhaps even encouraging them to learn the other unofficial national language. As readers demand more of queer Latino writing and cultural production, we hope that the Latino Brazilian experience also makes its way into the futures of Latino literary and cultural production.

Finally, we hope you enjoy reading *Ambientes: New Queer Latino Writing*. Please visit the book's website for research ideas, additional readings, links to authors' websites, as well as teaching suggestions and class projects based on *Ambientes*: www.myambientes.com.

Preface

FELICE PICANO

The two young men at the back of the library had been there early, and they dawdled after everyone else at my reading and talk had left. They'd been silent and attentive throughout, almost extra-alert, but now that they were standing before me they relaxed and they gushed. Among the things they said in their enthusiasm was this: "We're so proud to have someone of Latino extraction as an openly out gay writer."

I looked at them more closely. This close up, I could see that both appeared to be Latino. Clearly, they thought that I, with my vowel-filled name and my large brown eyes, was also Latino. And, in a way, I am. My father was born in the town of Itria in an area of Central Italy about forty miles east of Rome, the area known as Latium, from which the Latin tongue took its name. So, in fact, he, and I through him, was an original Latino.

Only I'm not Latino the way those young men thought: they felt proud of having a Latino gay man so out, so prominent, to represent them. A few generations ago, I might have been one of those young men, attending a rare reading of an Italian American author. Those certainly were rare in the past, and people of Italian heritage were mostly unassimilated into the American mainstream until the middle of the last century, in a way similar to how many younger Latinos feel to not be part of our wider culture today. As the result of discovering an unsolved murder in my family—through being a writer—I've been delving into my own family history. In New England in the 1920s and early 1930s, anti-Italian sentiment reached an all-time high, especially after the farce of the Sacco-Vanzetti trial. Elderly people in Rhode Island told me in interviews that as teens they would have to go to church and school in groups no smaller than ten because they were so often physically attacked. While still a youth, I personally remember experiencing anti-Italian prejudice, including at an Ivy League school. During an interview for a Woodrow Wilson graduate scholarship at Princeton in 1964, as I was discussing Henry James's middle-period fiction with one professor, another interrupted to ask if I was sure I wouldn't rather be a barber.

So, clearly, correcting those young men who thought I was Latino made no sense at all at the time, and I immediately changed the subject to a more general one. But in the months and years after that encounter, more readers, other writers, and several interviewers have all made the same assumption or outright asked if I was Latino. Why they did so has become increasingly clear. There was, there is, an exploding gay population with Iberian heritage, and they're on the lookout for role models, seeking people to identify with, to help build a queer Latino community and culture.

That's one very important reason why this anthology exists: to provide those two young men and other readers, writers, and interviewers with queer writers of quality who will provide significant writings about the U.S. Latino queer experience. Writers like Achy Obejas, Elías Miguel Muñoz, Susana Chávez-Silverman, and Emanuel Xavier, writers whose work—whether in stories, novels, poetry, memoirs, or plays— are, in effect, leading the way, writers who are represented here by an intriguing and wide-ranging variety of shorter fiction each representing a fresh Latino voice, looking from a queer Latino perspective into a slice of our life.

Ah, but the knowledgeable and the academic (not always the same thing) will instantly reply that we already have Latino gay literature. Look at Jaime Manrique, whose wonderful novel about Colombian emigrants living in Queens, *Latin Moon in Manhattan*, was published in 1992. And before him, there was the Argentinean novelist Manuel Puig, whose *Kiss of the Spider Woman* and *Who Betrayed Rita Hayworth?* were a unique collusion between his Argentine culture and Hollywood. And what of the more dour Cubano novelist, Reinaldo Arenas?

And, how many people are aware that even before them we had John Rechy? John is a Tejano, originally from El Paso/Ciudad Juárez. Rereading his now-classic gay novels *City of Night* and *Numbers*, it's clear how the elements of the Latino culture that he inescapably grew up with are reflected in and deeply inform the adventures, the choices, and yes also the ethics of his often nameless "youngmen" protagonists. Their outsider status is a double one, queer and Latino, providing an enhanced, more brightly colored distancing lens from which he so brilliantly examines, exalts, and critiques the Manhattan and Los Angeles gay life of his time. Also, let's not forget that at least one of his books, *The Miraculous Day of Amalia Gómez* (1991), is directly about the

Cal-Mex way of life. Then there's also an entire generation of Chicana and Chicano writers who have paved the way for contemporary queer Latino culture and writing, not to mention the important work of Nuyorican writers and poets such as Emanuel Xavier in his collection *Americano*, or the many other Nuyorican writers who came before him.

All well and good, I answer. But it's obviously not enough. In fact, when Manrique wrote his *Eminent Maricones*, he focused on Puig, Lorca, Arenas, and himself! A short and, yes, eminent list. But obviously not enough, because on March 4, 2007, a certain Johnny Díaz wrote on that book's Amazon.com website: "Where are all the Hispanic American gay writers? I don't mean those from Central and South America, I mean those in the United States?" And it was obviously not enough for those sincere and proud young men at my reading, or they wouldn't be out there eager to co-opt me and my work.

Besides, it's the twenty-first century, and it's time that a twenty-first-century literature about being queer in America existed and acknowledged the large number of Latinos in this country. Latinos, although not necessarily queer, are all over our contemporary popular culture: Jennifer Lopez, Ricky Martin (recently "out"), Daddy Yankee, and Santana in popular music; Osvaldo Golijov and Astor Piazzolla in classical music; Ana Alicia, Chita Rivera, and Fernando Bujones in dance; Selma Hayek, Elizabeth Peña, Cameron Diaz, Andy García, Benjamin Bratt, George Lopez, and Jimmy Smits on the silver screen and stage, plus many more behind the cameras, and that's just off the top of my head. American performance art, painting, and sculpture are all brightened and enriched by Latino artists as well. These artists all bring to their work passion and temperament, individuality and uniqueness, high spirits and deep longing, a certain spiciness and a playful mischief, a kind of old-time glamour and a dark intensity of purpose, not to be found otherwise.

But for contemporary "Latin" literature of any kind, we seem to have to go directly to Central or Latin America to writers whose work must be translated—Gabriel García Márquez, Laura Esquivel, Paul Coelho, and Carlos Fuentes, most popular among them. None of them write about being Latino in the United States. Few of them even mention, never mind explore, what it means to be gay, lesbian, bisexual, or transgendered. Isn't it time we had our own? While we recognize the works of Judith Ortiz Cofer, Junot Díaz, Sandra Cisneros, Gloria Anzaldúa, and Cherrie Moraga, only the last two Chicanas really address queer issues. Indeed, Chicana and Chicano queers have led the way but we need more. Quite simply, there is still an absolute need for art that is representative and responsive to the Latino queer experience.

What the young authors collected in *Ambientes* bring to us are many different ways of being queer, of being American, of being Latino. Intriguingly, the writers hail from all over the landscape. Some were born in the United States, some in Mexico, others in Central America, others still in the Caribbean. Their writing addresses what it means to be a queer Latino: not only how the color of your skin, or your accent, or any of a dozen of perceived differences affect not only how you may be treated—demonized, vilified, adored, iconized—but also how you come to perceive yourself. And what happens when, because of your sexual desire, you add yet another layer of difference on top of that.

Of course there are many other themes explored in these stories. If you're hoping for one story, or one author, to sum up what it all means, you are in for a disappointment. However, if you can accept, enjoy, and even revel in difference then you are in for a treat. These stories range from the poetry of Janet Arelis Quezada's "La Fiesta de Los Linares" and Lucy Marrero's "Arturo, Who Likes to Shave His Legs in the Snow" to Daisy Hernández's deliciously funny "Shorty." If you prefer the so-called exotic, then Myriam Gurba's "Malverde" and tatiana de la tierra's "Porcupine Love" fill the bill, while Steven Cordova's "Six Days in St. Paul" belongs in any U.S. queer fiction anthology. Just as you're about to conclude that queer Latino literature is one thing, the next story you read forces you to totally reconsider, since it's all so rich.

So much to read. So much to think of. I hope you'll be surprised and impressed by the works included here and impelled to demand more.

Acknowledgments

In preparing this book, Felice and I had tremendous support and cooperation from many writers, friends, colleagues, and institutions. We are grateful to have labored so intensely and productively with the writers whose work is included in *Ambientes: New Queer Latino Writing*, as well as those whose work could not be included in this anthology for reasons of space, timing, or deadlines. The University of Wisconsin Press's support for the project was exemplary and we were fortunate to have, and consistently count on, the fine stewardship of Raphael Kadushin. Raphael's reputation as a fantastic editor, writer, and reader preceded him; we can only concur, add to the accolades, and simply say, gracias. Also at the University of Wisconsin Press, we'd like to thank Katie Malchow for her able assistance and Sheila McMahon for her spectacular editorial skills. The Press secured two thoughtful external reviewers and we are grateful for their invaluable suggestions.

It has been a pleasure for me to direct the Program in Gender and Sexuality Studies at Bryn Mawr College. The Program and the Department of English helped bring Felice Picano to campus, where we had the opportunity to talk and refine the project through the thoughtful feedback of many motivated and simply brilliant students, especially the program's ever intrepid representative, Rebecca Farber. Many colleagues and friends were responsive with thoughtful suggestions and constructive criticism. I especially wish to thank Anne Dalke, Pim Higginson, Bethany Schneider, Rosi Song, Kate Thomas, Michael Tratner, and Sharon Ullman. The Bryn Mawr, Haverford and Swarthmore Tri-college Consortium's Mellon Queers of Color group has provided sustained support and I am fortunate to count on the intellectual camaraderie of Israel Burshatin, Homay King, Luciano Martínez, Jerry Miller, and Hoang Nguyen. I especially wish to thank Israel for the contributions to the field he helped to carve and the doors he continues to hold open. My involvement with the DC Queers Theory Group has also served as a resource for critical input and lively engagement. I especially wish to thank Marilee Lindemann, Dana Luciano, Robert McRuer, Ricardo Ortíz, and Tom Ratekin for the vibrant community they've helped create in the capital. David Conway, Rob Falk, and Gina Livermore both encouraged and distracted me at all the right moments and the book is better for it. I am also grateful to Cristina Beltrán, Oliva Cardona, Miguel Díaz-Barriga, Margaret Dorsey, Dara Goldman, Elena Gorfinkel, Zilkia Janer, Yolanda Martínez-San Miguel, Lydie E. Moudileno, José Esteban Muñoz, Israel Reyes, Juana María Rodríguez, Richard T. Rodríguez, Azade Seyhan, Todd Shepard, Nicolás Shumway, Heather Sias, Ben. Sifuentes-Jáuregui, Richard Torchia, Antonio Viego, and Tina Zwarg for their continued intellectual generosity and sheer good will. I wish to acknowledge the Office of the Provost at Bryn Mawr College, in particular Provost Kim Cassidy, for helping to secure funding for the project.

Finally, I dedicate my work on this project to the memory of my mother, Caridad Ondina León, and my aunt, Felicia Troadia Gutiérrez, queridas.

Ambientes

Introduction

Genealogies of Queer Latino Writing

LÁZARO LIMA

"American" Historical Memory, or
How to Write against Oblivion

Latinos represent the largest "minority" group in the nation but they are
the least represented in the nation's institutions and the most disenfranchised in the public sphere.[1] Yet the diverse groups we today refer to as
"Latinos," or people of Latin American ancestry living in the United
States, have been in this country long before its founding after independence from Britain in 1776. The Spanish and Portuguese settlement and
eventual colonization of the Americas from 1492 onward should make
this assertion commonplace, but "American" historical memory has
relegated this fact to historic oblivion for too long. When we consider,
for example, that after the United States–Mexico War (1846–48), the
country gained almost half of Mexico's northern territories including
modern-day Arizona, California, Utah, and Nevada and parts of New
Mexico, Colorado, and Wyoming, as well as Mexico's claim to Texas—
which had been under U.S. occupation since 1836—we can begin to
better understand both the literal and the symbolic violence enacted
against Latinos by our national forgettings. And the annexation of
Mexican territories tells only part of the story. With the incorporation

of former Spanish dominions such as modern-day Florida and much of the states in the Gulf of Mexico region—not to mention the eventual colonization of Cuba and Puerto Rico in 1898—we are left with a literary historical lacuna that yet has to be fully accounted for. Put more prosaically, we would do well to remember that many Latinos did not come as immigrants or migrants to the United States but rather "the United States came to them in the form of colonial enterprises."[2] Yet how is it that American literary and cultural history has been unable to register this important incorporation of a people, their cultural history, and the literature that charts this cultural expression? Why do Latinos continue to be represented as a "foreign" imposition on the greater national largesse and as immigrants who are sacking the national treasure trove of economic generosity while refusing to assimilate?

Indeed, the consolidation of the contiguous United States only occurred after the end of the United States–Mexico War with the signing of the Treaty of Guadalupe Hidalgo in 1848. Mexicans living in the newly consolidated United States, along with various nationals from the Americas, found themselves in a quandary as they were classed as foreigners in places they had inhabited even before Mexico's independence from Spain in 1821. Despite the signing of the Treaty of Guadalupe Hidalgo that guaranteed the full rights of U.S. citizenship to Mexicans who remained in the newly consolidated territories—among many other provisions—they were increasingly treated as second-class citizens. For example, less than three years after the signing of the treaty, in the politically significant state of California, Latinos were dealt a deathblow to their political power with the passage of the Land Claims Act of 1851 that unwittingly led to the loss of lands that had been in their families for generations. Even when the original Spanish and Mexican land grants were translated for the courts from Spanish to English, the act made it possible for litigants to continue to appeal their cases to the point that only the wealthy could prevail after costly court battles. Indeed, even if Latinos won the right in the courts to keep the lands that had belonged to them prior to the United States–Mexico War from the encroachment of Anglo-American squatters, many lost them to compensate the lawyers who had defended them when they could not pay their legal fees. Additionally, poll-tax laws further disenfranchised Latinos after losing their lands since one had to be at least a landowner and in many instances functionally literate to vote. Not surprisingly, Latinos increasingly began to be racialized as "black" to the point that by the end of the Civil War (1861–65) the term "Mexican" became a racial

4

signifier for "negro" rather than a term of national origin or ancestral affiliation.[3]

The political disenfranchisement of Latinos after 1848 was also integrally tied to language. In California, for example, the state constitution was amended through an 1855 act that negated the constitutional requirement that had ensured laws would be translated into Spanish. That same year a state anti-vagrancy law was passed that prohibited Spanish speakers from congregating in public for fiestas, rodeos, celebrations, and many other culturally specific practices. The California anti-vagrancy act of 1855, commonly known as "the Greaser Law," institutionalized discrimination against Latinos as Spanish-language use in public effectively came under state control. Literature and, more generally, print culture provided one of the few forums for addressing these injustices when the state and its laws institutionalized discrimination and cultural disenfranchisement. One of the most important novels from the period to chart these injustices was María Amparo Ruiz de Burton's (1832–95) historical romance *The Squatter and the Don: A Novel Descriptive of Contemporary Occurrences in California* (1885). Though perfectly bilingual, Ruiz de Burton wrote the novel in English in order to painstakingly document how Latinos became second-class citizens after the war (the "Don" in the title refers to Mariano Alamar, a patrician rancher whose wealth was encroached upon by Anglo-American squatters). Ruiz de Burton's novel, one of a score of recovered literary texts written by Latinos in the nineteenth century, would have been relegated to oblivion if not for the Latino scholars who have made this recovery against national forgettings possible.[4] Regrettably, long after Ruiz de Burton's novel, the belief that Latinos are but recent immigrant interlopers is part of the fiber of a broader historical and cultural amnesia that Latino literary and cultural industries continue to counter.

The critic David Eng has remarked that "the ethnic literary text in the United States has often been said to function as a proxy for history. This has placed particular pressure and urgency on the literary to perform what is 'missing' in history and to represent otherwise unrepresented communities. Here the burden of authenticity and the evidence of experience inveigh against the bind and sting of injurious racial stereotypes and the lack of minority presence and power."[5] Add to Eng's prescient observation the question of sexual orientation, and we have a queer quandary indeed: how do we represent not only marginalized or "missing" communities from the national record but also the affective registers that mark some of the members from these communities as "queer"?[6]

5

The category of sexual and gendered diversity we call "queer" has, of course, been around for much longer than national literary traditions. Michel Foucault, for example, famously argued that "homosexuality" did not exist as a social identity before the eighteenth century but rather existed as a sexual act among many other sexual acts.[7] Following Foucault, we might best understand "queer," and not just "homosexuality," as a historically specific and socially constructed category. Indeed, both the terms "Latino" and "queer" mark a contestatory relationship to the state. The state continues to take an active role in enforcing the discrimination of Latinos and queers through laws and, less directly but no less influentially, through the stigma that makes both vulnerable to other slights that mark them with the scarlet letter of cultural and political inferiority. If the state did not confine privilege by racial, class, gendered, or sexual mores and norms, the identity practices of queer Latinos would not require elaboration. But when the country mandates linguistic and racial profiling through "ocular evidence," or by simply looking "illegal," such as is currently the case in Arizona, and does not allow same-sex or gender queer couples the right to marry or to receive the same benefits that heterosexual couples do, for example, then the groups in question, irrespective of their internal diversity, must invariably elaborate a relation to the state that contests such injustices.[8] That Latinos continue to fight for inclusion within the national body politic after 1848 is instructive of both the promise and the limits of American democratic institutions. That queer Latinos are doubly disenfranchised makes the need to write against oblivion all the more urgent.

Re-membering the Future:
Contemporary Queer Latino Writing

This brings us to a logical question. Does art have a sexual orientation? And if so, can we speak of queer Latino art or, more specifically, of queer Latino writing? Universalists will answer no. "Identity" is a contentious category for universalists because they presume that "difference" is not a given but rather an essentializing strategy that reduces people to "types" as opposed to a universal humanity that transcends time, geography, politics, and historical prejudice. The possibility for equality is simply diminished for universalists when appeals to ethnic, racial, economic, sexual, and gendered particularisms are stressed rather than an individual's relational "commonality" to others. But those who have historically been marginalized or defined through the prejudices of the majority culture, as Latinos have been since 1848—be it by the state, religion, or the reach of both through secular law or "moral" compulsion—cannot risk their identities being in anyone's hands but their own. "Undocumented," "legal," "illegal," "foreigner," "wetback," "spic," "greaser," or "queer" are identity markers that have very direct effects on the lived experience of Latinos despite protestations to the contrary by universalists who see equality as a condition of philosophical being beyond materially grounded history or religious mandate. And it is against this universalizing that queer Latino art and narrative refuses the false embrace offered by assimilationists who prefer to forget the heavy weight of history in their understanding inequality as a problem merely perpetuated by "identitarians," regardless of "left" or "right" political proclivities, rather than confronting the mechanisms that make it necessary for Latinos who are queer to forge bonds beyond these universalizing ideals. The act of constituting oneself as a subject of "the law" through appeals to equality or "citizenship" rights may indeed require attachments to our own subjection, as Judith Butler once reminded "identitarians," but it is also a strategy for entry into civic life and democratic enfranchisement.[9] The alternative, the abnegation of ethnic, racial, class, and queer affective ties, is both impolitic and unfathomable especially in our present cultural and political moment.

This is not to suggest that queer Latino literature, or other "minority" literatures, can or should be the necessary proxies for history or that it can by itself do the necessary political work of inclusion required in democratic systems through the critique of the nation's literary canon or its normative social institutions (e.g., education, jurisprudence, the church, etc.). But recent history has shown us that when a national culture despairs of adequate checks and balances, and the imaginative prowess to live up to its ideals, it turns to force, which it masks in ideology. Felice Picano perhaps said it best in one of the first and most influential anthologies of gay and lesbian writing, *A True Likeness: Lesbian and Gay Writing Today* (1980). He wrote in its introduction that the category of the literary "is perhaps the last forum in an increasingly divided and specialized world where diversity is not only welcome, it is essential, if we are not to have our art forms decline into elitist stratification. . . . Critics and reviewers who constantly insist that the only difference between our literature and that of the so-called mainstream lies in the

erotic realm are refusing to see this corrective aspect of gay/lesbian literature. The very representation of any other kind of sexuality, social and
domestic life is a critique of the norm."[10]

A True Likeness was groundbreaking (many of its authors went on to
forge what today is queer or LGBTQ literature), and its diversity of
expression was breathtaking even in its inclusion of Latino-related themes,
though no Latino writers were included. Still, beyond the critique of
normative understandings of American literary culture, it proved that
great writing did not need to be separated from one's identity, sexual
or otherwise, because aesthetic agencies always mine experience. The
more pertinent questions should be: Whose experiences are valued?
How, why, and to what ends? Unwilling to make culture in the image of
the master literary discourses at play, culturally and sexually marked
queer Latino literary and cultural expression resists assimilation and
reminds us that literature will always be what we read *as* literature—
national or otherwise.

The work of inclusion demanded by queer Latino writing and art—
not to mention Latinos writ large—can, as history has also shown, be
slow and arduous. Some would even claim that the terms "queer" and
"Latino" can derail that work through the embrace of positions marked
by marginality (as if majority culture did not already have a hand at the
very marginalization that a queer subject position seeks to redress
through a naming strategy of cultural and political resignification). But
a queer Latino aesthetic can labor against the normalizing regulatory
regimes of the state that delimit privilege and access to cultural, educational, and political power through the very markers we must redefine
in our own image on a national scale: gender, sexuality, race, ethnicity,
class, economics, and political inclusion. Queer Latino aesthetics can
help us map out a space of resistance to those regimes, not just to oppose
but creatively to construct, to reimagine, to literally *re-member*, and to
envision a different kind of national culture that more closely resembles
its unrealized democratic aspirations.

So, what is queer Latino writing? It is writing by lesbian, gay, bisexual, transgender, and gender queer people of Latin American ancestry
living in the United States. It is writing that proclaims a sense of place in
the national culture while affirming a transnational character that
transcends the primacy of national borders, class, ethnicity, race, caste,
gender, sexuality, and the linguistic norms that have delimited privilege
and access to cultural capital in the United States. Queer Latino writing,
understood as such, functions as narrative acts against oblivion. It is the

name we give to an archive of feelings, traits, desires, urges, behaviors, and aspirations in an "American" literary vernacular that can apprehend our relationship to the worlds we inhabit through our collective agencies. In the process, we may tie ourselves to words that make us feel more at home in the world, words we may perhaps need to eventually discard when we find other more palatable, urgent, and necessary words that allow us to feel more comfortable in our own skin as our current demands for a place at the national table come increasingly within our reach. But identity, and the arts of identity, are strategic places of affirmation we cannot latch on to for too long lest we remain in creative stasis—what we were, or have been, rather than what we can imagine—because identity is relational only through the subjective positions we experience in the worlds we inhabit.

Writing *Ambientes*

The contemporary queer Latino writing included in *Ambientes* evinces historically different types of linguistic, cultural, racial, gendered, and sexual forms of subjection than those endured, for example, by the likes of Ruiz de Burton as well as those who came before, or after her. Yet the stories in *Ambientes* also link the languages of Latinidad with a broader history of cultural, ethnic, and linguistic struggle that emerged after 1848 and, most importantly, with templates from which to understand Latino cultural survival *as* queer Latinos. The queer Latino texts in *Ambientes* continue an aesthetics of resistance that build upon past archives and insist on building more inclusive futures—beyond the operative monolingual, monological, and heteronormative demands that seek to remand us to national abjecthood—through the aesthetic agencies of culturally marked queer Latino literary expression.

Ambientes provides a series of narrative engagements with the question of belonging in and through aesthetic acts of community making by intervening in American literature and culture in the registers of Latinidad—registers that effectively *queer* language: English inflected by Spanish, Spanish inflected by English, Spanglish, and the possibilities for self-making afforded by the languages of Latinidad. The works included herein create alternative queer Latino archives through what Juana María Rodríguez has called self-constituting "identity practices" that reconfigure notions of American cultural identity. For Rodríguez, "the challenge becomes how to conceptualize subjectivity through both

9

semiotic structures (discursive spaces) and agency (identity practices) by investigating the ways these fields work to constitute, inform, and transform one another."[11] The "discursive spaces" instantiated in this anthology inflect American writing with the cultural, linguistic, sexual, and gendered specificities and possibilities for *being* that have made queer Latino life culturally and politically illegible to both majority culture as well as the transnational communities from where queer Latinos of every national stripe originate. These narrative identity practices are agential acts against queer Latino invisibility. They also provide alternative social imaginaries and templates from which to envision forms of national inclusion that establish greater continuity between the past, the present, and the futures of queer Latino communities and aesthetics. Despite the tremendous strides made by earlier generations of committed Latinos as well as queer Latinos and, particularly, the Chicana and Chicano queer cultural provocateurs and writers who have come before (as Felice Picano's preface to this anthology makes clear), we are still in a state of yearning for what we do not have: equality. And so we write ourselves onto the national body politic in our present by reclaiming our past *for* and *to* the future.

This is what José Muñoz has recently posited in *Cruising Utopia: The Then and There of Queer Futurity* (2010) when he notes, "turning to the aesthetic in the case of queerness is nothing like an escape from the social realm, insofar as queer aesthetics map future social relations. Queerness is also a performative because it is not simply a being but a doing for and toward the future. Queerness is essentially about the rejection of a here and now and an insistence on potentiality or concrete possibility for another world."[12] And it is toward that utopian future of democratic possibilities, beyond the national amnesias regarding queer Latino inequality and abjection with which I began this introduction, that the queer Latino writing included in *Ambientes* envisions versions of "home" *differently*, ways of being in our world that instantiate practices of queer Latino freedom for our present and our futures.

NOTES

1. According to the Pew Hispanic Center, "Hispanics are the nation's largest minority ethnic group. They numbered 46.9 million, or 15.4% of the total U.S. population, in 2008, up from 35.3 million in the 2000 Census," yet they are also the

least likely to graduate from high school not to mention college (http://pewhispanic
.org/reports/report.php?ReportID=121). These statistics also make the United States
the third-largest "Hispanic" country in the world.

2. Stavans, Acosta-Belén, and Augenbraum, *The Norton Anthology of Latino
Literature*, liii.

3. Lima, *The Latino Body*, 22–55.

4. For a fuller accounting of Ruiz de Burton's novel in relation to Anglo-
American encroachment, see my "Spanish Speakers and Early 'Latino' Expression."
The Recovering the U.S. Hispanic Literary Heritage (RUSHLH) project has been
responsible for much of the important archival and recovery work to unearth and
rediscover texts otherwise destined to oblivion in archives and individual collections
across the country. Directed by Nicolás Kanellos, the project seeks to "locate,
identify, preserve and make accessible the literary contributions of U.S. Hispanics
from colonial times through 1960 in what today comprises the fifty states of the
Union." RUSHLH is housed at the University of Houston, and the project's
important publishing imprint, Arte Público Press, has been responsible for
altering our understanding of the national "American" literary landscape (see
http://www.class.uh.edu/hispanicstudies/resources.asp and http://www.latinoteca
.com/recovery/).

5. Eng, "The End(s) of Race," 1484.

6. By "queer" I am following Alexander Doty's critically important use of
the term. He writes, "I am using the term 'queer' to mark a flexible space for the
expression of all aspects of non- (anti-, contra-) straight cultural production and
reception" (*Making Things Perfectly Queer*, 3). The initial critique of cultural
(hetero)normativity emerged in the United States in the 1990s. The standard texts
include Michael Warner, *Fear of a Queer Planet: Queer Politics and Social Theory*
(1993), Judith Butler, *Gender Trouble: Feminism and the Subversion of Identity*
(1990) and *Bodies That Matter: On the Discursive Limits of "Sex"* (1993), Annamarie
Jagose, *Queer Theory: An Introduction* (1997), and many others. Eve Kosofsky
Sedgwick's *Between Men: English Literature and Male Homosocial Desire* (1993) also
provided an influential critique of heteronormative power relations by charting
how "heterosexual" men bonded "homosocially" in order to perpetuate class and
heterosexual power while maintaining erotically charged intimacies. It was not
until the late 1990s and, more productively into the first decade of the twenty-first
century, however, that queers of color began to systematically imbricate questions
of class, race, ethnicity, gender, and language into the polemic. An exception that
proves the rule was Tomás Almaguer's important early essay, "Chicano Men: A Cartography of Homosexual Identity" (1991). However, the major book-length studies
to accomplish this in Latino cultural studies were José Esteban Muñoz's *Disidentifications: Queers of Color and the Performance of Politics* (1999), José Quiroga's
Tropics of Desire: Interventions from Queer Latino America (2000), Juana María
Rodríguez's *Queer Latinidad: Identity Practices, Discursive Spaces* (2003), and others.

11

7. Foucault, *The History of Sexuality*, 1:53–73.

8. On April 23, 2010, Arizona Governor Jan Brewer passed Immigration Law SB1070, which, in effect, sanctions racial profiling and discrimination. The Arizona law makes the failure to carry immigration documents a crime and gives the police broad powers to detain anyone suspected of being in the country illegally. Additionally, Governor Brewer signed House Bill 2281, which effectively prohibits schools from offering courses at any grade level that advocate ethnic solidarity, are deemed unpatriotic, or are considered to cater to specific ethnic groups. In effect, this literally erases Latino literary or cultural studies as well as related programs at schools, colleges, and universities. As of this writing, Arizona Republicans will likely introduce legislation in the fall of 2010 that would deny birth certificates to children born in Arizona—and thus American citizens according to the U.S. Constitution—to parents who are not legal U.S. citizens.

9. Butler reads Continental philosophy's relationship to power in decidedly ecumenical terms. In her analysis, "power that at first appears as external, pressed upon the subject, pressing the subject into subordination, assumes a psychic form that constitutes the subject's self-identity" (Butler, *The Psychic Life of Power*, 3). She continues, "If there is no formation of the subject without a passionate attachment to those by whom she or he is subordinated, then subordination proves central to the becoming of the subject" (7).

10. Picano, *A True Likeness*, xv.

11. Rodríguez, *Queer Latinidad*, 5.

12. Muñoz, *Cruising Utopia*, 1.

BIBLIOGRAPHY

Almaguer, Tomás. "Chicano Men: A Cartography of Homosexual Identity." *differences: A Journal of Feminist Cultural Studies* 3, no. 2 (1991): 75–100.

Butler, Judith. *Bodies That Matter: On the Discursive Limits of "Sex."* Durham, NC: Duke University Press, 1993.

———. *Gender Trouble: Feminism and the Subversion of Identity*. New York: Routledge, 1990.

———. *The Psychic Life of Power: Theories in Subjection*. Stanford, CA: Stanford University Press, 1997.

Doty, Alexander. *Making Things Perfectly Queer: Interpreting Mass Culture*. Minneapolis: University of Minnesota Press, 1993.

Eng, David. "The End(s) of Race." *PMLA* 123, no. 5 (October 2008): 1479–93.

Foucault, Michel. *The History of Sexuality*. Vol. 1, *An Introduction*, translated by Robert Hurley. New York: Vintage, 1990.

Jagose, Annamarie. *Queer Theory: An Introduction*. New York: New York University Press, 1997.

Lima, Lázaro. *The Latino Body: Crisis Identities in American Literary and Cultural Memory.* New York: New York University Press, 2007.

———. "Spanish Speakers and Early 'Latino' Expression." In *American History through Literature, 1820–1870*, edited by Janet Gabler-Hover and Robert D. Sattelmeyer, 1118–23. New York: Charles Scribner's and Sons, 2005.

Muñoz, José Esteban. *Cruising Utopia: The Then and There of Queer Futurity.* New York: New York University Press, 2009.

———. *Disidentifications: Queers of Color and the Performance of Politics.* Minneapolis: University of Minnesota Press, 1999.

Picano, Felice, ed. *A True Likeness: Lesbian and Gay Writing Today.* New York: The Sea Horse Press, 1980.

Quiroga, José. *Tropics of Desire: Interventions from Queer Latino America.* New York: New York University Press, 2000.

Rodríguez, Juana María. *Queer Latinidad: Identity Practices, Discursive Spaces.* New York: New York University Press, 2003.

Ruiz de Burton, María Amparo. *The Squatter and the Don: A Novel Descriptive of Contemporary Occurrences in California.* Edited by Rosaura Sánchez and Beatrice Pita. Houston: Arte Público Press, 1992. First published in 1885.

Sedgwick, Eve Kosofsky. *Between Men: English Literature and Male Homosocial Desire.* Durham, NC: Duke University Press, 1993.

Stavans, Ilan, Edna Acosta-Belén, and Harold Augenbraum, eds. *The Norton Anthology of Latino Literature.* New York: W. W. Norton, 2010.

Warner, Michael. *Fear of a Queer Planet: Queer Politics and Social Theory.* Minneapolis: University of Minnesota Press, 1993.

Kimberle

ACHY OBEJAS

I have to be stopped," Kimberle said. Her breath blurred her words, transmitting a whooshing sound that made me push the phone away. "Well, okay, maybe not have to—I'd say *should*—but that begs the question of why. I mean, who cares? So maybe what I really mean is I need to be stopped." Her words slid one into the other, like buttery babies bumping, accumulating at the mouth of a slide in the playground. "Are you listening to me?"

I was, I really was. She was asking me to keep her from killing herself. There was no method chosen yet—it could have been slashing her wrists, or lying down on the train tracks outside of town (later she confessed that would never work, that she'd get up at the first tremor on the rail and run for her life, terrified that her feet would get tangled on the slats and her death would be classified as a mere accident—as if she were that careless and common), or just blowing her brains out with a polymer pistol—say, a Glock 19—available at Wal-Mart or at half price from the same cretin who sold her cocaine.

"Hellooooo?"

"I hear you, I hear you," I finally said. "Where are you?"

I left my VW Golf at home and took a cab to pick her up from some squalid blues bar, where hers was the only pale face in the place. The guy at the door—a black man old enough to have been an adolescent

14

during the civil rights era, but raised with the polite deference of the previous generation—didn't hide his relief when I grabbed my tattooed friend, threw her in her car, and took her home with me.

It was all I could think to do, and it made sense for both of us. Kimberle had been homeless, living out of her car—an antique Toyota Corolla that had had its lights punched out on too many occasions and now traveled unsteadily with huge swatches of duct tape holding up its fender. In all honesty, I was a bit unsteady myself, afflicted with the kind of loneliness that's felt in the gut like a chronic and never fully realized nausea.

Also, it was fall—a particularly gorgeous time in Indiana, with its spray of colors on every tree, but in our town, fall held a peculiar seasonal peril for college-aged girls. It seemed that about this time every year, there would be a disappearance—someone would fail to show up at her dorm or study hall. This would be followed by a flowering of flyers on posts and bulletin boards (never trees) featuring a girl with a simple smile and an offer of a reward. Because the girl was always white and pointedly ordinary, there would be a strange familiarity about her: everyone was sure they'd seen her waiting for the campus bus, or at the commons or the bookstore, or at t\he Bluebird the previous weekend.

It may seem perverse to say this, but every year we waited for that disappearance—I'd grown up in town and it had been going on forever, it seemed—not in shock or horror, or to look for new clues to apprehend the culprit: we waited in anticipation of relief. Once the psycho got his girl, he seemed pacified, so we listened with a little less urgency to the footsteps behind us in the parking lot, worried less when running at dawn. Spared, we would look guiltily at those flyers, which would be faded and torn by spring, when a farmer readying his corn field for planting would discover the girl among the papery remains of the previous year's harvest.

When Kimberle moved in with me in November, the annual kill had not yet occurred—the butcher was late—and I was worried for both of us, her in her car and me in my first floor one-bedroom, the window open for my cat, Brian Eno, to come and go as she pleased. I had trapped the window sash so that it couldn't be opened more than a few inches—that's all Brian Eno needed—but that meant that it was never closed all the way, even in the worst of winter.

In my mind, Kimberle and I reeked of prey. We were both boyish girls, pink and sad. Her straight blonde hairs moved in concert and she

15

had features angled to throw artful shadows; mine, by contrast, were soft and vaguely tropical, overwhelmed by a carnival of curls. She was certain she could fight off any asshole, but I wasn't so sure. We both seemed to be in weakened states. Her girlfriend had caught her in flagrante delicto and walked out; depression had swallowed her in the aftermath. She couldn't concentrate at her restaurant job, mixing up simple orders, barking at the customers, so that it wasn't long before she found herself at the unemployment office (where her insistence on stepping out to smoke cost her her place in line so many times she finally gave up).

It quickly followed that she went home one rosy dawn and discovered that her landlord, aware that he had no right to do so but convinced that Kimberle (now four months late on her rent) would never get it together to legally contest it, had stacked all her belongings on the sidewalk, where they had been picked over by the students at International House, headquarters for all the third-world kids on scholarships that barely covered textbooks. All that was left was a tennis racket with broken strings, a few T-shirts (mostly black) from different political marches, books from her former and useless major in Marxist theory (one with a note in red tucked between its pages that read "COMUNISM IS DEAD!" which we marveled at for its misspelling), and, to our surprise, her battered iBook (the screen was cracked though it worked fine).

Me, I'd just broken up with my boyfriend—it was my doing, it just felt like we were going nowhere—but I was past the point of righteousness and heavily into doubt. Not about my decision; that I never questioned. But about whether I'd ever care enough to understand another human being, whether I'd ever figure out how to stay after the initial flush, or whether I'd get over my absurd sense of self-sufficiency—I was haunted by those questions.

When I brought Kimberle to live with me she hadn't replaced much of anything, and we emptied the Toyota in one trip. I gave her my futon to sleep on in the living room, surrendered a drawer in the dresser, pushed my clothes to one side of the closet, and explained my alphabetized CDs, my work hours at a smokehouse one town over (and that we'd never starve for meat), and my books.

Since Kimberle had never visited me after I'd moved out of my parents' house—in truth, we were more acquaintances than friends—I was especially emphatic about the books, prized possessions I'd been collecting since I had first earned a paycheck. I pointed out the shelf of first editions, among them Richard Wright's *Native Son*, Sapphire's *American Dreams*, Virginia Woolf's *Orlando*, a rare copy of *The Cook and the Carpenter*, and Langston Hughes and Ben Carruthers's limited-edition translations of Nicolás Guillén's *Cuba Libre*, all encased in Saran Wrap. There was also a handful of nineteenth-century travel books on Cuba, fascinating for their racist assumptions, and a few autographed volumes, including novels by Dennis Cooper, Ana María Shua, and Monique Wittig.

"These never leave the shelf, they never get unwrapped," I said. "If you wanna read one of them, tell me and I'll get you a copy, or xeroxes."

"Cool," she said in a disinterested whisper, pulling off her boots, long, sleek things that suggested she should be carrying a riding crop.

She leaned back on the futon in exhaustion and put her hands behind her head. There was an elegant and casual muscularity to her tattooed limbs, a pliability that I would later come to know under entirely different circumstances.

Kimberle had not been installed in the studio more than a day or two (crying and sniffling, refusing to eat with the usual determination of the newly heartbroken) when I noticed that *Native Son* was gone, leaving a gaping hole on my shelf. I assumed that she'd taken it down to read in whatever second I had turned my back. I trotted over to the futon and peeked around and under the pillow. The sheets were neatly folded, the blanket too. Had anyone else been in the studio except us two? No, not a soul, not even Brian Eno, who'd been out hunting. I contemplated my dilemma: how to ask a potential suicide if they're ripping you off.

Sometime the next day—after a restless night of weeping and pillow punching that I could hear from the bedroom, even with the door closed—Kimberle managed to shower and put on a fresh black tee, then lumbered into the kitchen. She barely nodded. It seemed that if she'd actually completed the gesture, her head might have been in danger of rolling off.

I suppose I should have been worried about Kimberle's whereabouts when she wasn't home, given the threat of suicide she'd so boldly announced. But I wasn't. I wasn't worried at all. I didn't throw out my razors, I didn't hide the belts, I didn't turn off the pilot in the oven. It's not that I didn't think she was at risk, because I did, I absolutely did. It's just that when she told me she needed to be stopped, I took it to mean she needed me to shelter her until she recovered, which I assumed would be soon. I thought, in fact, that I'd pretty much done my duty as a friend by bringing her home and feeding her a cherry-smoked ham sandwich.

Truth is, I was much more focused on the maniac whose quarry was still bounding out there in the wilderness. I would pull out the local print-only newspaper every day when I got to the smokehouse and make for the police blotter. I knew, of course, that once the villain committed to the deed, it'd be front-page news, but I held out hope for clues from anticipatory crimes.

Once, there was an incident on a hiking trail: two girls were approached by a white man in his fifties, sallow and scurvy, who tried to grab one of them. The other girl turned out to be a member of the campus tae kwon do team and rapid-kicked his face before he somehow managed to get away. For several days after that, I was on the lookout for any man in his fifties who might come into the smokehouse looking like tenderized meat. And I avoided all trails, even the carefully land-scaped routes between campus buildings.

Because the smokehouse was isolated in order to realize its function, and its clientele fairly specialized—we sold gourmet meat (including bison, ostrich, and alligator) mostly by phone and online, though our best seller was summer sausage, as common in central Indiana as Oscar Mayer—there wasn't much foot traffic in and out of the store, and I actually spent a great deal of time alone. After I processed the orders, packed the UPS boxes, replenished and rearranged the display cases, made coffee, and added some chips to the smoker, there wasn't much for me to do but sit there, trying to study while avoiding giving too much importance to the noises outside that suggested furtive steps in the yard or shadows that looked like bodies bent to hide below the window sill, just waiting for me to lift the frame and expose my neck for strangulation.

One evening, I came home to find Kimberle with my santoku knife in hand, little pyramids of chopped onions, green pepper, and slimy octopus arms with their puckering cups arranged on the counter. Brian Eno reached up from the floor, her calico belly and paws extended toward the heaven promised above.

"Dinner," Kimberle announced as soon as I stepped in, lighting a flame under the wok.

I kicked my boots off, stripped my scarf from around my neck, and let my coat slide from my body, all along yakking about the psychopath and his apparent disinterest this year.

"Maybe he finally died," offered Kimberle.

"Yeah, that's what I thought when we were about fifteen, 'cause it took until January that year, remember? But then I realized, it's gotta be more than one guy," I said.

"You think he's got accomplices?" Kimberle asked, a tendril of smoke rising from the wok.

"Or copycats," I said. "I'm into the copycat theory."

That's about when I noticed Sapphire angling in unfamiliar fashion on the bookshelf. Woolf's *Orlando* was no longer beside it. Had I considered what my reaction would have been any other time, I might have said rage. But seeing the jaunty leaning that suddenly gave the shelves a deliberately decorated look, I felt like I'd been hit in the stomach. I was still catching my breath when I turned around and saw Kimberle. The santoku had left her right hand, embedding its blade upright on the knuckles of her left. Blood seeped sparingly from between her fingers but collected quickly around the octopus pile, which now looked wounded and alive.

I took Kimberle to the county hospital, where they stitched the flaps of skin back together. Her hand, now bright and swollen like an aposematic amphibian, rested on the dashboard all the way home. We drove back in silence, her eyes closed, her head inclined and threatening to hit the windshield.

In the kitchen, the onion and green pepper pyramids were intact on the counter but the octopus had vanished. Smudged paw tracks led out toward Brian Eno's usual route through the living room window. Kimberle stood unsteadily under the kitchen light, her face shadowed. I sat down on the futon.

"What happened to *Native Son*, to *Orlando*?" I asked.

She shrugged.

"Did you take them?"

She spun, slowly, on the heel of her boot, dragging her other foot around in a circle.

"Kimberle . . ."

"I hurt," she said, "I really hurt." Her skin was a bluish red as she threw herself on my lap and bawled.

A week later, *Native Son* and *Orlando* were still missing but Kimberle and I hadn't been able to talk about it. Our schedules failed to coincide, and my mother, widowed and alone on the other side of town (confused but tolerant of my decision to live away from her), had gone to visit relatives in Miami, leaving me to deal with her cat, Brian Eno's brother, a daring aerialist she'd named Alfredo Codona, after the Mexican trapeze artist who'd killed himself and his ex-wife. This complicated my life a bit more than usual, and I found myself drained after dealing with the temporarily house-bound Alfredo, whose pent-up frustrations tended to result in toppled chairs, broken picture frames, and a scattering of magazines and knickknacks. It felt like I had to piece my mother's place back together every single night she was gone.

One time, I was so tired when I got home that I headed straight for the tub and finished undressing as the hot water nipped at my knees. I adjusted the temperature, then I let myself go under, blowing my breath out in fat, noisy bubbles. I came back up and didn't bother to lift my lids. I used my toes to turn off the faucet, then went into a semi-somnambulist state in which neither my mother nor Alfredo Codona could engage me, *Native Son* and *Orlando* were back where they belonged, and Kimberle . . . Kimberle was . . . *laughing.*

"What . . . ?"

I sat up, water splashing on the floor and on my clothes. I heard the refrigerator pop open, then tenebrous voices. I pulled the plug and gathered a towel around me, but when I opened the door I was startled by the blurry blackness of the living room. I heard rustling from the futon, conspiratorial giggling, and Brian Eno's anxious meowing outside the unexpectedly closed window. To my amazement, Kimberle had brought somebody home. I didn't especially like the idea of her having sex in my living room, but we hadn't talked about it—I'd assumed, since she was supposedly suicidal, that there wasn't a need for that talk. Now I was trapped, naked and wet, watching Kimberle hovering above her lover, as agile as the real Alfredo Codona on the high wire.

Outside, Brian Eno wailed, tapping her paws on the glass. I shrugged, as if she could understand, but all she did was unleash an even more high-pitched scream. It was raining outside. I held tight to the towel and started across the room as quietly as I could. But as I tried to open the window, I felt a hand on my ankle. Its warmth rose up my leg, infused my gut, and became a knot in my throat. I looked down and saw Kimberle's arm, its jagged tattoos throbbing. Rather than jerk away, I bent to undo her fingers, only to find myself face to face with her. Her lips were glistening, and below her chin was a milky slope with a puckered nipple . . . she moved to make room for me as if it were the most natural thing in the world. I don't know how or why but my mouth opened to the stranger's breast, tasting her and the vague tobacco of Kimberle's spit.

Afterward, as Kimberle and I sprawled on either side of the girl, I recognized her as a clerk from a bookstore in town. She seemed dazed and pleased, her shoulder up against Kimberle as she stroked my belly. I realized that for the last hour or so, as engaged as we'd been in this most intimate of maneuvers, Kimberle and I had not kissed or otherwise touched. We had worked side by side, a hyaloid membrane—structureless and free.

"Here, banana boat queen," Kimberle said with a sly grin as she passed me a joint. *Banana boat queen?* And I thought: Where the fuck did she get that? How the hell did she think she'd earned dispensation for that?

The girl between us bristled.

Then Kimberle laughed. "Don't worry," she said to our guest, "I can do that. She and I go back."

In all honesty, I don't really know when I met Kimberle. It seemed she had always been there, from the very day we arrived from Cuba. Hers was a mysterious and solitary world. I realized that one winter day in my junior year as I was walking home from school just as dusk was settling in, Kimberle pulled her Toyota next to me and asked if I wanted a ride. As soon as I got in, she offered me a cigarette. I said no.

"A disgusting habit anyway. You wanna see something?"

"What?"

Without another word, Kimberle aimed the Toyota out of town, past the last deadbeat bar, the strip malls, and the trailer parks, past the ramp to the interstate, until she entered a narrow, gravel road with corn blossoming on either side. There was a brackish smell, the tang of wet dirt and nicotine. The Toyota danced on the gravel, but Kimberle, bent over the wheel, maintained a determined expression.

"Are you ready?"

"Ready . . . ? For what?" I asked, my fingers clutching the shoulder belt.

"This," she whispered. Then she turned off the headlights.

Before I had a chance to adjust to the tracers, she gunned the car, hurling it down the black tunnel, the tires spitting rocks as she swirled this way and that, following the eerie spotlight provided by the moon . . . for a moment, we were suspended in air and time. My life did not pass in front of my eyes how I might have expected; instead, I saw images of desperate people on a bounding sea; multitudes wandering Fifth Avenue or the Thames, the shores of the Bosporus or the sands outside the pyramids; mirrors and mirrors, mercury and water; a family portrait in

21

Havana from years before; my mother with her tangled hair, my father tilting his hat in New Orleans or Galveston; the shadows of birds of paradise against a stucco wall; a shallow and watery grave, then another longer passage, a trail of bones. Just then the silver etched the sharp edges of the corn stalks, teasing them to life as specters in black coats . . .

"We're going to die!" I screamed.

Moments later, the Toyota came to a shaky stop as we both gasped for breath. A cloud of smoke surrounded us, reeking of fermentation and gasoline. I popped open the door and crawled outside, where I promptly threw up.

Kimberle scrambled over the seat and out, practically on top of me. Her arms held me steady. "You okay?" she asked, panting.

"That was amazing," I said, my heart still racing. "Just amazing."

Not even a week had gone by when Kimberle brought another girl home, this time an Eastern European professor who'd been implicated with a Cuban during a semester abroad in Bucharest. Rather than wait for me to stumble onto them, they had marched right into my bedroom, naked as newborns. I was going to protest but was too unnerved by their boldness and then, in my weakness, seduced by the silky warmth of skin on either side of me. Seconds later, I felt something hard and cold against my belly and looked down to see Kimberle wearing a harness with a summer sausage dangling from it. The professor sighed as I guided the meat. As she licked and bit at my chin, Kimberle pushed inch by sitophilic inch into her. At one point, Kimberle was balanced above me, her mouth grazing mine, but we just stared past each other.

Afterward—the professor between us—we luxuriated, the room redolent of garlic, pepper, and sweat. "Quite the little Cuban sandwich we've got here," Kimberle said, passing me what now seemed like the obligatory after-sex joint followed by the vaguely racist comment. The professor stiffened. Like the bookstore girl, she'd turned her back to Kimberle. Instead of rubbing my belly, this one settled her head on my shoulder, then fell happily asleep.

Kimberle, you've gotta stop," I said. I hesitated. "I've gotta get my books back. Do you understand me?"

Her head was buried under the pillow on the futon, the early morning light shiny on her exposed shoulder blade. With the white sheet crumbled halfway up her back, she looked like a headless angel.

"Kimberle, are you listening to me?" There was some imperceptible movement, a twitch. "Would you please . . . I'm talking to you."

She emerged, curtain of yellow hair, eyes smoky. "What makes you think I took them?"

"What . . . ? Are you kidding me?"

"Coulda been the bookstore girl, or the professor."

Since our ménages à trois, the bookstore girl had called to invite me to dinner, but I had declined. And the professor had stopped by twice, once with a first edition of Upton Sinclair's *Mental Radio*. Tempting—achingly tempting—as that 1930 oddity was, I had refused it.

"I'll let Kimberle know you stopped by," I'd added, biting my lip.

"I didn't come to see Kimberle," the professor had said, her fingers pulling on my curls, which I'd found disconcerting.

Kimberle was looking at me now, waiting for an answer. "My books were missing before the bookstore girl and the professor," I said.

"Oh."

"We've got to talk about that too."

Down went her head. "Now?" she asked, her voice distant and flimsy like a final communication from a sinking ship.

"Now."

She hopped up, her hip bones pure cartilage. She shivered. "I'll be right back," she said, headed for the bathroom. I dropped on the futon, heard her pee into the bowl, then the water running. I scanned the shelf, imagining where *Mental Radio* might have fit. Silence.

Then: "Kimberle? . . . Kimberle, you all right?" I scrambled to the bathroom, struggled with the knob. "Kimberle, please, let me in," I pleaded, imagining her hanging from the light fixture, her veins cascading red into the tub, that polymer pistol bought just for this moment, when she'd stick its tip in her mouth and . . ."Kimberle, goddamn it . . ." Then I kicked, kicked and kicked again, until the lock bent and the door gave. "Kimberle . . ." But there was nothing, just my breath misting as I stared at the open window, the screen leaning against the tub.

I ran out and around our building, but there was no sign of her, no imprint I could find in the snow, nothing. When I tried to start my car to look for her, the engine sputtered and died. I grabbed Kimberle's keys to the Toyota, which came to life mockingly, and put it into reverse, only to have to brake immediately to avoid a passing station wagon. The Toyota jerked, the duct-taped fender shifted, practically falling, while I white-knuckled the wheel and felt my heart like a reciprocating engine in my chest.

After that, I made sure we spent as much time together as possible: reading, jogging, cooking venison I brought from the smokehouse, stuffing it with currants, pecans, and pears, or making smoked bison burgers with Vidalia onions and thyme. On any given night, she'd bring home a different girl to whom we'd minister with increasing aerial expertise. At some point I noticed *American Dreams* was missing from the shelf, but I no longer cared.

One night in late January—our local psychopath still loose, still victimless—I came home from the smokehouse emanating a barosmic mesquite and found a naked Kimberle eagerly waiting for me.

"A surprise, a surprise tonight," she said, helping me with my coat. "Oh my god, you smell . . . *sooooo* good."

She led me to my room, where a clearly anxious, very pregnant woman was sitting up in my bed.

"Whoa, Kimberle, I . . ."

"Hi," the woman said hoarsely; she was terrified. She was holding the sheet to her ample breasts. I could see giant areolas through the threads, the slope of her belly about to burst.

"This'll be great, I promise," Kimberle whispered, pushing me toward the bed as she tugged on my sweater.

"I dunno . . . I . . ."

Before long Kimberle was driving my hand inside the woman, who barely moved as she begged us to kiss, to please kiss for her.

"I need, I need to see that . . ."

I turned to Kimberle, but she was intent on the task at hand. Inside the pregnant woman, my fingers took the measure of what felt like a fetal skull, baby teeth, a rope of blood. Suddenly, the pregnant woman began to sob and I pulled out, flustered and confused. I grabbed my clothes off the floor and had started out of the room when I felt something soft and squishy under my bare foot. I bent down to discover a half-eaten field mouse, a bloody offering from Brian Eno, who batted it at me, her fangs exposed and feral.

I climbed in my VW and after cranking it a while managed to get it started. I steered out of town, past the strip malls, the corn fields, and the interstate where, years before, Kimberle had made me feel so fucking alive. When I got to the smokehouse, I scaled up a backroom bunk my boss used when he stayed to smoke delicate meats overnight—it was infused with a smell of acrid flesh and maleness. Outside, I could hear branches breaking, footsteps, an owl. I refused to consider the shadows on the curtainless window. The blanket scratched my skin, the walls whined. Trembling there in the dark, I realized I wanted to kiss Kimberle—not for anyone else's pleasure but for my own.

The next morning, there was an ice storm and my car once more refused to start. I called Kimberle and asked her to pick me up at the smokehouse. When the Toyota pulled into the driveway, I jumped in before Kimberle had the chance to park. I leaned toward her but she turned away.

"I'm sorry about last night, I really am," she said, all skittish, avoiding eye contact.

"Me too." The Toyota's tires spun on the ice for an instant then got traction and heaved onto the road. "What was going on with your friend?"

"I dunno. She went home. I said I'd take her but she just refused."

"Can you blame her?"

"Can I . . . ? Look, it was just fun . . . I dunno why everything got so screwed up."

I put my head against the frosty passenger window. "What would make you think that would be fun?"

"I just thought we could, you know, do something . . . *different.* Don't you wanna just do something different now and again? I mean . . . if there's something you wanted to do, I'd consider it."

As soon as she said it, I knew: "I wanna do a threesome with a guy."

"With . . . with a *guy?*"

"Why not?"

Kimberle was so taken back, she momentarily lost control. The car slid on the shoulder then skidded back onto the road.

"But . . . wha . . . I mean, what would I do?"

"What do you think?"

"Look, I'm not gonna . . . and he'd want us to . . ." She kept looking from me to the road, each curve back to town now a little slicker, less certain.

I nodded at her, exasperated, as if she were some dumb puppy. "Well, exactly."

"Exactly? But . . ."

"Kimberle, don't you ever think about what we're doing—about *us?*"

25

"Us? There is no *us*."

She fell on the brake just as we hurled beyond the asphalt, but the resistance was catalytic: the car twirled a double ocho as the rear tires hit the road again. My life, such as it was—my widowed mother, my useless Cuban passport, the smoke in my lungs, the ache in my chest that seemed impossible to contain—burned through me. Then we flipped twice and landed in a labyrinth of pointy corn stalks peppered by a sooty snow. There was a moment of silence, a stillness, then the tape ripped and the Toyota's front end collapsed, shaking us one more time.

"Are you . . . are you okay . . . ?" I asked breathlessly. I was hanging upside down.

The car was on its back. In a second, *Native Son*, *Orlando*, and *American Dreams* slipped from under the seats, which were now above our heads, and tumbled to the ceiling, which was below us. They were in Saran Wrap, encased in blue and copper like Monarch chrysalides.

"Oh God . . . Kimberle . . ." I started to sob softly.

Kimberle shook her head, sprinkling a bloody constellation on the windshield. I reached over and undid her seat belt, which caused her body to drop with a thud. She tried to help me with mine but it was stuck.

"Let me crawl out and come around," she said, her mouth a mess of red. Her fingers felt around for teeth, for pieces of her tongue.

I watched as she kicked out the glass on her window, picked each shard from the frame, and slowly pulled herself through. My head throbbed and I closed my eyes. I could hear the crunch of Kimberle's steps on the snow, the exertion in her breathing. I heard her gasp and choke and then a rustling by my window.

"Don't look," she said, her voice cracking as she reached in to cover my eyes with her ensanguined hands. "Don't look."

But it was too late: there, above her shoulder, was this year's seasonal kill, waxy and white but for the purple areolas and the meat of her sex. She was ordinary, familiar, and the glass of her eyes captured a portrait of Kimberle and me.

Pandora's Box

ARTURO ARIAS

I didn't know Walker before this new life of mine. I only knew that he lived upstairs from my apartment in San Francisco. The city was not far from Redwood City, where I had been raised. However, for me to move there was like a Brazilian moving to China as far as cultural differences were concerned. And I had only lived in San Francisco for a few months, so I still acted more like a typical Latino immigrant of the peninsula than a "real" San Franciscan. I was still learning the foreign mannerisms and lifestyles of people living in the most special of American cities, the only one that could be mentioned in the same breath as Madrid, Paris, Rio, Rome. Walker seemed to be what others liked to call, for lack of a more poetic term, "a cool city person," always busy, always with a sense of purpose, always in control. I often heard his dazzling, raw music, like freshly made ceviche with a scalding bite of poblano peppers, blasting through my high, peeling Victorian ceiling like a sudden tropical thunderstorm. He favored Latin house, for the most part, artful rearrangements of tunes I had known since childhood but in an infinitely slower rhythm than that of my grandmother's mellifluous tongue.

Then, on a foggy weekday night a casual acquaintance of mine, Pandora, knocked at his door.

"I've missed you. Couldn't wait to see you again."

After Walker opened and let her in, I panicked, breaking rule number one, and, feeling unrelenting distress as if I were a windowpane suddenly broken by a drunkard's punch, I went into a jealous rage. Yes, I was jealous—of Pandora. Surprised? Perhaps you shouldn't be. After all, no one who ever saw me before could possibly imagine that I could act like a girl. To tell you the truth, neither did I. After all, well, not only had I been a boy, but, most of all, I was a Latino boy from Redwood City, even if I was born in Central America and only moved to the U.S. as a teenager, and I looked very much like the tough macho I indeed was not. Dark hair, a curly beard, cinnamon-colored skin, hairy arms, legs, and chest. I was always embarrassed by my bulbous nose and less-than-straight teeth, but somehow or other, none of these parts ever seemed to make a difference when dating girlfriends since, as I was to find out later, women do not necessarily look for handsome men. I never quite figured out why in that early stage of my life, but girls were drawn to me despite the glaring faults in my squarish anatomy. My outrageous laughter might have overwhelmed them, bursting always in the middle of a spoken sentence like a broken water pipe in the middle of the street, or perhaps it was simply my clever irony and, as others whispered later in the night from the other end of the pillow, my good disposition.

The point is, I was successful as a boy. I was popular, I did well in my work, I earned enough to get by, even in this most expensive of cities. Yet, somehow or other, it didn't quite seem enough. It could very well have been my boredom of living in a country that lacked all concern for my two favorite sports, soccer and politics, and where people had the horrible habit of eating dinner before the sun had set, without salt and picante to boot. Or else my increasing intolerance for the histrionics of pro-lifers and pro-prayers, who, incidentally, were all milky white, when not hot pink, under their blow-dried hair. It was, without a doubt, a certain ennui with always repeating the same meaningless gestures— work hard Monday through Friday, party just as hard Friday and Saturday nights, recover Sunday from a dazzling hangover that left my brain bubbly but perforated as if left under the steady punch of a constant drip of water, and my cerebellum tense and swollen. I didn't mind the partying. I was just getting bored with the repetition of the exact same motions: jostle with the cocky men with hairless chests and make silly smiles for the attention of the pretty women, make dumb conversation with them in the hope that a joke or two would filter through before inviting them out to dance, seductively squinting a little as I talked, then hoping they wouldn't lose attention before those thick legs of mine warmed up and my daddy-longleg arms succeeded in spinning them around with an effortless, debonair attitude dosed with a certain intuition for aesthetic elegance. Feel their warmth, then smile a lot until I drowned them in the gulping gurgle of the gushing waters of my humor, displaying a good array of eye movements that spoke for me, then let my hands find their way down their bodies with boldness and self-assurance, but without any sign of coarseness or vulgarity, hoping for the best. Never insist on sleeping with them on the first night, but never see them again if I hadn't by the third.

I had always both desired and envied Alexandra, which was Pandora's real name, though she went by the nickname her parents gave her when she was a shy, silent, mysterious child. She was naturally gorgeous, with dark hair flowing down to the middle of her back like silk, and a perfectly proportioned body, long legs, wasplike waist, the finest possible ankles and smallish breasts just erotic enough to make me blink as if struck by the first, red rays of the sun after a total eclipse. I had never gone out with her. She was too beautiful, too elegant, a body perfectly arranged for someone who fit her world as naturally as the avant-garde decor in the lobby of Davies Symphony Hall or the War Memorial Opera House. She was in that rarest of all categories: beautiful women I didn't even dare approach, bold as I was, but for whom I saved vehement doses of dumb devotion without redemption. In real life I settled for the ones with slightly more visible defects, from a pimple here and there, to a voice too loud or hysterical, to a fanatical political correctness verging on the pathological. Pandora belonged to that dreamt-of category of "goddesses" that I only saw from afar, from a distance, as if we were forever separated by an invisible barrier that kept mere mortals forever at bay.

Whenever I saw Pandora, my intestines would twist in knots not even a Boy Scout could untie. I'd tremble like a wet chicken, my IQ would drop eighty points in a free fall, and both my stare and tumescence would immediately betray a certain longing impertinence that could be neither hidden nor easily explained. But like a movie star used to being mobbed, showered with gifts, and given children to kiss, she remained entirely unaffected by whatever signs of unconscious bodily betrayal I unrolled before her divine feet like those rugs made with natural flowers used for Catholic processions in Antigua's Holy Week.

One day, an older woman saw me watching Pandora and walked over to my side. "And who are you, my boy, who seems bewitched by this lovely lady?"

"My name is Juan, madam, but most American friends call me Gianni."

"Ah, a famous name indeed, most famous, and yet you long so much for this beautiful lady that you would be better off being Juana or Juanita, so as to know and feel as she does, to understand the power of that gaze of yours, to feel the burning eyes upon your skin as if you were being tattooed. Wait and see how it feels."

She then broke into an outrageous laugh that startled me and sent me trembling as if I were about to faint, shaking as if in an epileptic fit or the throes of an orgasm too intense to bear. My mouth felt sandy, or full of sawdust. I was suddenly dying of thirst. My eyes got blurry, my nose began to itch, and next thing I knew, my head was spinning out of control as if I had just fallen into a red and white vortex spinning faster and faster, and it seemed, don't ask me why, as if mangoes were raining down from a purple sky.

When I woke up, I felt like a tennis ball maliciously soaked for a long time under an open faucet. A big pain in the back of my head spread from that point like a tiara that ended on the power points just above my eyebrows. My muscles were cramped, and I had black and blue marks on my thighs, as if I'd been playing soccer and gotten kicked in the groin. To say that it was strange would be the understatement of the year, pardon the cliché. I placed the flat, caked palms of my hands against the bruises, and felt their soreness. It took me minutes longer, enough time for a grain of sand blown by the breeze to settle in my eyes, and for me to blink hard to rinse them with a tear, to figure out that my bruised skin was uncannily smooth. I touched my thighs again as if to reconfirm their newfound smoothness and fully realized that I no longer had any hair on my legs. No hair. My vision was still fuzzy, so it was hard to see clearly, but the skin felt like polished mahogany.

Puzzled, I instinctively reached up to caress my beard. But then I was thrown for a loop, because when my hand reached my face, there was no beard to stroke, just very bare cheeks and jaw ending in a round chin that no longer felt like a goat's. The shock was such that I instinctively put a hand on my chest, above my heart. And then, it all became more than clear, more than shocking, more than a little exhilarating, because as I put a hand above my heart, I ended up touching, caressing, feeling with the tips of my fingers a breast, solid and shaped just like the biggest of those mangoes I might have imagined were falling from the sky. I looked down and yes, there it was, and there was its mate, since I indeed had two of them, one on each side. Amazement? Shock? Words do no justice to this most singular situation. More than dreaming or

30

comatose, I felt like I was dead and in heaven. I realized that I had become a woman. Juanita indeed. Ah, Juaaa-ni-tahhhh.

I was still wearing the same summer clothes as before, which were fortunately gender-neutral: a white T-shirt, khaki shorts, and white tennis shoes. But I was definitely not the same; now, there was no hair on my legs, nor on my face, and my hair was longer than before. And then there were the breasts, which were quite pretty actually, and a little bouncy. Their unusual movement and weight threw me at first, as did my rounded ass, which swelled swishingly behind me. A girl indeed. In a sudden fit of panic, I immediately put my hands on my crotch. Oh no. I put one on top of the other, disturbed by the incommensurable space. Sure enough, there was nothing there, an unrecognized emptiness, a vacuum hard to account for in my still-dizzy mind. I didn't have the courage to take a peek under my shorts, to pull them down and see. Any kind of glance would have been disconcerting enough in those circumstances. I simply looked around, as if embarrassed that someone would recognize me, but I saw nobody, not even a stranger, and I decided immediately to head home, to run like crazy for home, feeling the strangeness of running with bouncing weights on my chest and my behind, yet also feeling somehow lighter.

The first thing I did, once in the privacy of my home, was take my clothes off frantically and explore my body. I felt like a woman on the verge of a nervous breakdown, breathing way too fast for my own good, afraid of the nothingness between my legs, the dark universe where previously the phallus had ruled. And if it wasn't quite nothingness, it sure felt like it compared to the something that had been there only hours before, humbly offering me the best moments of my life. I touched myself with a shyness I had never had with any of my lovers. It felt strange. I couldn't find a hand mirror, so I had to settle for a compact that one of my lovers had left behind and that I used for shaving in airplane bathrooms on business trips. I put it on the floor and squatted over it. I could clearly see female genitalia, a familiar sight, but the mirror was so small that I couldn't see quite as clearly the connection between that erogenous zone and the rest of me, just two-dimensional images, pink and dark close-ups. I moved to the full-length mirror in the bedroom, leaned over, and peeked between my legs. What I saw made me tremble with fear, apprehension, and, why not admit it, some degree of excitement as well. A woman.

I began to explore my new body, testing all the possible tingling sensations, the vulnerability of the nape of the neck, the peculiar feeling when pressing the nipples of . . . my breasts (whew, it was even hard to

31

name them as my own), the singularity of sliding my own finger up my, my, what should I call it? My vagina? Way too formal. My cunt? Way too vulgar. Pussy? Conventional, but it would have to do for the time being. The important thing was not the naming after all, but rather the exploring of a new reality, an unexpected, surprising new reality that left me wordless, as sensations familiar from provoking reactions in others now evoked singular emotions in a body I could call my own. I was wordless, yes, inarticulate without question, but very much a woman.

My next thought was, of course, that I had no clothes suitable for this new body. Spaced out as I was, I did my best to remember what the balance might be on my ill-treated credit card, and, assuming that it would all work itself out, I jumped back into my T-shirt and shorts and headed for the mall. How girlish of me indeed, how conventional and ordinary, but I literally had no choice.

As I drove to the mall, I began to think of how I could fulfill on my new voluptuous frame my fantasies of the perfect companion, a model I used to impose on my girlfriends. I thought of short, tight dresses, red of course, of modish high-heeled sandals that left all the toes exposed, with the toenails just as fiery red, a vision of vicious vermillion. Phantom mirages and hallucinatory apparitions of gorgeous women, of multiple Pandoras in various fatuous outfits and extravagant hairdos, paraded through my porous head, suddenly more like a colander or a Swiss cheese quietly melting on a hot summer afternoon than razor-sharp or logical, and that had nothing to do with being a woman, but a lot with still being in shock. It was all too pretty, a brilliant flash of excitement punctuated by the boredom of actually trying on a zillion dresses, none of which fit, all of which looked God awful because they either made me look too fat, or too slutty, or else I simply could not move inside of them, since it was impossible to lean forward without showing my ass, which, I might add, didn't look half bad, or exposing my breasts, which were bursting out like jack-in-the-boxes. It would be simply impossible to pass anonymously when I wore them. I did enjoy the sensation of standing tall in my black high-heeled shoes with my ass protruding even more than usual. It excited my back in more ways than one. I felt—it's still a sensation hard to name for me—sexy and desirable. I also bought new pants, blouses, and—dare I say it?—even a bra. Strange, now that I had my own breasts to show off, I was infinitely shyer than when I virtually required my girlfriends to go braless in my presence, and I was embarrassed of my nipples swelling like bursting grapes and drawing like magnets the eyes of every passerby to their very tips. Yes, I was as embarrassed now as I had been excited by the same effect when the object of desire was not myself but the woman walking by my side. Anyway, I went home. Or tried to. On the way there, I realized I had forgotten to buy a handbag and I suddenly discovered that women's clothes had no pockets in which to keep your wallet, your pen, your change, or your lipstick, the bare necessities of everyday life. So I had to go back, and buy whichever purse didn't look too ugly since by then I was exhausted from shopping. I finally made it home and tried on my new clothes. Afterward, I went into a deep, bottomless sleep, dreaming that it was all a dream and I'd wake up as Juan again, plain Juan, the familiar shapes and hairs outlining my body. But no, even after I woke up, I was still Juanita.

As time went by, small changes began to be perceptible. My vague, rather obscure thoughts at the time overlapped and intertwined to the point of erasing all possible sense, generating a sort of hallucinatory virulence in my mind, which felt virile at times, if you can forgive the use of such a silly word under my new condition.

Sex, for example. I did have sex after I became Juanita. It was very confusing, when not actually embarrassing, to relearn but, to my surprise, even more exhilarating than before. Part of the problem was that even though I was now a girl, I still felt attracted to girls. To complicate things further, now I also felt a clean, neat, distinctive attraction to boys. Indeed, it was the first time I thought of Walker in, shall we say, a different light. Intangible images appeared in my mind, in which I saw at times myself still a girl with my new body, but with a penis, a penis and vagina, a pussy, both at once, fucking and being fucked and enjoying both and doing it all in one big swoop with both Walker and Pandora, slipping into both roles in a vertigo of amber-colored desire, grappling with both, feeling the exquisite pleasure, never imagined before, of being penetrated, my muscles opening themselves at first to receive the foreign object and then fusing with it in full, tight force, the singular swift sensation of bursting in orgasmic bliss as I felt split in two by the foreign wedge spreading me in opposite directions. I no longer felt bound by the limitations of a specific gender, as in fantasy I was both, and penetrating was no less exciting than before but profoundly more transgressive since I was also a girl, and my feelings were now more involved with my desire, so that a caress of the belly, a kiss on the nape of the neck alone were virtually capable of giving me an orgasm. These opaque feelings were completely unknown by the boy in me before, whose lonely transcendence was the spurting forth of sperm, prelude to a snoring, chorkling siesta. I came to appreciate the incredibly rich inner experience of eroticism that women possessed and that men, at least the men I knew, were simply incapable of comprehending, this incredible web of buried events, layers of feelings, transfiguration of the imagination in concave shapes and dizzying colors.

This story is even harder to write than I thought. It's my duty to describe to you what it felt like to be a girl, when in reality I want to fast-forward to the moment when finally Walker, Pandora, and I . . . But no. I'll stay true to my genre, and the art of writing stories requires me to depict daily life at its plainest, while credibly juggling suspense so that you, dear reader, don't find out what is going to happen until the very end. Endings are elusive? Middles are nowhere to be found? Patience. Let me carry on first with the daily doings of being a girl.

The first noticeable disadvantage, beyond the constant ogling of disgusting men with IQ's the size of peas, was when I began to feel something I had never felt before. It was a swelling of my entire body, as if I were absorbing all the atmospheric moisture and my body were becoming some grotesque water balloon, stretched to the limit and ready to burst. My joints ached, my breasts hurt now when they bounced, and my nipples were so sensitive that the fabric of my clothes felt like sandpaper. The worst part was the effect on my emotions, which also felt like they were ready to burst wide open at the slightest prick of a pin. The only benefit seemed to be the sensitivity in my clitoris. I thought I could come forever. In fact, I felt like I needed to desperately.

In the absence of constant sexual relief, the intense physical anxiety came out as anger, which might have seemed unprovoked to uninformed observers. Assholes, what did they know? I was in agony! And I was a walking landmine, wearing my short, tight red dress and high-heeled shoes, feeling the wind blowing up my legs and forming a whirlpool by my crotch, ready to slap the first man that crossed my path. As it turned out, he happened to be a very solemn and saintly looking homeless person who always sat meditating in the lotus position on the corner of Taraval and Sloat, with a hand-painted sign explaining in eloquent prose why he was out of work and detailing in precious scripture his list of daily needs. I scowled at him and muttered:

"Lazy jerk!"

Startled, he turned to me, half scowling, half staring with hurt eyes and wounded pride. Then, twisting his lips derisively in a cruel grin, he retorted:

"Bitch! If you were a man I'd punch you right in the face!"

I was flustered, and then furious. What was this nonsense that if I was a man he'd punch me in the face? I was a man, for goodness' sake! How dare he?

"Fuck you, macho asshole!"

The man puckered his face into an asterisk, denoting both genuine anger and amused irony. He walked slowly over until he stood right next to me.

"You were saying?"

"Fuck you, macho asshole."

It happened so fast I barely saw it coming. He lifted his right hand and with his open palm almost slapped me across the face, laughing ironically at the same time. But he held back before actually coming in contact with my face. At that instant he stuck out his tongue and rolled his eyes. Then he clapped to himself for a job well done before walking slowly away in a cloud of laughter.

"I could kill you, bitch, if I wanted, but I'm damned if I'll go to jail for you."

That night I got cramps so bad I had to take a hot bath in the middle of the night. In the morning I was greeted by a thick bloody stream oozing from my pussy. I felt muggy and slow, with a certain dose of laziness and melancholia I'll never forget. I bought my first box of tampons, embarrassed by my ignorance of the size I needed.

Peeing sitting down was another adventure. I had a hard time adjusting to sitting on the toilet instead of simply standing, parting my thighs, and feeling a feverish flush of hot water dazzlingly flow out while holding nothing in my hands. And then, of course, feeling the damp drip on my thighs and discovering the yellow droplets on the toilet rim until I remembered to dry myself regularly with toilet paper. I could not just shake the last drop anymore, and believe me, it was frustrating.

I painted my toenails red and the effect turned me on, but no matter how pretty it looked, the arches of my feet always ached when wearing my girl shoes. I began cheating by wearing tennis shoes on a daily basis and only switching to girl shoes when concrete actions required a girl disguise. For example, when employing the oldest trick in the commonest book I put on my kinky sleeveless red dress and went upstairs to Walker's to borrow a cup of sugar. I was nearly hyperventilating by the time my agitated finger found his doorbell, gingerly touching it as if I were fondling an undersized asshole. The sound felt loud as a fire alarm. Eventually I heard his deliberate, beefy footsteps approaching the door with impatient speed, and a voice yelling still from the other side in a sort of groggy manner:

"Yeah?"

I answered in a voice so dainty it surprised even me.

"I'm your downstairs neighbor, hi. Sorry to bother you, but, uh, could I, uh, borrow a cup of sugar? I know, I know, it's more than silly, it's boring, but I'm baking a cake . . ."

"No problem."

The footsteps went away like the aftermath of a hurricane for what seemed an eternity. I was standing there, in the hall, all alone, a little cold, and my shoes were beginning to ache. Had he sneaked out through the window and gone to the 24-hour supermarket to buy me a pound of sugar? Finally, when, discouraged, I was ready to head back empty-handed downstairs, I heard the mastodon footsteps once again. The door opened this time.

I could tell you that at that instant the air felt steamy, greasy, stained, chaotic, mad, but I won't because it would be embarrassing to employ language typically used to describe latinas locas. However, there he was, standing deliriously in front of me, making my head spin with his Aramis lotion. He was wearing a wrinkled white shirt with a few wine stains on it, opened down to the middle of his hairy chest, black pants, and, yes, he was barefoot. His provocative dark hair seemed rumpled, as if someone had just passed her fingers through it. His eyes, vacant, as if I weren't there at all, told me everything I preferred not to know.

"Here."

"Thanks a lot, I really appreciate . . ."

The door closed in my nose, nearly knocking the cup of sugar from my hands.

"Asshole!" I muttered, biting my tongue at the same time, and then giggling a little. Men were unbelievably selfish. I should remember. It was as if you weren't there, as if you were invisible; they saw right past you. However, of all his gestures, it was his refusal even to ogle me from head to toe, when I had put on my red dress and black shoes just to get this particular cup of sugar, that left me absolutely furious, depressed, insecure. From that point on I decided, in a stubborn fit of anger that thinly disguised my dejection, that I would be woman enough to make any man do whatever I wanted to. I went back downstairs and switched to my tennis shoes. I had finally understood why being denied a desire intensely longed for was infinitely worse than not knowing one's desires. I resolved to myself that no matter what, he'd be mine. Looking out my

36

forlorn window at the crescent moon with its dark shadows shaped like fish swimming on its surface, I decided to swallow my newly found fears, and, not without guilt, to become a new woman. With God as my witness, I swore, I'll never be hungry again, obviously not thinking of food. If I were writing a stereotype of myself, I'd say that after that moment I became a predatory feline that paced and hunted, that preferred to experience the night raw, hungry, and lawless. But my singular beingness matters to me, and I'm too proud to reduce myself to a cliché, even if I did dress like one—a carnivalesque cross of a beauty queen and a robot dressed in a leopard-print bra top and mini-skirt.

Because that's how I dressed the next time I saw him, even if I did need a penny under my tongue like when I was a shy child, out of sheer nervousness. But I acted out the slut beast role only to discover that he wasn't interested. "It's not you, really," he said in the end, when I struggled uselessly to get his face as close to me as possible. "I know," I said, suddenly wise. "You like somebody else." His silence and uneven tiptoeing away from me was a form of confirmation of what I had said. My skin was suddenly too tight to breathe as I slowly died. I didn't know, I failed to grasp or unconsciously refused to know, who it was he actually desired.

I ran into the goddess, Pandora herself, at the "Curl Up" Beauty Supply Store on West Portal Avenue. I no longer feared speaking to her, so I actually did approach her and discovered that she responded to me in normal tone, just as though she were speaking to another woman. I didn't tell her I was Juan but introduced myself as, well, Juanita, which indeed had become my name, while requesting her advice on which cold cream to buy. She rambled about this and that as if this were the only world she knew, baroquely slouching toward a concrete answer. I realized, however, that it was the longest conversation I had ever had with her. Or, for that matter, the only time I had actually cared to talk with this woman, as opposed to just fantasizing about her. Well, as I admitted before, I thought she was beyond my reach. But that was as a boy, hard as it is for a Don Juan to admit such a thing without singing an aria to underscore his angst at his failure to conquer. But now I was a girl, and therefore, the stress of putting up or shutting up was no longer mine. I could just do girl talk, cold creams or eye liners, and she would never be forced into her own self-defined role as the perfect body of dreams for the masculine gaze.

"Men treat me as if I have no life of my own," she said at one point of the long conversation, "but I do."

"A life of your own? What is it?"

"I'm a curator at the Museum of Modern Art. Did you see the recent photo exhibit of AIDS widowers? My doing."

"Really?"

"Don't you act like a boy on me; what do you think? I have a degree in museology, and I minored in comp. lit."

It had never actually occurred to me that she had a mind. She had always been just a body to me, and only now did it dawn on me that she fought the experience of being essentialized as a woman while paradoxically essentializing herself with her looks. She was the ultimate contradiction, the woman who chose the role of reified object of desire and then resented being perceived as such, all the while holding open her humid lips to welcome kisses like a noiseless, flowing river, her half-closed eyes drowned in pleasure, even more lost than her mouth appeared to be at times, while refusing blatantly to cast herself out from her chosen role. I understood the damage men like Juan had silently done to her, while burning with my own female anger at her sacrificial passivity. And as a Latina to boot, it offended me that she was more "half out of her mind and half out of her dress" than María Conchita Alonso. I laughed after this last reflection, of course, because I remembered she had chosen her iconic role precisely for the type of male that I myself had been.

Later, I ran into Walker at the supermarket. He was deftly choosing various liquors and placing them in his cart next to frozen food, Dannon yogurt, and a small pile of cans. I followed him silently, as I would have done with Pandora in my recent past. The surprises life gives us like spoonfuls of honey! I began to daydream. And daydreaming as I was, in an aura of pink and golden tones, I did not notice that, turning from one aisle to another, he had stopped in front of the vitamin section, unsure which of them to pick. My cart bumped into his.

"Oh, I'm so sorry."

He said nothing.

"You're my upstairs neighbor. Remember me? The cupful of sugar, the leopard-print bra and miniskirt? I'm so sorry . . ."

He half-smiled and I interpreted the ceremonial gesture as permission to perform. Before he could retreat in any civilized direction, I talked and talked, about his wonderful Gloria Estefan music seeping through my ceiling, about how we should get to know each other as neighbors, and how I promised to return his raw Hawaiian sugar that very evening with a present to thank him for his kindness.

"No, not tonight. I have a date."

Those words were devastating to this girl, but, pretending it was nothing, I chattered diplomatically about how the day after or the one after that would do. I introduced myself; he timidly agreed to inform me of his name; I gave him my phone number; he did not give me his. I promised I would knock on his door if he didn't call. He only smiled, said nothing, and we parted ways. That evening I was determined to spy on his door to find out who was the malicious witch who dared to steal my handsome knight, and that's how I found out his date was, you've probably guessed it by now, Pandora. I kept at a melancholic distance as they descended the enchanted staircase in a sort of perpetual communion; then, neither fulfilled nor requited, I dissolved into tears on my bed.

They came back later that same night, much earlier than I would have imagined. I heard them walking upstairs. Well, the truth is, I spied through the peephole as well, then heard the inevitable, recognizable noises coming from the apartment directly above mine. Heard them, or imagined them, as I tried to sleep, foolishly thinking that such an act could erase all traces of reality, until I heard the knocks on my door. It was a dream, I told myself, part of my fantasies about Walker, because I wanted Walker so badly I felt his image burned my skin, Walker walking all over me, but it wasn't a dream or a fantasy; the knocks were very real and very much on my wooden brown door. I realized I had dozed off, probably not for very long, and the knocks on the door were bringing me back to a certain reality, my female reality of being neglected by the only man I yearned for. I couldn't imagine anyone knocking on my door at that time. Before I even dared look at the clock, I instinctively rushed to the door to open it, possibly a foolish act, yet driven by my longing, by desire, by loneliness, nostalgia, never-ending hope. I did look through the peephole first, obviously. And, to my amazement, Pandora stood on the other side of the door. She looked embarrassed, impatient, about to walk away. I opened immediately and smiled.

"Hi. Funny time for you to drop by for a visit."

"I'm sorry, Juanita. That's your name, right? You do remember me, don't you? I'm really sorry, I know it's late . . ."

"No, not at all, I'm addicted to late-night TV, insomniac that I am, when not rereading Proust . . ."

"Proust?"

"A French writer."

"I know, dear, I read him in the original. Comp. lit. major, remember? Anyway, I don't want to make a nuisance of myself . . ."

"You're not. Don't be silly. I'm always longing for a stranger to knock on my door late at night."

"Well, Walker kind of sent me, 'cause he was too embarrassed to come down himself."

"I see . . ."

"His corkscrew broke, just when he was about to open a bottle of wine, and he was wondering if . . ."

"He could borrow mine."

"Yes."

"Sure. I'll bring it up in a jiffy."

"What?"

"You heard me. I'll bring it up in a jiffy."

"You're coming upstairs?"

"Tell Walker I'll be there in just a minute."

I closed the door in her face. I dashed to the bathroom, washed my face, dried it, and clumsily, still feeling sweet and humid like a tropical night in the Caribbean, began drawing a long snake of a shadow with the eyeliner, fearing more the trembling of my own hand than the opportunity I was profiting from. I still confused the glittery powder with the other one, the one chosen this night, drier, like pancake mix, and of course lipstick, my favorite part, painting my lips as if I were sucking the man of my dreams in that image reflected on the high altar of my nights, my bathroom mirror. I jumped into a very short dress with no underwear underneath, slipped on my high-heeled shoes, dashed upstairs, backtracked because I had forgotten the damn corkscrew, pulled it out of the kitchen drawer, and dashed back up in those damn shoes, fearing I'd break my neck on every step, arriving breathless at Walker's door, where I rang rang rang the bell while pretending that not even an earthquake could disturb my stiff composure.

The door opened. I smelled incense, heard Gilberto Gil in the background. As I had guessed, it was Pandora who opened it. Walker was nowhere to be seen.

"Thank you."

Before she knew what was happening, or even had time to register that I had changed and made myself up, I darted inside toward the living room.

"Which bottle should I open? Is it in the kitchen?"

I balanced in my shoes as gracefully as possible while dashing toward the kitchen with the corkscrew. There, in front of the kitchen table was a sweaty Walker with his shirt unbuttoned to the middle of the waist, as

I had already seen him before, a frenzied, shadowy déjà vu, white shirt and all, the smell of Aramis, a sacred symbol of a paroxysm I recognized and longed for.

"You shouldn't have come here. This is a private party."

"It still is, just with three, that's all. More fun, no? Here, let me do it."

I took control of the situation as best I could remember from my boy days, dancing and whirling around in the middle of the kitchen like a chicken with its head cut off. By being fast, swift, masterful, opening the bottle quickly, getting a third glass out of the cupboard, passion defeating prudence, pouring all three, calling Pandora into the kitchen, toasting to this miraculous accident that brought all three of us together before Walker could think straight, if he could ever think without seeing red like most men, I had fully succeeded in inserting myself into the party with the people of my dreams. I made an elaborate, boastful, bloated, belligerent toast, then, dismounting reality even further, suggested we all dance.

"I don't dance," said Walker with a fiery frown.

"Fine. I'll dance with Pandora."

I pulled Pandora by the wrists. She let herself be led like a lamb to the slaughter, while I changed the music from romantic to house, and started dancing crazily, as if I were about to have a seizure, or be electrocuted for my crimes of passion. From the corner of my eye I could see that Walker, his clumsy imagination limited by his male's gaze, couldn't believe what was going on. He drank his wine in one big gulp and rolled up his shirtsleeves. I got into dancing with Pandora. She had rhythm, even if she was somewhat tentative in her ability to follow me, surprisingly shy, perhaps because I was a girl. Suddenly I felt protective toward her, very maternal of me, though mixed with a tingling sensation in my prickly skin and a rush of unexpected warmth surging from within my own inner body. I pulled her closer to me and could feel very distinctly her body heat. The air was steaming, amber sweat gliding down my eyes so that everything looked as if we had stayed too long in the sauna, deaf shapes deformed and colors more alive, chaotic, our scents tangling like a magical blood rite, deliriously dancing, mad, howling like melancholic wolves. We were holding hands. I began to swing in one direction, then the other, squatting on my knees as far down as I could, then sticking my leg between hers as we went back up. My bare leg in contact with her lacquered thighs sent shivers of pleasure throughout my entire body, eventually coalescing in my throbbing pussy. The pace and rhythm accelerated. I grabbed a glass of water and poured a third of it down my back to cool my stained, camouflaged emotions, then took advantage of this melodramatic excuse to holler my hallucinatory pleasure, leaned over to turn off the light, so that we were left only with the dim one coming from the dining room, and then immediately placed the glass of water on a little table forlornly abandoned against the wall near the light switch. By that point, I had forgotten Walker, my true object of desire, my sweet, my love. I touched the back of Pandora's neck. She crumbled, contracting her entire body like an accordion closing, but in the same gesture stretched her magnificent neck and half-opened her mouth, the mintlike moisture on her lips clearly visible in those indirect rays of light hitting us from the side. I squatted again, pulling her leg between my own. As we both went down, her leg was in the middle of mine, so I sat, literally sat, abandoned to my lubricity and my imagination, on her thigh, just above her knee, and I could feel my moist pussy coming into contact with her skin, our legs like two boas twirled one within the other. She felt it too, like burning ice, and her eyes doubled in size, amazed, shocked, I should say, but by then I was in full control, drowned in pleasure, and she was lost. She tensed somewhat, with the old unconscious memory of a shy stiffness, entwined as she was with me. We went back up, I smiled, winked an eye at her; she smiled nervously, unveiling some of her mental labyrinths, curious, with innocent doe eyes. I provocatively stuck my viscous index finger in my own mouth and sucked it while holding her with the other hand. She raised her marvelous head, weighing infinitely more because of her bedazzlement, and her eyes opened on a scene of madness.

All of a sudden it felt as if we had been caught in the middle of the street by a car that had lost its brakes. Walker charged out of the kitchen in full force. I swear I thought I saw horns on his forehead. He was so sweaty it looked as if he had taken a shower with his clothes on, his open mouth a very black and fearsome cave. He had the opened bottle of wine, now half empty, in one hand.

"Leave my girlfriend alone, you lesbian bitch!"

I was startled, then started to laugh. I had been a girl for such a short time, no one had ever called me a lesbian before. I was both shocked and pleased at the same time. Then, things began to move as if in slow motion, with the inexplicable acuity of horror. Walker screamed unintelligible phrases, having lost all sense of boundaries after stumbling onto the cutting edge of perversity. It almost felt as if he were speaking outrageous French, or maybe even Basque, shrieking, raving, and howling in the loudest voice I had ever heard. His entire stance was like a boxer's, and I realized he was ready to punch me, so I went into a crouched position, letting go of Pandora's hand at that instant. Pandora was entirely silent, paralyzed, like a Greek statue, but her eyes betrayed deep-seated panic. Walker advanced menacingly toward me, vociferous, breathing fire, looking like a hairy warthog, a chain with a cross dangling from his neck. As he raised his left arm in condemnation, a spurt of ink-red wine escaped from the bottle and flew in my direction. I instinctively ducked behind Pandora, still paralyzed, and Walker must have interpreted this in his furious rage as a gesture of protection on her part. Because all of a sudden, from within the river of unintelligible words erupting from his foamy mouth I did recognize the phrase "so you too, bitch," and then his hand flew in her direction. The woodlike palm of his hand was open but it still hit her with full force on her left cheek, sending her flying across the living room. She collapsed in a heap at the foot of the sofa, where she remained, trembling and convulsing in ripples of fear and shock.

I must have screamed, but I don't remember. I do remember my mouth open, my eyes staring into space as if they had fled from my body and could see me from afar. Then Walker's attention turned to me. He came in my direction, flailing his arms about wildly, shaking, chortling and gulping horribly. I leaned against the wall, trying to feel with my arms, hands, legs, any avenue of escape through the wall, and found the glass of water. He was rushing at me now, and I could see his left hand shooting wine with the extreme intensity of the solar blaze. I grabbed the glass of water and instinctively threw it in his face. He was so astonished at my sudden counterattack that he covered his eyes with his hands and dropped the bottle of wine to the floor. Swiftly, as if I had practiced that nifty move for years, I darted under his arms, picking up the bottle in the process, and ran in Pandora's direction. She was whimpering in rhythmic sobs, short, intense, modest, ladylike. I tried to pick her up, and she instinctively covered her head with her arms before realizing it was me, then gave me a frightened look that made me realize this had not been the first time. I turned around in time to see Walker charge once more. I remembered I had picked up the bottle of wine, and I threw what was left of it in his face, staining his lily-white shirt in the process. Then I grabbed Pandora's hand as hard as I could.

"Come on! Let's get the hell out of here!"

"My purse!"

Somehow or other, while Walker kneeled on the ground like a wounded boar with wine in his eyes, or like a squire about to be knighted, trying to pull his eyes out like Oedipus but without any sense of punishment or guilt, I managed to find Pandora's purse on the sofa, grab her by the wrist so hard it turned pearly white, and pull her out of the apartment, slamming the door behind me as if its noise upon closing were the beginning of an earthquake. We ran down the stairs to my place. I felt the warm exaltation of urine flowing down my thighs and smelled its acrid acidity as I closed the door and immediately called the police. They showed up in five minutes, calmed us down, and talked to Pandora, whose swollen face was now bruised and scary, deforming her beauty in unexpected and surreal ways, and tried to convince her to press charges. Then they paid a visit to Walker. I never found out what happened to him, but that night the police did insist that we should not sleep in the same building as him. So, Pandora offered to put me up in her place, and we were driven there in a patrol car, of all things.

Now, life has taken an entirely new twist for us. I live with Pandora. I'm her first, and I hope last, woman. Life being its own ironic self, when I desired to look at, to penetrate, Pandora's box as a boy, she was my unbearable, forbidden desire. She has been revealed to me, a woman, as this and more, as we forever repeat this refigured primal scene, our mouths mingling together in a storm of saliva, my lips foaming with love. I have never dared tell her I was a boy before, nor that I desired her as one, nor that I slept with many women in my previous manly life. She certainly did not believe me at all when I tried to hint she was my first lesbian affair. She insisted that I just admit it was either the first time I fell in love or lived with my girlfriend, that I should not exaggerate about never having done it before, since my technique was sufficient proof of my acquired expertise. I have also given up trying to become a boy again. Resplendent with happiness, I have learned to put up with PMS, a feeling of powerlessness, fear of men, not being listened to, having to help everyone all the time without being helped myself, impotent and all powerful at the same time, while enjoying my multi-orgasmic chain and the pleasure of not falling asleep, but on the contrary, being reenergized every time I come, as if I had snorted a thin, white line of coke. I've also discovered that my PMS and cramps are stronger than other women's, including Pandora's, who barely changes her moods over the course of time. The only problem I have now is that Pandora, who has since mastered her German, is tired of being a shy, passive girl perceived by all men, and even by many lesbians, as a princess with nothing in her head. She wants to become a boy!

Shorty

DAISY HERNÁNDEZ

I meet her at Julie's. It's Saturday night, and that means every tristate Puerto Rican lesbian is dancing salsa and having too many Coronas at Julie's in Manhattan. I've always wondered about that club. I mean, how many Latinas do you know named Julie? Julissa, sure. Julia, yeah. But Julie?

So, there I am on the dance floor with my buddy Marisol showing off my best steps when all of a sudden I do a little spin and I'm staring straight at some woman's tits and I'm not talking about the kind of cleavage where it's two droopy tetas propped up with a wired bra. This is the real stuff. Two round, large breasts squeezed together in a baby tee. Just as I'm about to bend my neck back to look up at the homegirl, Marisol spins me around, laughing. "Oye loca, careful before you get some old butch kicking your ass for staring at her woman."

I lean into Marisol. "Did you see the cleavage on that girl?"

Marisol's short, curly hair smells like oranges, but I know it's just that nasty anti-frizz gel she uses. She shakes her head. "Lou, she's too tall for you. La Cleavage wouldn't give you the time of day."

That's why I love Mari. We met at some gay parade years ago, and she's the perfect friend, la hermanita who nicknames the new hottie "La Cleavage." That's how well she knows me.

After three more songs, Marisol runs off to kick it to some cutie in high heels, but I stay on the dance floor, dancing solo and watching the old dykes do the best salsa you've ever seen. I also want to see who La Cleavage is with, but she's just hanging with friends. Homegirl has some seriously pin-straight highlighted hair. You know she's Dominican and she gets that shit worked on every week at the salon. Straightened, pulled, tormented. You gotta love her for it.

I'm heading to the bar when she steps up to me and puts a hand on my shoulder. "¿Quieres bailar?"

I start nodding because I'm thinking but she takes that for a yes and grabs my hand. I'm thinking, "what the fuck?" but girlfriend starts dancing and leading me. *Leading me.* I wouldn't put up with that shit except I'm at eye level with her tits and I'm a little buzzed from the gin and tonic I had earlier, and it's La India that the DJ's playing. By the end of the first song, though, I'm back to myself and I'm trying to lead her but it ain't working. She's too tall or I'm too short. Whatever. I thank her for the dance and say I've got to go. Which I do. I need another drink. She nods and goes back to her friends.

From the bar, I check her out. She's got the tight pants, the bright lipstick, the big, gold hoop earrings. I'm feeling pretty good about myself. "I could get that if I wanted," I tell Mari, who's buying her new girl a drink and shoots back, "Right." But what does Mari know? She likes playing it safe. Not that this matters. La Cleavage is too tall. We can't even dance together. So, fuck that.

An hour later, I'm in line at the coat check when I feel a tapping on my shoulder. I turn around and it's cleavage. No, I mean really: it's tetas. That's all I see for a second until I hear La Cleavage ask, "Are you gonna give me your number before you go?"

It's hard to know what to say when you want something you probably shouldn't have and come close to getting it. "Huh?"

"You speak English?" she asks.

"Sí," I say. "I mean, yeah."

The coat check girl asks for my ticket and disappears behind the jackets. She's chuckling, I notice. Is she laughing at me?

At the bar two old butches are doing shots and hollering, "Pa' las mujeres!" The song "Fruta Fresca" is playing and I see Cleavage's friends standing against the wall, shaking their hips and watching us. That bugs me about lesbians. You can't do anything on your own. Always gotta have an audience.

"What's your name?" Cleavage asks.

"Luna, but people call me Lou." I make a point of staring at her pointy chin. "And you?"

"Peggy. Peggy Edison."

At that point, it's over. I'm sorry. I don't care how much tits there are. I ain't dating no girl named Peggy Edison. What kind of name is that? Probably some white girl with a tan passing for Puerto Rican.

But then, coat check girl's handing me my jacket and Peggy places her hand on the counter like she owns the bar but is being polite to her employees and says, "Hey nena, you got a pen?"

Something about the way she says "nena" and I know she's Nuyorican. Or at least Dominican. I can hear it in her Spanish. She says it easy, quick, sin duda, like every letter belongs to her.

I don't expect her to call or I figure I won't call her back. It's just crazy how tall she is. Tall girls go for other tall girls, or they should. But when Peggy leaves me a message with her number, I call my girl Mari.

"You think it'll be weird?"

"What?"

"C'mon bitch, you seen how tall she is."

"Yeah, that girl's all piernas. Your five-foot ass is gonna have to do some climbing, mi'ja." Marisol is laughing.

"I'm five feet two inches."

"Right. Remember that white girl from upstate? The one I went with last year? She went climbing rocks and shit. That bitch had this bag—I'm talking like a suitcase of stuff you gotta take with you when you go climbing." This makes Mari laugh so hard that she puts the phone down.

"You drunk?" I ask when she picks up the receiver again.

"I smoked a little but I'm just thinking of your tiny ass with rock climbing gear, making your way up Mount Pegoña."

"Mount what?"

"Your girl Peggy. Pegoña. Don't you think that's better? A little more flavor to it?"

I hang up the phone. I ain't calling Peggy back. Mari's right. It's crazy. Climbing gear. Fuck. Not that I couldn't do it. I can bench press eighty pounds. But shit. Why did the girl have to be so tall? We'd look like freaks. I mean I've seen it once. I'd seen this Costa Rican chick, four feet eleven inches, and I swear she was kicking it with her girl who was six feet like Pegoña. They looked like freaks. Cute, you know, but freaky. I mean, how did they have sex? How could the little one top?

47

I call La Cleavage two days later. I don't believe in passing up hot girls. At the end of the day, I tell Marisol, it's that. I don't care how tall Pegoña is, you just do not pass up a girl like that.

"She could do porn with those tits," I tell Mari.

"Now that you mention it, maybe I saw her—"

"Fuck you, Mari."

The first date's good. Actually it's much better than I expected because we're sitting most of the night, watching a movie then getting something to eat on Bergenline, and honestly I do spend the night trying to figure out why we're the same height sitting down. Finally, I blurt it out. "You ain't that tall sitting down."

She laughs. She has this way of laughing where all of her shakes: boobs, shoulders, tummy, even the pin-straight hair. This bitch does not giggle. I hate girls that giggle. It's so fucking fake, like somebody trying not to fart. I'm always like, "Just laugh. Don't giggle." Not that I have to tell Pegoña. She's laughing her ass off.

"You ain't so short sitting down," she says, smiling. She reaches across the table and rubs my head. Generally, I hate it when people do that, like I'm some five-year-old. But with Pegoña, it's OK. I close my eyes and she doesn't take her hand away. "It's my legs," she says.

"Your what?" I ask, opening my eyes.

"I'm all legs." She lifts the edge of her long red skirt. "My torso's short. I'm five feet eleven inches but it's all legs."

After that, I have to fuck her. I don't care what anyone thinks of me going with a tall girl. I have to at least see her buck naked. I have to go down on her.

I take her home after the second date and it's not what I expect. I mean usually I don't get nervous. I've been a butch all my life, started dating girls when I turned twelve and I'm twenty-six now and I've never been nervous. But with Pegoña, it's different. Maybe it's the height thing. I stand there in my kitchen handing her a Corona and thinking: how am I going to pull this off?

Or maybe it's something else about her. The girl wears these low-cut blouses and the black pants are so tight on her so she's definitely femme but she's not girly. It's like she's about to kick your ass the way she walks. When she comes into my apartment, she starts thumbing through my CD collection and pulls out what she wants to play.

She makes the first move when we're sitting on the sofa, which is just fine by me, and I'm cursing myself 'cause maybe I should have had more than one beer. I'm too sober. But then we're kissing and it's good. She kisses the way she walks: like she owns everything. And then home-girl just kicks back and takes off her blouse in one move. Here's the crazy part: I don't notice her porn star tetas. I mean I see them and the lacy maroon bra, but there's this tattoo across the lower part of her belly.

"Fuck or fight," I read aloud. When I look up, she's just smiling. "What does that mean?"

"Why don't ya find out for yourself?"

I don't remember what answer I gave 'cause next thing I know we're wrestling on the Andean rug my mom brought back from Peru. And this ain't like some fake wrestling. The girl's strong and even though I can hold my own and beat her, I realize after a few minutes that we're not going to have sex unless I give up. So I do.

Sex with a tall girl ain't nothing like doing it with a short one. That's what I tell Mari a few days later at the bar in Hoboken, where we go for happy hour on Fridays. "It's like you can't get enough." I take another swig of my beer. "Every time you turn around there's more of her. It's fucking great."

"You're seeing her again?"

"Tonight."

Mari shakes her head.

"What?"

"You always get like this," Mari says, waving the bartender over to us.

"Like what?"

"Remember Great Adventure two years ago? You couldn't hit the biggest roller coaster just one time. No. That ain't enough for shorty. You weren't satisfied till you'd gone on it five times and you're so sick that you're face down puking saliva and they gotta call paramedics. It'll be the same thing with Cleavage."

"Shut up," I say, looking for the cigarettes in my bag and grinning. "And don't call her Cleavage. Have some respect."

Pegoña and I hang mostly at my apartment in Jersey because she's not out to her family in Washington Heights and she shares an apartment with her sister, who, she says, sort of suspects but nothing's been said, so you know how that goes. Now usually I wouldn't put up with that shit. If you love me, you gotta love me everywhere. You don't have to go down on me in public, but I'm not down with that "Let's act like we're hermanas in case your mom sees us." And anyway, most people guess about me so it ain't usually an option.

But this time, with Pegoña, I'm like, "Sure, that's fine." Actually I'm goddamned relieved. I mean the sex is good. Real good. But you know it's one thing to spend all your time lying down in bed. You don't really notice who's short, who's tall, and there's just so much of her. But it's another thing to be standing up. The first time I tried to hold her from behind, I ended up with my face in her armpit.

It's just weird. It's bad enough being gay. My mom is cool with it but I still have a tía that won't talk to me and . . . I don't know. I guess I like looking normal with my girlfriends. Life's hard enough so why make it harder?

My mom thinks we look like freaks. She told me so when I introduced her to Peggy. Mami just smiled and nodded and when homegirl was out the door, she was straight up. "That morena's made for the Amazon." She shook her head. "What are you doing? Going up a ladder each time?"

I roll my eyes at her. This is one of those times I wish I lived someplace else. But my mom and I split a house in Jersey. I got the basement, she's got the top floor and we rent out the first level to eight Salvadoran guys. Usually it works. She doesn't see who I bring home and I don't have to know what loser she's found. But on the downside, when she says stupid things, all I can do is go down to my place.

She turns on the TV in her kitchen. "You haven't been with anyone since that other morena dumped you two years ago."

"I been 'round."

"Is this one Dominican too? 'Cause I never seen a Dominican that tall."

I nod. "You think Pegoña and I look weird?"

She shrugs her shoulders. "I don't know about that stuff. But I guess nothing matters when you're lying down. Like my brother used to say, 'Who cares what the girl's legs look like? You just push them aside.'"

"Ma!"

"¿Qué?"

"I like this girl. Show some respect."

Being tall doesn't bother Peggy. It used to. She lived in Union City for a few years when she was young and the kids had names for her and jokes too. "I took it for two weeks," she says, grinning. "Then I realized I could beat them up and it was cool. You just gotta get the respect."

I know that too because I've always been the runt, even back in pre-K when you're supposed to be small. The teacher almost didn't take me the first day. She thought my mom was lying about my age. And then when I got into the school, the kids started on me. But I was tough. I didn't take crap from anybody. By the time I was done with pre-K, I'd fought every kid, even a tall one too. When it came to time with the trucks, I had first dibs.

Peggy kisses my cheek and then my earlobe, which tickles the shit out of me. "You're so cute," she says, "I wouldn't have beat you up."

I roll my eyes and, in one move, flip her over and I'm on top and it comes out my mouth: "I love you." She tells me I'm crazy, so I say, "I still love you." She says it too and I forget what we were talking about.

The more time we spend together, the more often we go out. It's crazy. I don't want people to think we're together, because . . . well, maybe we *do* look like freaks, but at the same time, I want people to know we're together. And sometimes they need to know. Like the other day, we go to the mall and we're standing in line waiting to pay for Peggy's new jeans and this asshole just starts talking to her. *Starts talking to her.* Motherfucker doesn't even look my way and when she ignores him, he just keeps kicking it to her.

I go to put my arm around Peggy's waist, but she grabs me by the wrist and narrows her eyes at me. I think she's about to say something to me, but she cuts into the guy. "Leave me alone, OK? I'm not interested."

"Whoa, mamita," the guy says, putting up his hands. "Chill. I just wanted to give ya some love. Damn, girl."

The register lady is now waving her hands and I'm pushing Peg's jeans on the counter. "Will this be all?" she asks but I don't get to answer because Peg says, "Excuse me but do you have a store policy to let guys harass women while they're waiting in line?"

The register chick apologizes but Peggy mutters "whatever" and pulls out her credit card.

Walking back to the car, she goes on and on about all the shit women gotta take from men. When we're in the car, she's done complaining about the guy and is on to me. "Are you crazy grabbing me like that? I told you my tía comes to this mall all the time. She could have seen us. What were you thinking?"

I grin. "That you were my bitch." I'm hoping the joke will calm her.

She puts the car in park. We're in line waiting to exit and the car behind us starts honking. "Are you intentionally trying to piss me off?"

51

I stare out the passenger window. She can actually be such a bitch sometimes, making little shit into big arguments. But it's cool. I've already figured her out. Just let her yell, agree with her, and then it's alright.

Things are good between Peggy and me for something like three months. We spend every weekend together. On Sundays we stay in bed and watch movies from Blockbuster. We eat food ma makes and Peggy organizes my CD collection and takes over half the closet.

Life's good.

But I know it's going to fuck up sooner or later. I just don't expect it to go down at the Javits Center.

I take Peggy there because it's the gay and lesbian business convention and I've got tickets from a friend. I've been before and I know it's a damn good place to drink free booze and stock up on free camisetas, water bottles, pens, and get entered into those prize getaway vacations nobody ever wins.

Peggy and I walk in and find a bunch of white boys glued to the booth for vacations in Mexico. The guy behind the table is wearing khakis and a white T-shirt and saying, "The hotel will be closing down for a full weekend in February and opening itself to the gay community."

I'm looking at a brochure, thinking maybe I should save up for this shit, when out of nowhere Peggy takes my hand. I don't notice it at first 'cause she's just dragging me away from the table. But then she keeps holding it and I look at her like "what the fuck?" and pull my hand away.

"Lou, I wanna hold your hand," she says. "It's OK here." She gives me that "I don't wanna fight—I wanna fuck you" smile and then starts walking and there I am getting my brown ass dragged down the aisle of gay and lesbian dot-com companies.

People stare at us. Actually, they stare at Peggy. She's a looker, but I'm there attached to her like a small dog. I don't know what to do. This hasn't happened before. So, I do what I can to avoid holding her hand. I get us shopping bags and start filling them. Free Post-it notes, free key chains, free water bottles. "Why are you taking that?" she asks as I throw in a magazine of naked guys.

"It's free."

She laughs and hugs me. Usually I love her hugs, the way she grabs me up into her body and my face gets squished in that space between her tits, but this time I just pull away.

"What's wrong?" Peg asks.

I point like an idiot. "Enter us in that contest." She puts our names in to win face lotion, hand lotion, lipstick, a car, a Hawaii vacation, a new CD. She signs us up to get information on condos in the Poconos and bed and breakfast places in Provincetown. I follow her, holding the bags.

We get back to the stage where a black drag queen's joking with the audience and introducing a band. Drag queens. At that moment, I wish more than anything to just be a drag queen. They get up on stage and because everybody expects them to be freaks, they ain't freaks. Like here's this six-foot-tall homeboy in stiletto heels and a long dress and nobody in the room thinks he's a freak. But you know when that boy goes home, he goes home to a six-foot-tall boyfriend.

I tell Pegoña that I need a drink and go for the vodkas. They have this long-ass rectangular table with vodka in every flavor. We're talking raspberry, strawberry, vanilla, chocolate, and still it's all vodka. At first it's Pegoña and me taking one shot of strawberry. I'm not a big drinker and it burns my throat. Pegoña says, "I'm going to the beer table." I nod and tell the guy who has thick blond-dyed hair to give me a real shot, not these tiny-ass tasters.

"Testers all we got, hon," he says, pouring me another.

I taste two more flavors of vodka, but when I get to the chocolate I can't stop. I wouldn't have stopped either if the tester fag hadn't put up his hand and said, "I can't serve you anymore."

"C'mon man. Don't be like that."

"You've had enough."

"I'm fine." I get up and the room doesn't spin. "See?"

"Then go for free hits at another table."

Fine. As I walk away, I realize the room's tilted and my head feels swollen. I try focusing on a group of white dykes at another stand drinking beer, but they keep moving, blurring almost. I've got bags in both hands when Pegoña grabs me by the shoulders like she's my girl or like I'm her girl and I catch that group of dykes laughing at us. Laughing. They ain't pointing. They're just looking at me and Peg and laughing. Maybe I'm imagining it. I drank too much. But no, they are laughing. I can tell when somebody's laughing at me. I pull away from Pegoña.

"What's wrong?" she asks.

"Nothing. I'm tired. You wanna go?"

That's the wrong shit to say. Pegoña lifts my chin. "Ay, pobrecita. ¿Estás cansada?" and she kisses me. Kisses me. I pull my head away and she asks in a loud voice, "What's wrong?"

"Peg, lower your voice."

She narrows her eyes at me. "What's going on?"

"Nothing. I'm just tired."

"Since when have you been too tired to kiss me?"

"Lower your voice."

"I'll talk as loud as I want."

Pegoña turns around and walks away fast. I mean that kinda fast that says "I'm going to fuck you up in a bad way the minute I calm down." She walks past the white dykes and when I pass them, they pucker their lips and make kissing noises and one of them says, "Kiss and make up, shorty."

I throw both bags at them but miss and the shit just goes all over the floor. Who cares? I'm too dizzy to run after Peg, but I can see the top of her head. She heads straight for the bathroom and goes in one of the stalls. The glare of the lights is crazy in there and makes me wince. My head feels bloated. How much did I drink?

Pegoña comes out and washes her hands. She checks her eye makeup, wipes the corner of her lips, and walks past me like she doesn't know me. I follow her. "Peggy, stop walking away from me."

She spins around outside the bathroom door and points her hand to her chest. "You talking to me? I know you ain't talking to me till you ready to explain to me what bug is up your ass."

"Just calm down, OK?"

"This is calm. You ain't seen nothing if you think this is not calm."

"I'm just tired. I drank too much. I just want to go home. Can we do that?"

"I ain't going home with you when you just stand there in public and diss me like that. What was up with that?"

"Baby, look, I didn't mean it that way. I drank too much."

She narrows her eyes at me and I can tell she's thinking that one over. "You're full of shit," she says. "I've seen your ass drunk. This ain't it."

I cover my face and listen—along with every other homo that walks by—as she says, "You haven't wanted to hold my hand since we got here. What the fuck's up with that and you'd drunk nothing then. So how you explain that? And you haven't wanted to be anywhere near me. What's up with that? You think I'm blind?"

She had a point. Bitch had a point. In private I'm always hanging on her. I can never be near her without touching her.

"What's going on, Lou?"

I shrug my shoulders. My mouth still tasted like chocolate and vodka.

"Are you messing around?" she asks. "Do you got another girl that's here?"

"No. No, I'm not cheating."

"Then what is it?"

"I just wanna go home."

I see a look on her face I haven't seen before. I can't tell if she's gonna scream again or what, but she mumbles, "Let's go," and starts walking.

In the car, I kick back in the passenger seat. It feels good to rest my head, which is still feeling like it's full of water. Shit. I hate getting drunk. You just end up wasting a day. Like now. It's six thirty on a Saturday but the night's shot.

And Peg's still angry. I try holding her hand but she puts it on the steering wheel, curling her fingers and acrylics. As we're going through the tunnel, I know she's not going to stay tonight. She just stares at me when we pull up in front of my house. She doesn't say anything.

"Look, baby, I just wasn't feeling well." At this point, it's not a lie. The vodka is fucking with my stomach. "C'mon inside. Let's just forget today."

She looks at the car stereo. "You know I don't do that. I don't go kissing girls in public like that, not even in gay places. That took a lot for me today." She looks at me now. "And you fucked it up."

I lean back, put my foot on the glove compartment. Shit. "I'm sorry. I fucked up but I'm sorry, alright?" When she doesn't say anything, I add, "I just felt weird. I mean didn't you feel weird?"

Her face softens and I think, I'm winning her over to my side. "Peggy, people were looking at us the whole time. It's just a little uncomfortable when you're in a gay place and even the gay people are staring at you."

She doesn't say anything and I think, keep going. She's getting it. "Peg, it was like people were staring and going 'look at that short girl with the tall one.' They were laughing at us. I'm sorry. I just felt weird."

She frowns but nods her head and stares straight ahead. "People were looking at us because you're short and I'm tall." She repeats it then. "Because you're short and I'm tall." She says it a little louder that second time. And then, she repeats it again. "Because you're short and I'm tall." She says it another two times until finally I'm like, "Yes. Will you lower your voice?"

"Get outta my car," she says.

"Peg, don't be like that."

"GET OUT!"

"C'mon, don't—"

She closes her eyes. "You are such a freak."

She's joking. Either she's fucking with me or I drank too much and ain't hearing her right.

"You're a freak, you know that? You are the only person on this fucking planet that gives a shit how short you are. You are so full of yourself to think that your five feet matters to anybody but you. You need to get a life, you know that? And you need to get out of my car."

I jump out of the car. I hated that car anyway. It's an SUV that belongs to her uncle. The shit's so big and high you need a forklift to reach the seat. Fuck it. If that's the way she wants it, then fine. Fuck her.

Outside the car, I stand there, looking at the ground. I start to feel how sick I am. There's that extra saliva in my mouth, the kind that comes before you puke. But I'll be damned if I'm going to throw up now.

I glance up at Peggy and she's wiping her face with the back of her hand. I'm about to reach for the door when she starts up the engine. I stick my hands back in my pockets. Fine. If that's what she wants, fine then.

Puti and the Gay Bandits
of Hunts Point

CHARLES RICE-GONZÁLEZ

Puti sat in the window of her first-floor apartment facing the auto glass shops on Garrison Avenue. The South Bronx streets below her rumbled with people dealing, mothers pushing baby carriages, kids sucking on sweets, men inhaling, bibles thumping, and guys watching girls watching guys watching girls checking out girls with slick faces wearing clothes wrapped around curves and swells. The sun spilled along the street, creating long, skinny shadows stretching the length of the block. The tinkling music from a Mister Softee ice-cream truck offered Puti a trip back to a simpler time when she would forego the vanilla cones with toxically bright sprinkles in favor of performing fellatio on a cherry popsicle because it created a red pucker. BMF, Before Max Factor.

Now, Puti's hair needed tending. Her nails needed a visit to the Salome Ureña Salon. Her eyebrows needed plucking. Her face needed a half hour of undivided attention at the Clinique counter at the Macy's in Parkchester. The housedress she wore belonged to her mother and smelled of chuletas.

But she sat. She watched. The bodies of the shirtless auto glass guys glowed in the sunset. She sighed. She thought if Cuketa and Betty La

China, the Gay Bandits of Hunts Point, could see her they'd gasp, swarm on her, and restore her former glorious glamour. But they weren't with her now. They weren't leaning on her, trying to push their heads out the window to see the newest auto glass guy. They weren't rummaging through her closet, asking to borrow clothes. They weren't incessantly changing the radio station trying, to find a tune to which they could dance. There were no shouts of "nena" or "mija" or "girrrrl" or "miss thing." She turned to look at her room, but no spirits hovered in the dark corners. The old bedsheets had the colors washed out. The dresser was chipped and lopsided. The bare wood floor was flat and dull. She saw her image in her mirror. She mock gasped but genuinely felt frightened by what she had become and turned her attention back to the street. Watching. Life. Pass.

Puti's family moved to Hunts Point in 1973, when most people were leaving and when landlords were burning their buildings to collect insurance. Right outside her window, drug dealers and prostitutes conducted business at all hours of the day and night while police cars rolled by and did nothing. Puti couldn't do anything about the grimy streets or the black smoke pouring out of the trucks rambling down Garrison Avenue, but she tried improving her life in the tenement in which she lived. She complained to the landlord.

"Hey, the lobby is dark."

"There's still light in it."

"But only one light is working and there's supposed to be four, and the steps are cracked and loose; it's not safe."

"Maybe if you were more of a man, instead of a girly boy, you wouldn't worry so much about being safe."

"I can take care of myself, but you can't take care of this lobby." Twelve-year-old Puti put her hands on her slim hips and walked to the landlord, who was old but big and stared up at him. "Gimme the fuckin' bulbs and this girly boy will change them."

The landlord moved closer to Puti and shoved her. "I gotta order the bulbs."

Even when they moved in, the apartment in which Puti lived with her mother and uncle hadn't been painted in years. She fell asleep looking at a chipped, cracked ceiling and dreamed of a better life.

Puti met Betty and Cuketa at Junior High School 125 in the Bronx. That year, all the boys were placed in the home economics cooking class and the girls in wood shop. Back then, Cuketa was Máximo Hernández. He wore thick glasses and bright corduroy pants. Betty La China was Lei Lee Jones, a slight boy who was short for his age and never talked. Puti was Pedro Sánchez, who insisted everyone call him P, and was often called faggot—something he got over after the third grade.

"Today we are making cupcakes from scratch." Mrs. Ellis passed out warped cupcake pans to each section. They all went up to get eggs, butter, sugar, flour, and vanilla. The trio coordinated their efforts, but like all the other boys they made a mess and produced lopsided, partially baked cupcakes. But from recipe to recipe they created a bond and a force field against the abuse hurled at them daily. Sissy! Faggots! ¡Patos! They made a pact that if one was sick she would call the others so that they could stay home too. It was all for one and one for all.

At sixteen years old, the summer after her second year in high school, Puti began her quest to personify glamour. Cuketa and Betty joined her on her crusade. They'd all go to Puti's house to study fashion magazines. They'd steal makeup from their respective mothers and experiment on each other. They spent most of the summer of 1977 perfecting their craft while studying reruns of the first season of *Charlie's Angels*.

"I hate you, Betty." Puti continued to apply honey-plum lipstick to Betty's full lips. "You look so real."

Betty La China was the product of an African American father and a Vietnamese mother. She was the youngest of four kids—three females and Betty. All four children looked like their mother, but Betty had more of her father's richer, creamier, darker skin color and she had wild, curly hair. She was slim and petite.

"Don't hate, Puti. You turning out real fierce too. But it's Cuketa we gotta work on."

"Fuck you both." Cuketa pulled out a blonde wig from her knapsack and placed it over her head. "What do you think? Blondes have more fun, right?" Cuketa was Dominican and Puerto Rican. She had dark copper skin and shoulder-length hair that was considered pelo bueno. She was short, just over five feet. And she learned to skip before she learned to walk.

Puti picked up Cuketa's knapsack. "What else you got in here, nena?"

"My tampons."

"You wish. Let's go shopping."

"You got money?" Cuketa stuffed her mother's blonde wig back into her knapsack.

Puti shook her head. "Leave your mami's wig here, we gonna need the space."

Betty's afro bounced as the three scurried across Garrison Avenue on their way to all the stores on Southern Boulevard. They were wearing men's polyester shirts with wild prints, zipper pants that were snug on the buns with super bell-bottoms, and women's platform sandals, all in fashion in the late 1970s. Puti's hair was tied back in a ponytail and Cuketa had cornrow braids that streaked from the front to the back of her head. The instant they were spotted, the guys on the corners began hurling comments. "Hey patitos, you don't have to run. Nobody's gonna hurt you . . . today."

"Fuck you!" Puti spit in their direction.

Three of the six guys on the corner charged them and quickly caught them. Freddy, who was their age, sixteen, but about a half foot taller, grabbed Puti by the neck and pulled her toward the spot where her spit had landed. "You gonna lick that shit back up. Don't go polluting our neighborhood."

"Leave her alone!" Cuketa and Betty shouted and squirmed while the other two guys held them back.

Freddy shoved Puti to the ground. "Lick it up, faggot." He pushed her face into the spit.

"Yo, Freddy, leave him alone, already," one of the guys from the corner shouted.

Freddy raised his hand as if he were going to punch Puti. Puti stared up at him. The spit and flecks of dirt stuck to her face.

"Get the fuck out of here, you little faggot. You better watch your step."

Freddy waved the two guys across the street back to the corner. Puti got up and wiped her face. She crossed the street to her two friends. "Let's go shopping."

Discotheque 1 Boutique had a big, mirrored ball spinning in the middle of the store, with lots of track lighting to keep the store dim but the clothes lit, and a small wooden platform where customers danced the hustle. The large mirrors throughout the store reflected shiny halter-top dresses, satin blouses, loose silk-blend skirts, and jumper suits with thick, sequined belts.

"Can I help you?" The sales rep had a feathered Farrah Fawcett hairstyle and glitter eye shadow.

"It's my sister's birthday; we just want to look around." Puti picked up a multicolored sequin tube top.

"Let me know if you need help."

The tube top along with halter-top jumpsuits, blouses, and skirts were rolled up and slipped into their knapsacks while two young women did the Latin Hustle to Tavares's "More than a Woman" and the customers cheered.

"Let's go." The sweat in Cuketa's armpits was camouflaged by the print of her shirt.

"I checked out a size 2 miniskirt I want to get first," Betty said as she pulled Cuketa and Puti over to the rear of the store. The security guard watched and walked in their direction.

"Let's go," Cuketa repeated.

"I'm gonna go dance." Puti winked and snapped her fingers. "Then you go get your skirt." She walked to the security guard. "Can anybody dance over there?"

He looked past Puti and nodded.

On the platform, Puti spun around and her bell-bottom pants flared out. She pointed to the sky with her right hand, stared into the store, and pumped her pelvis. A crowd formed around her. In the middle of the song, Cuketa approached the small platform and mouthed, "Let's go." Puti saw Betty heading toward the exit, then bowed to the crowd and hopped off the platform.

The Farrah Fawcett sales clerk congratulated Puti. "Come back and dance any time. Do you hustle?"

Puti nodded.

"Next time we should hustle. There aren't a lot of guy partners to dance with here."

"Next time, linda. I love your hair."

"Thanks."

The trio slipped out of the store. "Now we need shoes." Puti eyed the piles of shoes in the bargain bin outside of Fabco Shoes.

Their last stop was the makeup aisle at Del Sol's Pharmacy. When they reached the checkout counter, Puti purchased a pack of gum, Cuketa bought *People* magazine, and Betty bought a bar of soap for fifty-nine cents. They walked out with fifty dollars in makeup.

"That was so easy!" Betty held up the size 2 miniskirt back in Puti's room.

"Let's try everything on," Puti said. "We have to hem the jumpsuits. I know it."

Over the next several months, they expanded their operations outside Hunts Point and visited department stores. They stole bedsheets and curtains to decorate Puti's room. They kept their parents' shopping bags from Alexander's and would bring them in the stores empty and walk out with them full.

Puti's room was crammed with lace and satin, and her closet bulged with the clothes they swiped. She hung framed posters of Da Vinci's *Mona Lisa*, Van Gogh's *Starry Night*, Picasso's *Guernica*, Munch's *The Scream*, Monet's *Water Lilies*, and Frida Kahlo's *Self-portrait with Thorn Necklace and Hummingbird*. Puti created a plush rug by sewing together fluffy, white bath mats, and she painted the dresser she'd had since childhood a shiny, metallic gold. The trio's favorite piece of furniture was a small chaise lounge Puti found on 33rd Street (on her way home from "shopping" at B. Altman's), carried home on the subway, and re-upholstered with red velvet fabric.

"Welcome to our palacio." Puti outstretched her arms and turned around and around.

"English please, English." Betty snapped her fingers.

"You need to learn Spanish."

"Why don't you just speak English?" Betty curled up on the lounge and sipped a Tab through a slim straw.

"Because, I don't *just* speak English."

"Damn, Puti, you and Betty always gotta be in each other's face, jodiendo, just call it our palace y ya."

"Well, if y'all gonna speak Spanish then translate shit."

"OK, and when we translate you better remember and get with the program, China."

"I am not Chinese."

"Oh, you understood that; you a fast learner. You Chinese are always the smartest in the class."

All through high school, they were weekend divas. They'd dress up and listen to music in Puti's room. When it was time to go home, Betty and Cuketa cleaned up. Puti stayed in her dress and makeup. She walked past the television and sat in the living room with her mother and uncle. She fluffed her hair and smoothed her dress, but they kept their eyes on the screen.

For school, they had to dress like boys, but since it was the late 1970s, they grew their hair long. Puti's and Cuketa's hair was shoulder length and Betty let her hair go natural into a big Angela Davis afro. They wore dashikis and bell-bottoms that came down over their platform shoes.

"I can't wait to turn eighteen so I can take some hormone shots and grow my tetas," Puti said as she stuffed her bra with two small balloons she had filled with warm water, double bagged, and wrapped in a ripped stocking.

"I'm not taking no hormones." Cuketa adjusted Puti's bosom. "I'm a natural woman."

Betty lay across the chaise lounge. "I'm thinking about it, too. I mean this is all fun, but I feel like I want to be a whole woman and get a real man."

Cuketa began brushing Puti's hair. "A whole woman? You getting snipped?"

"Maybe."

"Me too," added Puti. She and Betty high-fived each other.

"You two are crazy. I'm not messing with my shit. Besides, we look real enough." Cuketa pulled Puti's hair back to make a ponytail. "And there ain't a operation to fix our voices."

"True." Puti examined her newly manicured nails. "Oh, what if we took sign language so that way we don't have to talk?"

Betty got up from the bed and stood next to the other two. "I know sign language." She gave them the finger.

"Hey, you two, don't start," chided Cuketa. "I have some news. I'm in love with David Maldonado."

"Cuketa, everybody's in love with him, right, Puti? But he likes pussy. Real pussy. That's why I'm gonna get snipped."

Puti shook her head. "For David Maldonado?"

"Not him, but to get a real man." Betty blew kisses at her reflection in the mirror.

Cuketa stopped brushing Puti's hair a moment and pointed to Betty. "I'm not getting snipped over no man. I'm not getting snipped, period."

"We hear you, Cuketa. Me and Betty La China will do it together." Puti and Betty danced around the room chanting, "We gonna be re-al, we gonna be re-al."

"You two are stupid. Can I change my outfit?" Cuketa pulled a black, strapless gown covered in diamond rhinestones out of Puti's closet.

"Do what you want." Puti looked out the window. "Check it out. Hector took off his shirt. Damn, he looks good."

Cuketa joined her at the window. "Why do we torture ourselves with those assholes? Zip me up."

Betty obliged. "To land a man like that, you gotta be a woman. Full out."

"Then forget men like that. I want a man who wants me as is. How do I look?"

"Cuketa, girl, you look like a beautiful boy in a dress." Betty snapped her fingers. "Be prepared to be alone for the rest of your life, because gay boys want guys, straight guys want women, and nobody wants us."

Puti watched Hector. "We got each other, muchachas."

Betty put an arm around her two friends. "Yes, but even with all the love I have for you two, I still want a man."

Hector notices them and gives them the finger.

They weathered high school, then attended the Wilfred Beauty Academy right after graduation but quit after six weeks because of all the math and biology classes they had to take.

"Well, muchachas, we're all eighteen. It's Saturday night. I think we should go out." Puti sat at the console table that she'd converted into their three-person vanity table. She'd nailed a long, slim mirror, meant for the back of the door, horizontally to the wall above the table. For seats she had three plastic milk crates with square pillows attached to cushion their bottoms.

Betty applied plum-colored eye shadow. "Where would we go?"

"I'm not going out." Cuketa stopped applying makeup and sat on the lounge.

"Then stay here, but I need to be a woman here and out there." Puti pointed out her window.

"I'm with you. We talk about getting men and being fierce, but it's all talk." Betty applied passion-plum lipstick then leaned back to take in her face.

"Those guys fuck with us when we're boys. Imagine if we go out like this."

"Then when?" Puti asked. "I feel like a woman 24/7; I am sick and tired of switching back and forth. We had to for high school, but that's done."

"I can't wait for my mother to see me like this." Betty spun around to show off her miniskirt. "My parents will kill me. They gonna kick me out. I know it."

"Then you come live with me, Cuketa." Puti slipped her arm around Cuketa's shoulder. "My mother would let you. Shit, you practically live here already. Oh, then we can get jobs and get our own apartment." Puti snapped her fingers. "Hairspray. Please."

"Who's gonna hire us?" Cuketa stood up, fluffed Puti's hair, and sprayed Final Net liberally. The fumes from the spray reminded Puti of beauty school.

"Maybe we could get jobs at a salon."

Cuketa slammed the can of hairspray on the console table. "We quit Wilfred's. We don't have certificates."

"Puti, she is so negative. If you don't want to go out, nobody is forcing you. But I am way ready."

Puti and Betty finished dressing up.

"I don't want to stay behind." Cuketa adjusted the dial on the radio to WKTU.

"Great, muchachas, then it's all for one. We're beautiful and badass. Charlie's Angels are hitting Hunts Point."

"But where are we gonna go?" Cuketa sat down at the vanity table and applied eye makeup rapidly.

"The village, I guess. We can't get into clubs without fake IDs." Puti picked up a hair blower and styled Cuketa's hair.

Betty worked on Cuketa's face. "And we need good ones, which cost money. We're beautiful, but broke."

Puti put a barrette on either side of Cuketa's temple. "So as long as walking in the village and hanging out on the pier is free, that's where we headed."

"We gonna take the train?" Cuketa looked at Puti in the mirror.

"How else? Either of you got money for a cab?"

They walked arm in arm out of Puti's building onto Garrison Avenue. Their cloud of musky perfume was an invisible force field. The streetlights had just popped on and the auto glass shops were closed. Freddy and several of the guys were drinking beers on the corner. Freddy shouted, "It's not fucking Halloween, you faggots." And all the guys on the corner laughed. Freddy crushed his empty beer can and tossed it in their direction. It landed with a dull clank in the middle of the street.

They walked across Southern Boulevard. The shops were all closed or closing. They passed Fabco Shoes and Discotheque 1 Boutique and climbed the stairs to the Number 2 train. They rode silently down to the village and even though they relaxed when they were walking down Christopher Street toward the pier, their hearts never stopped pounding against their chests.

When Betty arrived at her apartment, her mother was sitting at the kitchen table sipping tea, hair wrapped in a towel.

"You were out late; don't make it a habit to . . ." Betty's mother laughed.

"What's so funny?"

65

"You look good. I almost didn't recognize you." She continued to laugh.

"I don't see what's funny."

"I'm sorry Lei Lee . . ."

"Betty. My name is Betty."

"OK. Betty." She stopped laughing. "I expected you to be gay, but not this."

"This is who I am, and this is just the start." Betty cried because the pounding of her heart had not stopped all night.

Her mother slid her tea cup across the table. Betty sipped it. She loved the taste of her mother's tea. It was strong and lightly sweet with a hint of lemon. Betty's mother placed her hand on her back. "Your father is gonna have a tough time with this. He gets back in a week. Let's figure out how to let him know."

Betty sipped the tea and her heart slowed to a steady pace. She looked at her lipstick stain on the cup and rested her head on her mother's belly and sobbed quietly.

How'd it go with your parents?" Puti sat in bed with the phone pressed to her ear with her shoulder as she removed the nail polish from her toes.

"They were asleep when I came in so I just went into the bathroom and cleaned everything off. My brother was watching TV, but I slipped past without him seeing me."

"Betty said her mother laughed. Her dad is out of town. But this is it, Cuketa. I'm not wearing men's clothes again."

"I'll admit the village was fun; it's just getting there and coming home that's tough."

"This is my life, so I gotta do it everywhere."

"I hear you, nena. I feel it, too, but it's fucking scary. I don't want to get my ass kicked and my brother has already made my life hell. This might be too much for everybody, I think."

"As far as I'm concerned they need to get used to it. I'm going 'shopping' on Fordham Road tomorrow with Betty. Are you in?"

While they "shopped" on Fordham Road it started to rain, so the trio ducked into a liquor store. A young Latino security guard about twenty-two years old stepped up to Betty. "Hey China, you looking sweet."

Betty smiled and looked away.

"Damn, do you taste as good as you look?"

Betty shrugged.

As the guard flirted, Puti took a bottle of Bacardi that was on a display and slipped it inside the sleeve of her jacket.

By the time the security guard squinted his eyes and knitted his eyebrows to get a closer look, the three had darted out into the rain. They were glad to have followed Puti's advice to not wear heels when they shopped in drag, in case they had to make a run for it.

Safely in Puti's room, they all laughed and unloaded their knapsacks, revealing the booty from their latest venture, and sipped rum and Tabs.

"We're too young for bars, and swiping this rum gave me an idea."

Puti cased out a liquor store on Castle Hill Avenue. It was near the Bruckner Expressway and after 11 p.m. there was not a lot of foot traffic. There were usually two guys who worked behind the bulletproof protective casing, but on Tuesdays and Wednesdays there was only one. The taxi pulled up close to the liquor store and faced the direction they needed to go for the escape. Betty, the most "real" looking of the trio, got out of the cab and entered the store to flirt with the worker.

"I just want a little pint of Bacardi, but I ain't got no money, Poppy. But I can pay you in other ways." When he let her into the bulletproof casing, she left it open and went in the back and kept him busy. Puti and Cuketa came into the store with two large canvas bags each and filled them with top-shelf liquor—Bacardi, Johnny Walker, Hennessy, Tanqueray, and Glenlivet. They brought the rear bottles to the front of the shelf so that the shelves looked stocked. They came and left in less than two minutes. When Betty was done, she accepted the pint from the man she'd just blown and jetted out to meet her cohorts in the cab.

"That was too easy." Puti twisted the cap off a Bacardi bottle and inhaled the rum. "Delicious."

"I was so scared we were gonna get caught." Cuketa looked out the window and watched the Bronx flash by them—streaks of light, a White Castle, an empty school yard, and a gas station.

"We didn't get caught, and Betty here got some dick in the process."

"He was alright. Nervous as hell. I swallowed. He wanted my number. I gave him the phone number to Happy Garden takeout."

Betty and Puti laughed. Cuketa continued to look out the window.

"This should last us a while, right?" Cuketa looked back at her friends. "A month or two, right?"

"I have an idea," Puti said. "Let's have a party. On the roof."

"I love it!"

"But people are gonna drink all of our liquor."

"We'll get more," Puti and Betty said simultaneously.

When the trio got back to Hunts Point with the liquor, they called and invited their friends from the pier to party on the roof. Their friends arrived in cabs with food and mixers. House and disco music played low out of the portable 8-track player. Religious candles lit the ground and the moon lit the sky. Some of the building residents, local roughnecks, and guys from the corner joined the party. Puti was surprised at what free liquor could do.

For the next several years the rooftop parties became a ritual on Saturday summer nights, and it was one of the ways in which the threesome kept good standing in Hunts Point and bought their freedom to be "women" 24/7. A highlight of the party was "Showtime," when guests lip-synched to their favorite songs.

One evening, during the second summer of parties, while salsa music played and couples danced, Freddy sat next to Puti.

"I know you ain't buying this liquor. Where you getting it from?" Freddy took a long drag from his cigarette and blew the smoke into the night air.

"We have our ways."

"I bet. There's been talk about liquor stores being robbed by three chicks."

On the surveillance cameras they looked like women, and most of the men were too embarrassed to report the robbery, instead silently taking the loss of twenty or thirty bottles of booze.

"Talk?" Puti looked over to Betty, who was talking to a guy she'd met in the village.

"Yeah, talk. How much money you takin'?"

"None of your business, nene."

Cuketa was doing a show for the crowd as she lip-synched to Gloria Gaynor's "I Will Survive."

"You ain't takin' money, which is why you gettin' away with it."

"How do you know so much?"

Freddy winked at her. "But you better watch your asses, because word is out, and maybe Betty La China might be better off charging for her blow jobs than risking your asses for a couple of bottles of Bacardi."

"Since when do you give a shit about us?"

"These parties are cool, and regardless you fags are from our 'hood. You one of us, I'm just sayin'. So if you need some added protection, I can help you out." Freddy winked again. "Maybe I could join your team; you might need some muscle."

"We don't need no one else on the team."

Freddy nodded to the music and surveyed the small crowd dancing on the rooftop. "I would hate for the Gay Bandits of Hunts Point to go down without any protection. I could hook you up with a piece for extra protection." Freddy pointed his finger at Puti, as if it were a gun, and fired.

"Gay Bandits of Hunts Point?"

"Gay Bandits is what the police call you. I just added the Hunts Point part because I figured out who you was."

They didn't hit the same store twice unless the ownership changed, and hit only one store a month. They branched out from the Bronx to lower Westchester and Washington Heights.

"I got us a present." Puti reached into her bra and pulled out a Kahr PM9, an automatic 9mm pistol with a Black Diamond finish.

"Is that real?" Betty reached for the gun. "Shit! It is real."

"We may need some protection. We've had some close calls, and the Bandits can't continue to get over on charm and deep throating alone."

Betty aimed the gun out the window. "I'd love to shoot every mother-fucker whoever gave me shit."

"Careful, nena, that shit is loaded. I'll show you both how to use it."

"I ain't touching it," Cuketa said. "I think we do just fine with our charm, and this one gets to suck all the straight dick she wants."

"Excuse me, Miss Thing. I'd like to have a little more choice in the dicks I suck, and most of those guys are disgusting. It would be easier if once they let me past the security gate I just pulled out a gun and said, 'Don't move.'"

"Oooh, you look very Peggy Lipton from Mod Squad." Puti winked.

"I was going for Kate Jackson."

"You two keep playing, but I am not down with that gun." Cuketa sat on the chaise lounge and looked out the window.

Puti put the gun away in the top drawer of her dresser. "OK, Cuketa. You don't have to deal with the gun. Me and Betty will."

"I just don't want anything to happen to any of us."

Puti put her arm around Cuketa. "The gun will help protect us."

Cuketa shoved Puti's arm off her shoulder. "Or get us killed."

"Nobody is gonna get killed. And Betty had the right idea. She gets in. Holds up the guy. We move in and take our shit, but we need to be taking money, too, because our jobs suck."

They had all gotten minimum-wage or off-the-books jobs. Puti was sweeping floors and washing hair at the Salome Ureña Hair Salon on

Hunts Point Avenue, Betty was a floor girl at Discotheque 1 Boutique, and Cuketa worked as a cashier at the fabric store.

"So what?" Cuketa said. "We get some spending money. We swipe our clothes and we get the liquor for free and party as much as we want."

Betty shook her head. "You are so small time, Cuketa."

"Right! We have to think big. So listen up, the meeting of the Gay Bandits of Hunts Point is called to order." Puti opened a box of Prada shoes—black, two-inch heels, tight smooth leather.

Cuketa raced toward them and touched the shoes. "Did you pay?"

"The Yolandita Layaway Plan."

"For real? Tell me. 'Cause security is fierce at Prada. May I?" Cuketa took one shoe from the box and slipped it on her stockinged foot. "I live for Prada."

"Yolandita from Faile Street works at the store in SoHo and she gets a discount. And I gave her fifty dollars a week to hold these for me, and once I had enough . . . Prada!"

Cuketa walked the room, as she did through life, as if she were on a runway. Now, as a young adult, she was always impeccably dressed, dripping in fashion. She made up in style and grace what she lacked in face. Her eyebrows were meticulously plucked, her lipstick always had a frost, and she wore green contact lenses. She believed that blue lenses would be too white girl, and her Puerto Rican grandmother had green eyes, so she was just adding what nature skipped. She dyed her hair blonde because she liked to have fun. Cuketa stood at about six feet tall, lifted by Prada and pride. Cuketa paused and turned. She pointed her foot, kicked up her heels, then sat on the bed and crossed her legs.

"You want to try them on, Betty?" Cuketa slipped one shoe off and offered it.

"No. I think they look too big for my feet. I'm surprised Prada makes shoes in that size. You sure Yolandita didn't buy some knock offs and just put them in a Prada box? You know you can't really trust those straight girls to do shit for us." Betty took a sip of her Amaretto Sour served in a crystal martini glass.

"Perra." Puti barked and took the shoes and put them back in the box.

Betty laughed. "Well, we need hookups at Dior or de la Renta, because I'm not a Prada bitch."

"OK, so we need hookups at the vieja clothes for Betty," Cuketa said.

"English please." Betty slipped off the chaise lounge and walked over to the pitcher of Amaretto Sours.

"Oh, you understand me, don't play. Vieja is old lady. You like those old designers." Cuketa rummaged through Puti's closet.

"Ain't nothing new in there, but 'chachas, we either got to keep up the schemes or we need to improve our cash situation."

Cuketa gave up looking in the closet. "Well, it's a smart hookup, especially in those stores where we can't swipe shit. They see us coming and they focus all the security cameras on us. So we should just find more hookups. At least it's legal."

Betty finished off her drink and set the glass down next to the empty pitcher on Puti's night table. "I say we start taking cash and liquor."

Gay Bandits of Hunts Point Nabbed

Bob Kaptstatter, *New York Daily News*

June 11, 1989

Police apprehended three homosexual men dressed in women's clothing who robbed liquor stores at gunpoint in the Bronx and the surrounding area. They were caught on surveillance cameras, but the masters of disguise changed their looks and evaded the authorities for over ten years. All three lived in the Hunts Point section of the Bronx.

They were stripped of their glamour and their heads were shaved. Lipstick and street clothes were considered a privilege at Rikers Island, and gender reassignment hormones could only be had through the black market—so Puti and Betty went without.

Puti and Cuketa each received a sentence of five years in jail, with possible parole after two years, and Betty got a mandatory ten-year sentence because she was carrying the gun. Cuketa only survived a week.

"Puti! You heard?"

"No. What?"

"They got her. They got our girl." Her eyes were nearly swollen shut from crying. A short fuzz was beginning to grow back on Betty's head, and her prison garb was several sizes too big. "They cut her throat. Those motherfuckers raped her and slashed her throat."

Puti wailed and collapsed. Prison guards rushed over to separate the two Bandits. Cuketa's assassins laughed.

Puti got a knife to protect herself and survived until she was paroled in 1991. She was raped and beaten several times. Her left cheek bone was fractured and caused her left eye to have a permanent squint; several of her teeth were punched out, so she stopped smiling; and a stab wound to her right shoulder severed nerves that left her right arm weak and palsied.

"Take care, Betty."

"Paco takes care of me. He ain't gonna let nothing happen to me. 'Sides, you know how fast time flies in here; I got, what, another eight years."

Puti embraced Betty.

"I'll be cool. My man got my back." Betty smiled sadly.

"Your man?"

"I always wanted a real man, right?"

Paco was the leader of the Bloods, and he made her his "woman." He got her makeup and women's clothes and treated her like a trophy wife and punching bag. She always had to be with him or within view. He would hit her if she talked back to him, if she laughed at any other man's joke without his permission, or if she soiled any of her dresses. She had to make sure his laundry was done, clean his cell, wash him, and sit on the floor next to him whenever he commanded. Each night he fucked her and liked to fall asleep while still being inside her.

"He ain't a man, he's a cabrón."

"English, please." Betty laughed quietly and took Puti's hand. "Maybe I don't want a real man. I'm better off with my girlfriends. I miss Cuketa and I love you, Puti."

"I love you too, you beautiful, crazy China."

"What are you gonna do?"

"I'm thirty. I'm busted." Puti held up her palsied arm. "I'm gonna collect a small disability check and I'm going home to my room, mija." Puti cried through her tight-lipped smile.

Betty wiped away Puti's tears. "I can't wait to go to your room."

"One good thing about not being able to wear makeup is that I can cry and not have my mascara run."

"I get waterproof, girl."

The pillow that cushioned Puti's bony elbows as she sat at her window was covered with dust and soot. She looked at it and thought of washing it. She thought of changing out of her housedress. She thought of washing her hair. She looked back out on the street. There were different cars. Different people passed her window. The sun was lower. The fellas were assembled on the corner to sip Hennessey and "philosophize" about life, pussy, pot, and money. The auto glass shops were closing.

The ice-cream truck had turned the corner, taking away its tinkling music and memories of a simpler time, and the subway, a block away, had delivered a whole new group of neighbors, strangers, and possibilities.

"Puti, you so ugly. Jail done fucked you up," a young queen on her way to work the trucks spit out.

"Hola, Mrs. Einstein, you look great, mama. Ten, five, three . . . ten dollars for the shoes, five for the skirt, and three for the blouse—you look exactly like what you will earn tonight, eighteen dollars." Puti painstakingly unfurled her long, slim arm and snapped her unmanicured fingers.

"Oh, you can count; that must come with age."

"Yes, dear, along with wisdom."

The queen mouthed "fuck you" to Puti and ignored the "dirty faggot puta" remarks from the auto glass guys.

"Hey, nena, don't let those stupid assholes talk to you like that. They gonna just walk all over you."

The queen spun around on her heels and gave Puti the finger.

"Do that to them!"

The young queen kept her finger raised to Puti. She reminded her of Betty, whose prison release was finally coming up.

Now thirty-eight years old, Puti pushed herself against the dirty pillow and strained to get up from the window. Her shoulders were cramped and her legs asleep. She limped across her room and realized she didn't need to pee. Wasn't hungry. Wasn't sleepy. She returned to the window.

"¿Qué pasa?" Her mother came into the room and leaned on Puti to look out the window.

"Ay, mami, get off my back."

"You should clean this room. It smells, and you smell too."

Puti sniffed her underarms and cringed.

The warm water washed over her. She felt her slim hips and ran her hands over her nipples. The hormones she had taken before prison made them expand and swell, and even though her small breasts deflated when she stopped, the nipples remained large. She felt her slim legs and squeezed her spongy dick. She sat in the tub and cradled her weak arm. She thought about Cuketa and Betty. She wanted to melt into a puddle of tears and disappear down the drain.

But Puti got up, wrapping her hair in a towel and herself in a terry-cloth robe. Betty La China would be expecting her. She walked to her room and was going to apply lipstick for the first time since she was arrested ten years before. She stopped. She put the lipstick back in the drawer and wondered what kind of woman she could be if she was a woman who didn't wear makeup.

She swept and mopped her room. Threw out garbage. Cleaned the mirrors and changed the bedsheets. Then she put on a blue dress. No low cuts. No splits. Her shoulders were covered and she liked the way she looked. She brushed her hair and tied it back in a ponytail. She thought she looked like a Pentecostal woman so she put on a pair of black patent leather pumps, a black patent leather purse, and a black felt hat that had a net veil she pulled over her face. She smiled at her reflection and took the van to Rikers Island to pick up Betty La China.

Porcupine Love

TATIANA DE LA TIERRA

if they spy on me they will discover that i am loving you.

I want to fuck her via e-mail but the spam filters at my job won't let me. She suggests that I open another e-mail account, but I am a one-e-mail type of girl. She wants us to go to a chat room but I am not so high-tech.

have been thinking/feeling you very close lately. of you and your body and everything about you.

She is in Auckland, New Zealand, and I am in Buffalo, New York. That's 2 continents, 3 oceans, 8,643 miles, and 31 airplane hours between us. It's been fourteen years since we were together. Fourteen years since I drove her away, out of the country, all the way to those remote slivers of island, New Zealand.

mmm, and i of you. it's amazing after all these years not seeing you and all this distance between us, you still have the same effect on me, on my body, as if you were right next to me.

When I met her she had a shaven head and wore a cunt bead around her neck. I was at a lesbian event at Our Place, a vegetarian restaurant in

75

Miami Beach, where she was the head chef. She worked as a waitress on Wednesday nights, which were reserved for lesbians.

"Wow, a cunt bead!" I said. I had seen them for sale at a womyn's music festival. They were ceramic thumb-sized cunts that looped onto a leather cord.

I was hungry, but she had turned away without asking me what I wanted. She reappeared with a warm plate of food—crunchy brown rice with miso tofu and vegetables, and a potato puff. "This is on me," she said. "No one's ever acknowledged my cunt bead before." Then she winked and went off to do her job.

I kept my eye on her the whole time. Watched her glide from table to table. Noted the feather tattooed on her breastbone, the firm muscles and hairy armpits, the nipples that stretched into the fabric of her tank top, the long legs and the ease with which she moved about. Her quick laughter. How she was all there, in the moment.

I took her home that same day, to my apartment on the beach. We sat on the balcony, overlooking the water, and told each other our life stories. She was from Portland, Oregon, and she had been traveling around the world for years. She would stay and work in a city in the U.S. long enough to save a few thousand dollars. She had lived in Provincetown, Seattle, San Francisco, New Orleans. She spun pizzas, invented soups, framed artwork, brewed coffee, did odd jobs. Then she would travel overseas, to Nepal, Machu Picchu, the Swiss Alps, and walk in the cities and swim in the rivers and hike in the mountains. She was unattached and had few possessions, save for her mountain bike. She lived in an art deco apartment in Miami Beach, where she slept in an old enamel bathtub on top of a wad of wool blankets.

Our throats ached at the end of the night from talking so much.

I served us some Colombian coffee liqueur and pulled her onto my futon bed. We both relaxed in the darkness. She took off her glasses and I began to stroke her whole body, starting with her shaven head, which was rough with invisible stubble. That's when I decided that, tall and lean with a knobby head, she looked like an antenna, and I told her so.

"Antenna, you have to stop traveling now." I said this after I'd taken off all her clothes and while I tugged at her pubic hair. "Because all those trips were just detours. I am your final destination." Her pussy was wet and wanting, and she was weak, I guess, since she agreed on the spot to be mine, my fingers already fucking her, her sex song cooing into my mouth. I explained that if she wanted a Latina lover, she had to do what I said. She giggled. She was so sweet, I remember, so lovable. She was like water in bed, going with the flow, coming like a small and steady current.

I liked her.

She moved in with me the very next day, and was at my side for nearly two years. But it wasn't much fun, not in the long run. We loved each other, but I would suddenly turn cold on her, not quite understanding why. Once, we went to Key West and I barely spoke to her during the whole trip. We went snorkeling together and hovered over coral reefs as schools of tiny fish darted between us. I clenched the snorkel with my teeth and listened to my breath, which was magnified underwater. Antenna, who was just an arm's length away, pointed at a huge golden brown starfish moving at the bottom of the ocean. But I turned my back and kept a distance while I gaped at the sea grasses, mollusks, and sponges nestled in the pink corral reefs. Meanwhile, the sun warmed our backs and the ocean water held us in a salty embrace. A few days later, when we got back to Miami, I had a postcard from her waiting for me in our mailbox. There was a photograph of red coral reefs on the front, and "Wish you were here. Love, your Antenna" on the back.

i'm sorry i was such a bitch to you.

Porcupine love, as my therapist called it, is a symptom of my emotionally fucked-up self. By the time I met Antenita I had a well-established pattern of loving and fucking and then turning cold and mean to my unsuspecting and in-love victims.

On another trip, Antenna and I journeyed to Colombia. At first we stayed with my aunts, where we had to be covert about our relationship. Then we went traveling through the countryside and rented a hotel room. Finally, we would be able to be together any way we wanted. We went horseback riding up a mountain road in the morning and found a spring along the way. There, we took off our clothes and climbed into the warm mineral waters. We talked and held hands for hours, breathing in the pure Andean air and the pungent smell of sulfur, and marveling at the verdant landscape. Then we got back on the horses and found a waterfall, where we dismounted and disrobed again. The cold mountain waters rushed down, pelting our heads and invigorating our bodies. The waters had purified us and jolted us into our senses. Our nerve endings were pulsing. We kissed before getting back on the horses, our tongues thrusting into each other's mouths. I grabbed her crotch—I could hardly control myself—unzipped her jeans, and rammed my fingers into her. She was wet and desperate for my love. "I'm going to fuck you all night," I told her, yelling over the loud, gushing waterfall. She bit my neck and protested when I pulled my hand out. But by evening, I had shifted to my icy self, ruining the warm connection we'd had throughout the day.

Our hotel room had two beds. I took the big bed for myself and made her sleep on the small lumpy mattress on the floor.

i don't remember you as a bitch. what i remember about you are the sweet things. your laugh, the way you made me laugh. the way you loved me, the way you touched me. the delicious food you cooked, how you made me family.

Antenna offered me her love. She held it out to me in her hands and she wanted me to kiss her fingertips and become intoxicated with it. I wanted it at first but then I would feel repulsed. It was nauseating. It was thick and sticky and cloying. A turnoff.

"The coldness is a protection from your feelings," explained my therapist. I had to have her spell it out for me because it was too important an issue and I wasn't able to verbalize it on my own. "You avoid being vulnerable because it scares you." Anger was my mode for masking fear. And porcupine intimacy was the result of my attempts to love and to be loved. I could only get close for so long before the quills were activated. The harder anyone tried to love me, the deeper the quills penetrated, the greater their barbs expanded. The quills weren't deadly to their victims but they were painful and impossible to remove.

I couldn't accept Antenita's love and I wanted it to go away.

Finally, it did. She left me and, after visiting Australia, she ended up in Auckland, for good.

And now, fourteen years later, she is back, electronically at least, wanting me, courting me. I found her on the Internet while looking for European adventure tours. She is the webmaster for a New Zealand site. The photo gallery grabbed my attention—it's full of stunning images: emerald lakes, wide-angle scenic mountains, vibrant forests. I found her as I clicked on the pictures. She was underwater, scuba diving, posing next to a seven-foot snapper and a cluster of prickly sea urchins wedged in the rocks. Smiling. *Is that you?* I sent her an e-mail; we hadn't been in touch for a while.

i still love you. i've never stopped loving you.

How many times can love happen? I've had a lot of love in my life, but I've repelled every bit of it. All my girlfriends, including all the ones who loved me most, eventually stepped off my path and found someone else to love. Meanwhile, I continued with fuck after fuck, love after love, enjoying each one for just so long.

I am not sure that I really want love, even now. Or that I can handle it. Or that I can get it. But I've had years of therapy and I understand why my love life has been dysfunctional. And I have set up an altar for Ochún, the spirit of pleasure. I offer her flowers, oranges, and honey and light yellow candles for her. I wasn't looking for love when I found Antenita on the Internet. I was looking for a vacation spot, a getaway plan, a back-to-nature place for a few weeks.

But I found her. And the memory of her love found me.

Of all the love I repelled, Antenna is possibly my biggest regret. And now my biggest hope. It is foolish, a near impossibility, a sign of insanity— or maybe proof of some sort of faith in the goddesses and the spirits— in Venus, in Aphrodite, in Tlazoltéotl, in Ochún, in Changó.

We are calling to each other across continents, scheming a reunion.

crazy fantasy: what if there was another chance?

New Zealand, 2 continents, 3 oceans, 8,643 miles, and 31 airplane hours away. New Zealand, those two idyllic islands with volcanic craters and rainforests, with dramatic coastlines and cliffs and glaciers, with opalescent pools of water and mountainsides covered with sheep. New Zealand, with an underwater fantasy world, with triplefin and flounder and orange golfball sponges, with crayfish and blue cod and jellyfish, with anemones scattered like daisies in the bottom of the sea. The place where my Antenna found a home. The place that is far away, like love. New Zealand, with black butterflies and water birds and orchids and buttercups. New Zealand, where I will go and eat my own flesh if I have to. New Zealand, where she is wet and writing me, where she is wet and calling me, where she is wet and whistling for me.

i can feel the heat in my ears as it travels from my c u n t all the way up. i feel it strongly when it's going through my abdomen and my chest. then my ears get really warm and my head kind of spins a little.

79

My boss rejects my request for a three-week vacation over the Christmas holidays. I want to go to New Zealand to be with Antenna. I want to quit my job, even though it's a good job by most standards—a secure full-time position with health benefits and a retirement package. But I want out. I want freedom. I want love—the possibility of it, anyway.

I want to let go of everything and fly to New Zealand but I'm scared that I'll fuck everything up for a fantasy. I think I can hop on a plane and see where it takes me. I am checking fares every day. She is calling me every day. We are e-mailing every other moment. The only thing I know for sure is that traveling will deplete my savings.

i'm getting excited now, travel excited, that is :) been the other excited for a while :)

I am the fool ready to plunge off the cliff and see where I land, the soul who will journey with migrating birds across continents and seasons, the traveler who pines to be buried in hot, black volcanic sand, the seeker who will walk barefoot on hot embers and thorns. I am the one who will lie down in the nude and let the acupuncture needles into the center of my heart. I am the wino who will cackle and dance until I drop, the musician who will play for pennies for the joy of it.

I am unhappy at work and I call in sick, pretending that I have a sinus infection. I spend my days masturbating and walking in circles. I imagine all the ways that life can be different. I imagine quitting my job, getting evicted. I imagine a new life. I imagine love. I imagine hiking through the woods with her, finding a lake and swimming in the nude like we used to, and hanging a hammock from the branches of an ancient tree. We will swing in the hammock and she will wrap her limbs around my body, hugging me like a vine. I will fuck her like she hasn't been fucked in fourteen years. I will let her love me, I swear it; I will let her.

There is a little voice that wants to tell me how stupid I am even to consider any of this. I tell the voice that I believe in Antenna, that she is a magical being who stirs up the stars when she walks. That she planted an herb and vegetable garden with me in the mountains of Colombia years ago and the garden is still producing. That she is a lizard, fast and intuitive and transformative. That she is a vegetarian, a computer programmer, an artist, a deep sea diver. That she promised that one day she would make me a water fountain carved with goddesses. That she promised me that if I go to New Zealand she will take me swimming with the dolphins. And I want her stars and artistry and I want the gardens and the goddesses and I want to swim in her waters.

i have a picture of you—of us—up on my wall. i am kissing your neck and you are receiving my kiss. i think we took it in a bathroom stall in bogotá, do you remember? i held my arm out and pointed the camera at us.

The little voice persists. I call my therapist—whom I haven't seen in forever—to set up an emergency session. The recording informs me that she is out of town, on vacation.

I panic. What was I thinking? I am drowning in fantasies. I need help. I need wisdom.

I need to stop masturbating. My clit is becoming a snooze button, going off and waking me up for barely a moment before it makes me sink back into the bed, back into the dreams, back into the wanting. My clit has sedated me and has made me think all these crazy things. My clit has made me a cookie monster, and my cunt is the cookie jar. My clit is always to blame. Once again, as I have been throughout my life, I am a victim of my clit.

I keep my hands off my pussy just long enough to put on some clothes and stumble out of the house. The drunks sitting out on the front porch next door give me mischievous smiles and I realize that they have been the unintended audience for my screaming orgasms.

"Fuckers!" I curse as I stomp off toward Elmwood Avenue.

I lunge into Spot Coffee, order a cappuccino, and pore over the notices on the bulletin boards: "Loving Couple in Search of a Child to Adopt." "Celebrate World Literacy Day." "Democracy is Free Speech: Use it or Lose it." "1-888-MEDITATE." "Don Juan del Corazón de Jesús Seeks Spanish-English Translator for Private Mystic Sessions."

I found it.

I rip the announcement off the board and run home to make the call. Don Juan is a Santería priest from Costa Rica who is traveling throughout the U.S. He is raising funds for his village, which is on the verge of economic catastrophe due to the plummeting trade value of coffee beans. He will be in Buffalo for a day, offering private sessions for $200 an hour. If I translate for him, I can have a session for free. My mind is racing with the cappuccino still fresh in my bloodstream. I'll do it, I tell the man who is coordinating the sessions at Rust Belt Books.

The back room in the bookstore, normally a site for poetry readings and art installations, is set up with an altar for the Orishas. Atop a white cloth is a feast for the gods—fresh fruit and flowers, salted codfish, feathers and candles, coconuts and corn, water and rum. There is a fishbowl in the center. I am watching the tiny fish, marveling at their vivid metallic colors while Don Juan prepares himself for a day of ceremonies. He is a small man, lean and strong, with intense eyes, dressed in white. He sprinkles the space with scented waters and chants in Lucumí.

I sit on a straw mat on the floor. I close my eyes and breathe deeply.

I am in Cuba now. On the terrace of a spirit house in Old Havana, meeting with a Babalao. He is puffing a cigar and the smoke is all around me. I come to inquire about my brother, who is gone from Earth. I am in the Barrio Jesús María, looking up at a balcony on the second floor. Someone throws a rope down with a key dangling at the end. I snatch it, open the door, walk up a hot, dark circular stairwell and into a house ruled by Yemayá. A santera is cleansing me with flower water, speaking to the spirits on my behalf. I am in Buena Vista, nighttime, at a drum ceremony. Spirits are all around me, dancing, laughing, flirting. I am in Matanzas, wearing white. It is dusk and the batá drums are calling me to the spirits. I am dancing. I am outside of myself. I am one with the spirit. It moves into me swiftly, sweetly. I am in bliss.

I am in Miami. A santera is sweeping my body with branches. I am in Miami Beach, whiffing the fresh blood of a dove. It is intoxicating. I am in Bogotá, meeting with a curandera, in an apartment near Seventh Avenue, downtown. She is burning dried herbs and I am cradling a coconut in my hands, praying. I am in Gainesville, Florida, calling the four directions, casting a circle with a group of women. We are all in the nude, bound together by a red cord. It is dark and there is a fire and a goblet with wine being passed around.

I am at Niagara Falls, throwing sacred collares into the rapids. I am in Buffalo, talking to a medium. My brother is with me, she tells me. I have found him.

I am at home in Buffalo. Here is my altar for Ochún. Above the altar is a photograph—I am kissing Antenna on the side of her neck. Her hand is in my hair; she is pulling me into her. Beneath us is a color photograph of two mermaids underwater. They are seducing each other.

i really really miss you now and long to see you.

I am at home, surrounded by Frida Kahlo and ponytail plants and la Virgen de Guadalupe and Audre Lorde and the Chibchas and Shakira and la Patasola and beaded curtains and smoking prayers and San Antonio and the tree of life and pyramids and pussy willows and flamenco dancers and good-luck bamboos and chunks of rose quartz and clusters of amethyst crystals. I am burning sage. I am splashing myself with Florida water. I am offering libations to the spirits. I am hitting the Chinese gong. Clanking on the energy chimes. Clicking the castanets and dancing around the house like a wild woman.

I open my eyes. The cobalt-blue fish is still and seems to be looking at me. Seven candles are burning on the altar. Don Juan has made markings on the floor with white powder. He will cast sixteen shells and divine my future. He will converse with spirit guides in an ancient language and translate their messages for me. He will give me recipes that require specific herbs and sticks.

When I get home I will set up a new e-mail account and an instant messaging system so that I can fuck Antenita electronically, like she wants. I will put a map of New Zealand on Ochún's altar and ask for her blessing and guidance.

I will fuck all I want, and love all I want, and live all I want. Here, and there. So mote it be. Aché.

The Unequivocal Moon

ELÍAS MIGUEL MUÑOZ

You're still working on that?" he asks. "Still," I reply, as I sip the margarita he just made for me. It's my second one already, and he's only been here for an hour. His wife knows that Ray is getting high with me. As usual, I'll give up an evening of writing, he'll give up three hours of sleep. Our occasional tête-à-tête (my word) is always a blast (his word), a place created by and for the hombres amigos that we are. He brings the booze, I provide the entertainment: food, music, and a late-night rerun of *Star Trek: The Next Generation*. It's a show we both enjoy for different reasons; predictably, Ray likes the ships and gadgets, whereas I go for the mind trips.

He tells me that there'll be a full moon in two weeks, on the fifteenth.

"We should make plans," he suggests. "Like the last time . . ."

"Oh, Ray," I say in jest. "The moon is such a hackneyed symbol."

"Hackneyed?" he mispronounces.

"Trite, overused, meaningless."

"It's not meaningless."

"The moon is a parasite," I decree, feeling playful. "It depends on the sun for its light."

"Bullshit!"

"The moon belongs in the Land of the Dead, amigo mío."

"You don't know what you're talking about!"

"Wrong. I know everything. Have you forgotten?"

"Not everything."

"La Luna is a treacherous monster, both a loving mother and a demon."

"Maybe the moon is all those things you say . . ."

"It is."

"But you sure loved it the last time, up there, with me. Didn't you?"

His eyes are retelling the story of one recent night, when up on the roof of my condo we got high on weed and Dos Equis. And we almost kissed.

"It was a full moon," he recalls.

"So beautiful. We toasted to its light."

He's laughing. "And you wanted my body!"

"No, I didn't," I lie.

"You kept touching me, holding me."

"I was cold!"

"Yeah, you wanted some heat, that's for sure."

"Are you drunk, Ray? So soon? How about some quesadillas?"

Ignoring my questions, he decides to lift the coffee table with his legs, as he lounges on the futon, his favorite spot. "Ándale," he boasts, "sit on the table. I can take you!"

"That's OK," I say, unwilling to comply. "I know you could take me."

He lets go of the table and touches my thighs. A timid caress.

"Other men," I tell him, "are afraid of this kind of intimacy."

He smiles. "But we're not like those other men."

"You know what makes us different, Ray?" I'm right on cue.

I imagine he'll say something like . . . the fact that we worship the moon. But his response doesn't surprise me.

"The size of our dicks," he replies.

I seize the opportunity: "Let's compare."

Ray sticks his hand in his Bermuda shorts and fondles himself. "Like the baseball players," he says. "They shift their dicks around all the time . . ."

I make an effort to stay cool, not to let my ganas—longing, hunger—show: "Their pants are too tight." And I go on, nonchalant, "Mine is seven point five."

"Seven point five? What kind of a size is that?"

"You know what I mean. Seven and a half. How about yourself?"

"I've got a big verga. And I don't need no comparison to prove it."

"Who cares, anyway."

Ray's not deterred by my indifference; he can tell I'm faking it.

"You know, last weekend," he announces, "on our way to Big Bear Lake, Luisa sucked me off while I drove. For two whole hours! You know she gets wet just looking at my dick?"

He looks at me, between my legs where my hand is moving back and forth. I'm sitting on the wicker chair. Ray stares, "Is that your boner, what I'm seeing?"

I must disappoint him: "No. It's my thumb."

"Big thumb."

"You're drunk."

"Is your verga bigger than your thumb?"

"I told you my size already."

"I forgot."

"No more margaritas for you."

"Come here." He grabs my wrist, pulls me to him. I trip and fall on his lap. He's fondling himself again. "You can help." He seems annoyed by my inertia. "Get into it," he orders me.

It's my turn for some teasing: "What do you mean get into it, Ray? You mean grab your big brown verga and suck on it? Suck on it hard and hungry for two hours?"

"Maybe just one . . ."

"Sorry, querido. I'm not your Luisa."

I pull away, walk to the kitchen. He follows me and touches my ass, rubs himself against me. "You like the fact that I'm strong, don't you?" he says. "You dig my muscles."

I should tell him that I find his strength—or, rather, his fixation with it—boring. But I won't. Instead, I'll let him impress me. "Yeah, I'd say you're very well built."

"Hit my arm," he demands. "You'll see that it's like hitting a wall."

I hit him. He reacts with a wrestling maneuver, swiftly, pulling my right arm behind my body, twisting it, and placing his right leg between my legs. I can't move; my left hand is free, though, and I use it. I touch his left thigh and his buns.

"What do you think?" he asks.

"Yeah, you've got muscles of steel, Ray."

"Do they turn you on?"

"Yes. Now let go of me."

"Not yet . . ."

"Now!"

He does as I say. I'm free of him. But I didn't want him to let go, not really. In fact, tonight I'm envisioning a perfect fantasy, a story without a happy ending for Ray, because it could obliterate his wife and his domestic bliss. It must happen at the stroke of twelve, under the moonlight, when and where I can become who I want to be for him . . .

He takes me. I fight back, but he's stronger. I am, after all, his delicate mujer, the frail Caribbean queen of his Aztlán kingdom. As he invades me—ay, his thrusts!—I realize that the fantasy has gone beyond its truest form, that a man who feels this pain will never fear the moon.

It's past midnight. We're sprawled on the futon, having just watched a first-season episode of *The Next Generation*. Ray seems satisfied, relaxed, filled with booze and quesadillas.

He turns to me: "I always feel like a king here."

I react, again on cue: "Indeed, Your Highness, under this humble roof you're wanted and loved and well fed by your faithful servant." He smiles, stares at the blank TV screen.

His servant, not his queen—she's waiting for him elsewhere. No, I'm something else. His courtier? The court's buffoon? I've let myself be pushed, I've played weak. No: I am the scribe. My strength—*he* has decided it—lies in the mind. Mine is the power of words.

The king brings out a binder he carries with him everywhere. This multilayered notebook organizes his life. *Work*: he's a land surveyor for the Colina Company. *Build shelves in garage*: he owns a brand new tract house. *Fix truck*: he's a part-time mechanic. *Dinner out*: at Denny's or Chili's. *Movie*: on cable. *Mass*: he's true to his Catholic roots.

Every eight or ten pages there's a short vocabulary list, with many entries culled from our encounters. Tonight Ray enters *unequivocal*, a word Captain Picard used in the episode we just watched, about desertion and the escalating threat of war. The captain, Ray's hero, pronounced it in his customary way—male essence and wisdom teleported to us from a distant future.

"What does it mean?" Ray asks. "Do you know?"

"Yes, I do. When something—a word, a thought, an idea—is unequivocal, it has only one possible meaning or interpretation. It is clear and unambiguous, to the point. Absolute."

He tries to use the word but fails. Too drunk. I provide an example, "Your masculinity is unequivocal," and he nods in agreement. Now I should challenge him, wrestle with him, and immobilize him: What is the absolute meaning of your masculinity, Ray? What is so clear, so unambiguous, about your desire? How does your manliness fit into our moon ritual?

Hard questions. Not a fair match. "It's getting late," I tell him.

He scrambles to his feet, heads for the door. "Buenas noches," he mumbles.

In minutes he'll be gone, and I'll beat off, imagining the love he'll make to his wife, the sex we could've had, our long hour . . . Then I'll tell myself that this, whatever it is, has to end. For good. Because I'm supposed to be older and wiser. Time to go again, it seems. I know I'll never grow roots in this unreal city. Colina, a place where Ray stands out because he has a dark Mexican face, and where I sort of fit in because I'm a white Cuban American.

He helped build many areas of this Orange County town and was tempted by its beauty and safety. So he left his native Santa Ana and poured his savings into a down payment. Ray can barely afford the mortgage, but he wants to belong here. In his impeccable home on a verdant hill, he has a full-time housewife. Ray likes being the bread-winner, the ship's captain. He'll stay in Colina and have children, enjoy BBQ grills on Sundays, picnics at Colina Lake, soccer games with his boys at Verde Hill Park. And I'll renounce our friendship because it must be done.

"There'll be a luna llena on the fifteenth," he reminds me.

"I'm sick of the moon, Ray."

"Yeah. But you'll be here all the same, waiting for me."

"Ray," I say as I hug him. "What you have with Luisa . . . is it important to you?"

"The most important thing in my life."

"You'd never want to hurt her . . ."

"What are you telling me?"

"I think you know."

"We haven't done anything bad," he says like a niñito caught in the act.

"Not yet," observes the old sage who can see the future.

Ray walks out the door, turns to me. "I always feel great when I'm with you," he admits. "There's nothing wrong with wanting to feel that way."

"I agree."

"So you don't want me to come back?"

"No, I don't. Not until the next full moon, anyway."

Dear Rodney

EMANUEL XAVIER

This summer promises to be our most adventurous. My available sister of sin, Leo, and I will be away just about every weekend and even had to pencil in our movie schedules. God forbid I actually start seriously dating anyone. They'll only get dinner, rentals, and walks in the park from me—at least until the fall. And we all know how cold it gets in New York during the winter. I have met someone who lives just a few blocks away. It's much sweeter than phone conversations with guys who live in Kentucky. It will be nice to ask questions like "Would you like to meet up for lunch or a stroll in the neighborhood?" rather than "What's the weather like down there?" However, we did meet on Adam4Adam.com, and he lured me with his cock pic. At least I know we are sexually compatible and I know he is also a Madonna fan from the framed photographs throughout his apartment. He also happens to be a yoga instructor. This is definitely one of the pros of gentrification. I used to have to travel into the city to meet hotties like this.

Of course, there was the tall blond who was into a lot of foreplay and the whole daddy-son role-playing. He really enjoyed spanking me and cuddling. He also asked a lot of questions about my first time. It was only weird when he asked me to imagine myself as a ten-year-old boy. Then it got a little creepy and I told him I had to be up early the next morning for school. He finally got his dick in me, molested me or whatever, and I got him to leave. In the end, it was kind of hot. However, I think I scared him off afterward. When he asked me, "Do you know what bad boys get?" I looked at him blankly. He then proceeded to spank me on the ass really hard. I then asked, "Do you know what bad daddies get?" He pondered the question for a minute before I answered it for him: "Five to ten years!"

The next day, I found out my ex-boyfriend, a police sergeant, was arrested for allegedly having sex with a now-twelve-year-old boy over the course of five years. His arrest happened after we broke up so I suppose now I know why it didn't work out between us. The whole time we were dating, I was thinking that as a police officer he couldn't imagine being seriously involved with a former drug dealer and hustler. Turns out it was because he may have been a pedophile.

So we went back to Hillside Campgrounds for Memorial Day weekend. As the person who introduced us to camping, you were totally missed. Everyone asked about you, to which we replied, "He's away with family this weekend." The usual hedonism of men and alcohol ensued. Leo blacked out and doesn't remember how we almost got eighty-sixed from the campgrounds after he decided to whip out his dick and get a blow job in the middle of the strip by some guy worth completely forgetting. The next evening, we crashed Cumalot's "Rocky Horror Picture Show" party by showing up with hoodies and pretending we ended up at the wrong party. When asked, our response was cued as, "I thought this was the 'Rocky' party!" I went as "El Rocky," Leo went as "Rocky Road," and we christened Mark "Rocky Feather-boa." We were a subtle hit among all the sweet transvestites and got drinks poured into our mouths, as we couldn't hold any cups with those giant boxing gloves. My package was quite revealing in those boxing shorts and, as expected, I got so laid.

After kicking Doug (or whatever his name was) out of my tent, that's when the revelry truly began. I ventured back to Rec Hall by the bonfire to meet up with the other Rockys, only to get totally trashed and taken advantage of by a guy you messed around with and envisioned a life together with before finally meeting Dave and settling down for a while. Okay, so I was an easy target after several rounds of Peach Schnapps (aka the devil's nectar) offered by some short daddy trying to lure us back to his hotel about half an hour away for a "party" with him and his friends. I probably should have given into being gangbanged if only to avoid running into Mikey at the end of the night. Mikey has always hit

90

on me, and his Richard Gere looks made a pussy out of me—literally. At least now I know why you liked him so much. Of course, the next morning I felt like the complete slut that I am (and my ass hurt!). I left you several messages and thank God we eventually spoke and we were still cool after a few tears and laughter. I guess, in the end, both Leo and I had regrets from that weekend. Our most valuable lesson here—stick to the vodka!

The following week we schemed our way out to San Francisco and stayed at the notorious and classy Beck's Motor Lodge in the Castro District. The first night out I picked up a young aspiring daddy bear that I had lots of fun with while Leo ended up with an Adam4Adam piece he ran into at Badlands. That bitch ended up in Twin Peaks! Apparently, that piece was real good because Leo also ended up back at Twin Peaks the following night. This was after we picked up Enzo, a hot daddy off the streets on our way to the Eagle. He was visiting from L.A. Needless to say, we never made it to the leather bar, and I proved my hospitality by providing him with a comfortable bed at Beck's Motor Lodge to spend the night. We didn't have sex, only cuddled, at his request. Either he thought he had found true love or he was incredibly drunk. As soon as he left in the morning, I went online and invited a hot, hairy, and horny Arab/Italian daddy to come over and complete the unfinished business. On the third night, after Leo was back from his misadventures at Twin Peaks, we went to an underwear party at 404, where I picked up a delicious young Mexican who turned me out back at the ho-tel.

However, it was on our last night that we broke all records. Leo met the man of his dreams (or of his trip to San Francisco) online and kicked me out of the hotel to enjoy a few hours of lovemaking (or great sex). Alone on the streets of the Castro, I met a hot, young Latino hustler carrying around a paper bag full of crystal meth that he had decided not to deliver and enjoy instead. Not into drug addicts and afraid he was only after my olive-green Castro sweater (which I bought on sale at Walgreens because it was quite chilly out there, and he seemingly had his eye on it), we simply made out after I told him I was meeting my friend in a few. I wasn't getting murdered because he wasn't delivering the goods. I've seen that movie! Later, when Leo was done exploring the great insanity of temporary romance, he joined me at 404, where I was already sticking my tongue down a local comedian's throat. As soon as Leo arrived, it was my turn at the hotel room and we agreed to meet later at Badlands after I entertained this funnyman. I actually tried plunging him, only to be politely informed he was more of a top and couldn't take my cock. The nerve! The irony! I popped a Listerine strip in my mouth, laughed at the hilarity of it all, and spread wide.

By the time I made it to Badlands to meet up with Leo, he was already working his way into an orgy. Some hot Latin guy, who also happened to be staying at Beck's Motor Lodge, invited him back for a private party along with a hot young white boy (Leo's favorite!) and a muscle-bound Asian guy. My impression (or inner desire) was that I was also invited to join, but Leo and I have never had sex in front of one another and we weren't going to start now. Well, except for running into each other in the back of dark rooms and that one time I arrived too early to that hotel room in New Orleans. In any case, it was Leo's party and, though I did try to crash along with a friend of ours we ran into from Philly, I simply went back to our hotel room and had sex with the neighbor next door as his boyfriend slept naked in bed on the other side of the wall. After all, who am I to deny anyone some sugar?

Then, it was off to Philly—the city of brotherly love, Woody's, and 2 a.m. barbecue chicken pizza. Our friend, Roosevelt, joined in on this leg of the tour. However, on our first night, after I had already had sex with and kicked out some drunken papi chulo, it was Roosevelt's leg trying to take a tour of my body. Leo messed around with some guy he met at the pizza shop on what was supposed to be my bed and then fell asleep on it. I was left to share a bed with Roosevelt, who, in the middle of the night, dreamed I was some piece and proceeded to molest me until I woke up and giggled my way over to Leo. The following evening, Leo left us alone at the hotel room to hook up with a hot piece of Adam4Adam ass. My cell phone went off and it was him asking that we go to the window of our sixteenth-floor room and look at the top floor of the building directly across from Woody's. Well, wouldn't you know it? There he was waving to us like Evita from the balcony of the Casa Rosada after fucking Juan Perón. It was a building-to-building thumbs-up. A few hours later, we sweated our way through a jam-packed Woody's (it was Philadelphia Pride weekend) and, feeling hot and horny (my libido is wicked!), I broke down and made my way to the nearest sex club. I whetted my appetite with a sweet white daddy before getting fucked in the newly discovered "Glory Lane" on the third floor by a hot Latino go-go dancer. My only intention was to blow him, but he pulled out a condom. It was dark enough that I wasn't intimidated by everyone watching, and he gently positioned me bent over backward before thrusting into me like a piñata.

After resting up for a while (you do get six hours in a room), it was the juicy, well-built, tattooed Asian guy who dropped his towel for me and dispelled certain rumors and my own experiences with certain Asian men. It was a really nice size, and I simply had to make up for any time his parents might have spent in a refugee camp. I've single-handedly made up for all of our country's past mistakes. That night, I was like an ambassador of piece. Before I left, I messed around with another veteran of war and ended the night with a young black stud, which reinforced certain rumors and my own experiences with black men. The people of color movement had never been so empowered. I was a total whore that night but it was worth the $30, of which I would have spent $10 on breakfast at 2 a.m. My kind of hunger provided me with a full meal.

This is where the plot twist comes in and this letter comes to a close. About two weeks later, Leo and I meet up with our mutual friend Grant in Denver for Denver Pride (at this point we're all Pride-ed out). He comes to meet us at the airport because his other friends are arriving a bit later from Albuquerque. After acclimating ourselves to the surroundings and going through some travel guides during our wait, we had already determined that there wasn't much to do in this town. Grant had built it up to be the one city in the United States where Leo would finally meet his ultimate boy toy and I would finally meet the daddy of my dreams. Well, fuck me silly!

His friends finally made it after a slight delay, and we went over to say hi. Henry and I had already met at the Monster the same night Leo met Grant. It was Thanksgiving and Leo and I had laughed all the way home at the fact that Grant was a Native American Indian. As a matter of fact, I recall we had just come back from a previous trip to Philly before that ill-fated night and joked about how Leo should have bought that Pilgrim hat at the Betsy Ross museum to wear for his first dinner date with Grant. Leave it to him to pick up an American Indian on Thanksgiving. But I digress!

Now, back to that airport in Denver. After saying hi to Henry, we went over to meet the last member of our group for the weekend. He was at the conveyor belt waiting for his luggage. From the back, all I noted was a tall, bald, white boy. When he turned around to say hello to us, one look into his bright blue eyes and my world completely fell apart. Chris seemed rather shy and only made eye contact with me while shaking my hand. It was a strong handshake and I swear the earth moved when we came into contact. I was like, "Oh my God!" You could ask Leo. Slutty me was all over him like a cat in heat. At that point, I was only thinking about how he was going to be my piece for the weekend. I even clearly remember telling Leo, "Back up, bitch! He's mine!" after Grant revealed Chris preferred to be a top in bed. He was beautiful, and in my mind, I was already working my way into his room back at the hotel.

Apparently, the feeling was very mutual. Before getting to the hotel, we met up for lunch and, instead of sitting next to him, I sat across from him to stare into his gorgeous face. He sniffed his armpits jokingly to make sure he didn't smell bad, without knowing I was rumored to have an armpit fetish (I don't, but I joke around enough about this to invite the speculation). There was some casual small talk and apparent side notes that revealed a budding flirtation between us. By the time we checked into our hotel room, I already knew I wanted him and he felt the same. We were supposed to meet back at his room (just down the hall from us, at the end, because he had a reputation for being noisy) for drinks.

Grant had already set it up so that we both knew we were into each other and it was just a matter of time before everybody slowly made their exits and the two of us were left alone. I had been forewarned that Chris was just as much of a slut as I was. So I pretended to lag behind to unplug the iPod (seductively, of course!) and bring it back to our room. Once it was out of the socket, I fumbled my way over to Chris, who was sitting in bed staring back at me, almost begging me to stay. Without any hesitation, I simply stopped and kissed him. Tramp! It wasn't long before we were naked in his bed and having the most amazing sex, like ever!

I did make one stupid comment afterward that almost killed the moment, about how I didn't want to be cock-blocking him for the rest of the weekend. I had initially planned to be a complete whore for this trip and even had a pre-printed discount coupon for the local bathhouse (which I gladly passed on to Grant). Chris and I supposedly both had a penchant for traveling to other cities and falling in love, so I didn't want to keep him from anything or anyone. For me, there was Joe in San Antonio, Greg in Philly, Jose in Chicago, Ty in Louisville, and, most recently, Enzo from L.A. None of this kept us from pursuing this romance, and Leo got to enjoy the hotel room all to himself without the need for planning our schedules for hotel-room sexual trysts. I spent that entire Denver trip with Chris. We had the best sex every single night, held hands, and kissed in front of everybody and fell in love with one another during the course of one weekend vacation.

We've talked every day on the phone several times throughout the course of the day since then, written and texted each other, et cetera. He even sent me flowers and a specially made photo book with pics from our trip. He's coming to New York to spend several days with me in August and I hope to visit him in Albuquerque sometime this fall/winter. He's talked about moving from New Mexico and we've joked about getting him a job out here in New York. This all sounds absolutely fuckin' crazy, I know, but Rod—I think I really love him! I've been such a whore (and he knows this!) (and he has too!), but I think he may be *The One*. He makes me feel like no other guy has in such a very long time, and I can't stop thinking about him. It's sick, I know! How could this happen? I haven't even made it through the entire summer yet. I wasn't planning on this, but it only comes to prove that God is truly a sick bastard! I even feel bad saying that, like God exists or something and is smiling down on us. WTF?

I guess this seems like a good place to end this letter, manifesto, revelation, gospel, or whatever this is. I know you wanted to hear about an orgy or a bukkake or some other wild adventure, but this how it ends, my friend. The man-whore gets married and lives happily ever after with the man-whore of his dreams. The boy meets his daddy and we'll see how far we go before I have to write you another letter.

Your sister-of-sin,
Manny

P.S. You will be wearing taffeta to the wedding, bitch!

This Desire for Queer Survival

HORACIO N. ROQUE RAMÍREZ

These high-power street lamps can't burn out the gang-infested walls. Black spray paint letters fuse into unlit alleys. Parked cars are tombstones. The air is sewer-scented. I've been here before, time after time, told my mother where our old house would be buried, near the call box, under the fast lane. She knows when I ramble it's the virus. She questions me about what my doctor has said, ignores my response when I say, I'm just lonely.

Gil Cuadros

"My Aztlan: White Place"

Monday, 10:46 p.m. The taste of loneliness is the taste of toothpaste as I brush before bed on another Monday night. One more week has passed and my bed remains empty. Surely some colossal failure of connection has occurred that I should be so lonely. Loneliness is a motherfucker and, as Seal noted, a killer. We all know this and will endure much to keep it on the other side of the door. We will bide in our work and manias, bury our faces in the chests of inadequate lovers, or pretend our children need us more than we need them. Most anything is preferable to the crisp reflection in that mirror of loneliness.

Jaime Cortez

"Sun to Sun"

Almost Back in the Family Nest:
Spring 2001

I am one of those lucky gay men with a family most open to his life. My parents were probably ready to receive the official news about my gay self years before I came out to them, only months before completing my doctoral dissertation in 2001. I was thirty-one years old. They were more ready than I was, for sure. Apprehensive me, who had organized and written for years about gay Latino life and history, more public about my erotic life to hundreds of strangers than to them. Culture was too heavyweight an animal for me then, whether I wanted to acknowledge it or not. Then again, maybe I was just chicken shit about it all, good ol' male son privilege at work, not to show weakness, difference, outsideness. Or maybe it was the fact that I was soon to return to the nest in Los Angeles with a very queer PhD in hand, that academic privilege bestowed upon the family clan too obvious for its details and my desires to remain unknown to them. The unemotional conversation we had that morning when I finally confided almost in passing was reassuring, uneventful really, facts formalized about what they already knew for so long. But it was finally out, and that silly secret died in those moments of loving support and reassurances around the dining room table. There were no regrets about the disclosure, our lives that much closer after the telling. It took me ten years to finally have the courage to spell out for them in Spanish what I had been trying to make sense of openly in several cities, away from the family unit. It was time to begin returning home.

My parents began to tell me that morning that in El Salvador, lesbians, gays, and male-to-female transgenders—*vestidas*—were all around them. Years before I was born in 1969, and independent of one another, my mother and my father dissuaded folks in their town from harassing their queer kin. My parents were against what we now call homophobia long before any homosexual or gay movement, in this country or anywhere else. So for me, it's never been a question whether my family will accept me or not, their one and only son, the last child, the professional intellectual, the gay one. It's been more about the ability for any one of us in this interdependent family unit to survive without one another. Our economic, immigrant, and emotional histories are all intertwined in this thing we call familia. And thus the need to begin to try to end my silences.

Queer Latino Revelations:
Summer 2001

In those same months when I convinced myself that it was time for me to announce my queer self to my parents, I also secured a postdoctoral fellowship. In that oh-so-exaggerated academic culture of graduate school, even short-term financial security matters, especially when well-established senior faculty members try to convince us not to worry about the job market. With only weeks approaching the completion of my dissertation, I take a trip to sunny San José. I spend some time with a close friend and academic mentor. But I also get to catch up finally, after months of e-mails and gay Latino promises not to let our work get in the way of our lives, with a close, younger, gay Chicano friend, one of her star students.

For reasons that probably have to do with the way we each intensely live our lives, always juggling projects and commitments, our lunch date is not too long. But he slows down enough to do some telling of his own. Over lunch, he reveals to me that he recently has seroconverted, that he has become HIV positive. He seems calm about it, as a matter of fact. I am still not in the practice of hearing these words from close friends. Of the gay Latino immigrant posse that nurtured me when I began to look into the mirror of my homo-self in Los Angeles in 1991, only one of us has uttered these words to any other as far as I know. At age thirty-seven, I am still somewhat deaf to these words, more from circumstance than by choice, mostly by the fact that it's still yet another overwhelming silence in many of our lives. I know it's tough to speak this truth to one another, but it's not altogether easy to hear it either.

As I hear his words while we sit on the sunny cemented surfaces of gentrified San José, I wonder how he's reacting to this critical piece of news about his body and his life. I know well what he's like: motivated, driven, cute, fully bilingual, a writer, a leader, a doer, and a thinker.

But now, after hearing his confession, I lean back against my own historical self, still sitting, quietly overwhelmed with the news. I am pissed at what's happening to this young Latino queer and too many others like him. There are equal feelings of anger, guilt, and disappoint-ment, about him and about me. I sometimes feel responsible for not doing enough about the protection of others, as if I could, as tough as it is to secure my own. As we continue to talk about his seroconversion, he seems just as focused as ever, with determination to do his own graduate work as planned, to leave the family that was anything but nurturing once his sexuality was revealed, Latino religious intolerance standing firm. He decides to move on with his life, virus and all. Becoming HIV positive turns out to be just another queer challenge at his still young age, as he coordinates the plans for another stage of his life.

I can't help but think at that moment that his survival is mine, and that my survival is his.

He is barely in his early twenties; I am thirty-one. It's summer 2001.

Queer Losses:
Lionel, Spring 2002

I have just arrived at the University of California President's *Postdoctoral Fellows* retreat in gorgeous Lake Arrowhead, a meeting of up-and-coming academic minds of sorts. I am part of the new batch of hopeful intellectuals committed to the business of educational justice and more equitable racial, ethnic, and gender representation, and I have been invited to join because of the promise of my work. I am both apprehensive and excited about my first retreat with this group, because I get to meet Lionel Cantú Jr., fast-rising Chicano joto sociologist who's publishing like a mad man on gay Mexican immigrants. I am quite sure he had to have played some role in my getting to share some of the UC glory and funds to carry my own queer Latino visions further.

The well-behaved young scholar in me approaches him first but cautiously, Lionel my elder only by a few years. He's engaged in a lively conversation with several people around his table who are obviously just loving his company and his wit. I take this opportunity also to apologize to him again for not having been able to present at a conference he organized at his home campus in Santa Cruz; I remind him that one of my sisters' life-threatening cerebral hemorrhage kept me focused on family and away from all academic commitments then. He tells me not to worry, and shares his own story of a "little hemorrhage" he had, an eye hemorrhage his doctor detected, likely blood-pressure related. "God," I say, "you gotta be careful—so much work." He just smiles.

Lionel and I hit it off during those three days of intellectual support, a queer mentoring relationship beginning to take place: he, a UC professor, articles and books in progress, very popular as a teacher, and even with a partner living with him; me, aiming for all of that, farther behind, especially on the partner bit. Over coffee or wine we talk about strategies of all kinds. He tells me, for example, of the hilarious "anonymous" gay

Internet chat-room encounter he had once with someone who ended up being a well-established scholar and the tricky situation he found himself in then as the younger, more vulnerable one. He knew that once the electronic conversation had gotten into real-life details, including respective professional positions, chatting with his "buddy" became potentially risky. We agreed that the academic community can be a tricky thing, especially when it's mixed with the queer cyber kind.

Several weeks after the retreat, I turn on my laptop one early morning at my parents' home to read e-mail. I prioritize those related to work, ignore hundreds of others. In one of the first messages I open, Lionel's book coediting partner, Eithne, writes in the message subject heading: "deeply regret to inform." I am confused, without first reading the actual body of the message, because they had both told me days before over e-mail that they liked my essay contribution to their book, so it could not be about that. But "regret to inform"? Eithne writes to the other book contributors and me that Lionel died on Sunday, May 26, from cardiac arrest following a ruptured intestine. I just scream at the computer screen: "FUCK!" "This fucking sucks!" "No!" Selfishly, I am angry that I have one less connection in the world. I also think of Lionel's book that I could not wait to read, and all the gay Mexican immigrants he interviewed in Southern California. The ethical oral historian in me also kicks in with a vengeance. Could we get Lionel's interviewees together to let them know what happened? Would they care to know? I also think of Lionel's immigrant partner, Hernando, with no family in the U.S., whom I don't know at all, but write him a long card anyway, explaining to him what Lionel meant for me even in only the few weeks I knew him. I also let my parents know of his passing, and the important work he was doing. They feel bad and seem to understand exactly why this death is quite tragic for me. That night, tired from working all day and receiving the news of Lionel's death, I write in my journal before watching *ER*. I don't want the academic game to kill me. And when I am gone, I don't want my name to ring the loudest in an institution.

Around the time of Lionel's death, I am also monitoring and studying the coverage of queer culture in Spanish-language news media. Another project, yes, as if I don't have enough to do already: more stress, more work, and more lives to theorize about. I do it mainly because postdocs, as glorious as they are, just don't pay enough. So I successfully rent my bilingual gay Salvadoran academic brain and soul for several months to track and write about queers in print and television media in Spanish.

The work is tedious, often boring and predictable, rarely interesting. But as I watch and read more and more, it becomes painful and sad to realize, after digesting hundreds of hours of televised, pre-packaged Latino culture—my culture—that heteronormativity is deep. It's not the outright homophobia that freaks me out, the stuff that's actually easy to expose. It's the active writing and imaging out of me and my body and my needs that hurt. Watching so much, as if I didn't already know this, hits me, yet another reminder of queer loneliness at work. Damn, this project is gonna kill me, I tell myself, if I don't start to laugh about it. Again, I recommit myself, this time to being with my Central American queer writing gang on Monday nights, to continue hanging out and creating visions of our lives. Because I do want to stay alive; even in this heterosexual society I have to analyze and feel day in and day out. It's so easy to forget the basics of survival sometimes.

War Cries and Other Battles:
Winter 2003

It's early March, and the imperialist drums of war are getting louder. Because I am overworked and overstressed, and I have promised myself to get my academic work done and stay healthy by going swimming three times a week, I choose not to get actively involved in most of the antiwar movement. It's a decision full of conflict for a Salvadoran immigrant whose life story is all about the U.S. empire across the Americas. I try to resolve my internal conflict of noninvolvement by signing e-mail petitions as much as I can. But that's all I do. And yet, as much distance as I try to put between myself and the reality of living in the empire, our international catastrophe hits me close very often.

One early morning, with the first cup of coffee in my hands, it's an e-mail that fucks me up—again. This time, it's one of the regular e-mail pieces forwarded by Andrés Duque, the very active gay colombiano in the East Coast who keeps us informed of queer Latino lives and deaths here and in America Latina. The long note, an article from the gay *Washington Blade* about the rift among queer groups about the U.S. invasion of Iraq, makes me scream. I read about New York's Audre Lorde project taking the lead to condemn the war, a loud queer cry others join, many of color: The National Center for Lesbian Rights, Jews against the Occupation, *LATITUD o*—"o Latitude," the Ecuadorian gay organization with the coolest name—and others. Many others protest as well, actually dozens, but not the national Latina/Latino queer organization—they are not part of this queer stance against an illegal war. And its executive director, clarifying that they are "very concerned with the reality that our government's priorities are concentrated on a war," says that the organization "is morally opposed to the war because of the military's 'Don't Ask, Don't Tell' policy against gay men and lesbians." With this argument, it seems, their opposition to imperialism comes in part from not getting an invitation of equality to the imperialist table of the war machine itself. Damn, I think, if this is national gay Latino leadership and analysis in the times of global crisis, then we're really fucked. Immediately I also feel complicit, and embarrassed that I attended the organization's fun-filled 2002 gathering in sweaty and sunny Miami. I calm myself down, bitch about it with some of my friends, and recommit to my writing. I have to stay focused.

Days later at home I am having my usual rushed breakfast with my father and my mother—with my father actually, because my mother always privileges family men's needs first. And so she serves the food but rarely gets to sit with us to eat it at the same time, from beginning to end. But I am there talking with both about war—I, the hyperactive son, sit close to my elderly and slow-eating father while my mother keeps us nourished and listens in, traveling back and forth the short distance between the dining room and the kitchen. They remind me that El Salvador, that tiny little thing around other tiny things in Central America, has also lent its support to the U.S. I laugh, because it's so predictable, and insignificant, for a little national thing like El Salvador to support something as massive as the U.S. and its capitalist hunger for oil and business contracts. But that tiny Central American thing must do a little global kissing of some imperial ass if it wants its more-than-a-million-strong diaspora not to be treated less kindly in the heart of the Empire. So, immigrant diasporic me and gay me feel like there's no place to go: the nonprofit queer Latino nation wants to be at the military table of death on behalf of sexual equality, and the nation where my folks and I almost experienced this precise death has little power to make that fresh memory of violence worth anything. Things are pretty bad.

Queer Moves of Lonely Survival:
Into Spring 2003

Between rushed L.A. morning and evening commutes to and from UCLA, gyms, my writing group, and suburbia, I am trying to secure a salaried academic future. This is a good year for me, with more than thirty applications for jobs I can actually do, eight preliminary phone interviews, and four outright invitations to visit. My suit, suitcase, and curriculum vitae travel far and fast as I deliver my queer theoretical gospel to whoever wants to listen; many do, and some pretend.

Toward the end of these academic job talks, I tell my audiences that homophobia is as "American" as racism and patriarchy. I remind them toward the end because I want to emphasize that queer racial survival can be quite tough. By the time I invoke these words I have already talked to them about the life of the late male-to-female transgender ranchera singer Teresita la Campesina, a loud and proud mexicana, and how she mattered in history. I talk about her, the artist and the pervert; she and I were good friends for several years up to her death in 2002 from AIDS. I use her life in the best sense of the term to make history (and even a little theory) come alive. With my talk, in these most public forums when you're supposed to shine and dazzle and prove your theoretical stuff to strangers, I privilege gay Latino community history. Sure, community history that is contested and conflictive and fractured, but queer community history nevertheless: living, desiring folks who commit to life with others, for one another.

In these same job talks, before and after I try to dazzle my audiences through the power of oral history, I sit around many tables with administrators and senior faculty with the amazing power to give you benefits and teaching time release and travel funds as they consider welcoming you to their club. I handle them and their questions well, as honest as I can be when they ask about what classes I'd like to teach, what my second book would be about, where I'd like to live, why I applied there to begin with. I answer well, mostly because I need a job, and even add plenty more to their questions. I have to be on, engaged, sell my body and mind well. But the labor is heavy.

There and in their intimacy, I also often have out-of-body experiences. Because there I am seated around desks and conference tables, this short, young academic with an accent and a hungry desire to take my queer work far, and I suddenly begin to notice wedding bands: plain gold wedding bands around fingers, skinny, fat, and medium-sized fingers, usually white fingers. I have several out-of-body and out-of-mind experiences as I see these wedding bands, such innocent reminders of who I am and where I stand, this lonely academic queer leaving the suburban family nest four times in four weeks to land four jobs in four corners of this country, just to feel that much smaller in the company of wedding bands. After receiving one of the four job offers and taking a second visit to the campus in the Midwest, I feel confident enough to joke with some of the faculty that I am quite an inexpensive candidate, since, having no partner (then), they don't have to hire someone else as well. Instead, I continue, they could give *me* that money to *attract* someone once I take the job. Of course they laugh at my silly, inventive proposition. I am still not sure today how funny the whole thing really was. After giving my talk for a fifth and final time, as an example of a successful talk at a gathering of younger PhDs of color in this same academic pipeline, I realize the truth of my own words, what a weary maricón traveling down lonely academic roads has been trying to convince others about. Homophobia sucks, and it hurts, and there's no way to overtheorize that, because those wars are quite constant, often silent, even when we think we're done and we've signed on the dotted line. And because I try hard not to be silent about any gender or sexual closets, I know the road and the battles ahead will continue to get quite lonely.

Mentoring:
Summer 2003

After my successful job-hunting season, I get to reward myself with some light teaching, a weeklong writing course for hundreds of low-income and/or students of color at UCLA. One of these students, attending the residential program to help him transfer from a community college to the university, comes out to me late one evening. He does it carefully, only after hearing me discuss my research on race and sexuality in front of the classroom. He is a young mexicano, nineteen years old then, quiet and focused in class, observant, with the courage at that moment to mirror himself against an older gay Latino to verbalize this mostly hidden experience of his life. We talk outside the UCLA dorms at around 11 p.m. when both he and I have time, other students, peer counselors, and staff buzzing around us, maybe wondering why this student is talking to the openly gay professor. He confides that he's actually fine with his being gay, that he's been out to himself and a couple of friends in the San Fernando Valley since age fourteen. He believes his father suspects something, that his mother doesn't really know, and that his sister, who *does* know, is not too helpful. I ask him about gay support and gay friends, about relationships and sexual safety. He asks for general answers mostly, about what to do, what to read, where to go. Carless and young, he is stuck in the expansive dry Valley with not many options. So he searches for answers with professional gay me, and I feel like he's pulling teeth with little success. I tell him about several books and authors, remind him of my e-mail address to stay in touch, tell him to visit UC–Santa Barbara if he likes. But what else do you say to a young gay Latino, the young man of the family, asking about queer life when there's so much insecurity around him?

A couple of days after our conversation, the morning when the program ends, I see a family van driving close to the curb at the student dormitory. It's his Mexican family picking him up on time for their family trip, he tells me. I bid him goodbye with a handshake, very consciously, without breaking those well-understood protocols of the public closet. I also introduce myself to the family briefly—father, mother, and sister—as the Latino profesor. They seem happy to meet me, but even happier they have their son back in their midst. They drive around the curb, the family unit complete again, and take off.

I can't help but think at that moment that his survival is mine, that my survival is his. He's nineteen and I am thirty-three.

Survival and Risk:
Mid-Summer 2004

In July I finally muster the courageous push to return to that oh-so-routine and oh-so-nerve-racking queer event of HIV antibody testing. This one had to be at least my twelfth or fifteenth since 1991, when I first came out, such a basic practice for queer men in the age of AIDS. This time, however, I knew well that I had had more than one "slip" when having sex with others. "Slips" happen, my friend Ricardo reminded me years ago, so casually, to impress on me the simple reality of desire and needs. But I knew the occasional unprotected sex I had had the previous eighteen months or so had not quite been just slips, that they belonged to a new historical moment of rawness, of being tired of having to discipline the self, of lack of collective queer commitment to remaining negative. With all of that, at least on occasions, I slipped right in. Late in the night after session one of this latest round of testing, when my blood flowed freely into a clean, glass tube, and a week before I would get my results, I make a conscious point to remind myself in my journal where I have been and what I have done. The memory of the needle's prick in my left arm that afternoon still fresh on my mind, I try hard to put my anxiety in its rightful place for a moment. This is to be my most honest itinerary of risk, and it went something like this:

Moment Number 1. In winter 2003 one early afternoon, days after receiving my last HIV-negative result at a Pasadena clinic, between academic job applications, in the home of a handsome *hondureño* in South Central L.A., taller and darker than I am, trying to circumvent my loneliness that day. Likely no more than four and a half minutes of raw sex, his excuse being—as if I needed one that day—that he cannot remain completely hard with a condom on, even the larger ones; he feels very big, too inviting to refuse. As I take a sip of beer, soaked in emotional and erotic confusion, I slowly back off from his heavy, brown dick and remove myself from that warm space of conflict and pleasure. He is disappointed; I am confused. We compromise and end in mutual hand play, just. The instance is too important for me to forget it: he showed me and pushed and argued successfully to enter; I first gave in but then backed off, never to play again with him. Hardly any acknowledgment of each other's existence in years to come.

Moment Number 2. One or two weeks after, with a most perfect Persian fuck buddy in Westwood, a fellow alumnus, shorter and flirtier than I am. It had been until then an exciting and useful months-long sexual relationship. Every couple of weeks I'd come to his tiny single apartment after working late at the office, leaving files, bibliographies, e-mails, and professional insecurities behind for the night. I'd bring bottles of wine, and, after the perfunctory TV cable cruising and cross-cultural comparisons, he'd get up from the couch where I'd caress his hair and he'd turn on the stereo and select the song in his CD player, the one he always played, over, and over, and over. I'd make love to him for a portion of the night, our senses numbed and intermittently vaporized with the help of several of his small glass bottles of poppers, erotic time thus slowed down to match the tempo and make history that much longer. On more than one occasion he had suggested that I penetrate him raw—without coming, of course, he clarified—because it felt so much better. He reassured me of being HIV negative. Once, he even offered to pull the paper evidence out of a drawer across the cramped room; as he was going to reach for it, I told him I didn't need to see it, that I believed him, a most odd, on-the-spot negotiation of trust, I thought, unconvinced. I always rationalized nicely why we should not give in, taking the upper hand in the situation—literally—controlling his body and his hands, making sure lube and condoms were always around us, the reassurances close to me that I've always needed, not to feel alone with irresponsibility. Until this one night. Then, the wine, the fumes, the same song over and over, and the same body parts on the same section of the bed simply come together stronger and my insistence against the pleasure he has offered too many times before caves in. It is as if he has dared me one too many times, and I have called his bluff, perhaps my own. Of course I come inside after a forceful fuck, perhaps with a vengeance while disregarding his violent grunts as he holds on tightly to my torso, a rampage; I know he knows what we're doing, that he feels me deep inside, can't imagine that he wants me to stop, for us to end. The feeling of that closeness persists, its memory as fresh today as then. After my release I lie on my back next to him, until he gets up, and reassure him of the safety of *our* trespass—this wasn't just my doing. I have no paper documentation to offer, just my testimony. But neither one of us is entirely convinced. I shower later that morning and leave after we have a bagel sandwich nearby. We never talk again. I see him at a bar a year later in another city; I am not sure if he sees me, but I ignore him and our earlier history.

Moment Number 3. Sometime in the summer before I start teaching, at my favorite bathhouse in Los Angeles, right next to the freeway, sunbathing naked bodies caressed by the exhaust-filtered humming of the 101. Inside the multiracial maze, with safety all around us—lube, condoms, raggedy bleached towels, and a dim light in my tiny room close to the showers—he positions himself for me to enter. Fit, friendly, handsome, and hungry, he moans as we both control the rhythm, everything well placed, calculated, measured. I finish inside, reassured of its appropriate context, and he does too, loudly, both so satisfied, hearts beginning to slow back down. He remains lying on his stomach; I remain inside, lying on his back, total silence. And then, no longer needing him, I pull out and realize the artificial latex barrier between us was broken. Neither one of us cared to check in the process, which is recommended, and which is so easy to forget. After seconds of silent dialogue with myself, I choose not to burden him with this detail of our encounter. Later in the day, outside and under the brightness of the L.A. sun, I wonder if others have done me the same favor before.

Moments Number 4 and 5 in this itinerary. Different geographies and bodies and races and dimensions, but all similar moments of uncertainty, pleasure, and deep sadness over the loneliness of queer life and queer death, however I exaggerate it but can't ignore, of queer survival with dignity when you feel the weight of responsibility is all over you. And you feel that you can fail yet again, whether you want to or not. This was, actually, a very biased itinerary of the anxiety-ridden kind, for what I failed to do in that evening of queer sexual narrative disclosure to the self, and during that week of pre- and post-testing self-suspension, was to remind myself of the dozens of times I *did* privilege safety, when I ensured and experienced queer pleasure with others within the *modern* dictates of sexual conduct. Our culture of HIV antibody testing has generally failed to deliver the message of hope and faith, to recognize honestly human frailties as much as human agency. The cultures of shame, stigma, silence, and denial continue, some better than others, and I am often embarrassed to admit, sadly, how tough it has been to challenge them. And no amount of academic degrees can protect you against that. One week after the drawing of blood, now with the excitement of having reconnected with a man I felt so attracted to a year earlier (now my boyfriend), I drive to a Santa Barbara clinic to get my results. My routine during this week of waiting is rather surreal, again an individual silence around HIV testing as I choose not to share the process with anyone, that weeklong deep emotional reflection hovering over my writing, my speaking, day and night. Finally, I walk into the post-testing counselor's office quite self-assured, tired of feeling guilty, and rationalizing both a possible negative or positive result. It's been thirteen years that I've remained negative, I remind myself, not a bad accomplishment in queer time. He's quick in his delivery of the good news, almost too quick, given the exaggerated weight of its meaning on my psyche. I am more relaxed from that moment on, but not fully satisfied, as I know that I have been here before, in that nice, momentary state of assurance. Because I know that it's kind of going back to zero, the score cleared, with only my erotic history helping me move forward. The counselor asks me if I have any questions, if I need condoms (I take several packets), and is happy to hear that I do have some comments for him. The counselor is engaged and a bit surprised, it seems, for me to be so specific and matter-of-fact about a frustration I communicate to him. I explain how much I have thought, these months before this latest testing round, about sexual negotiation, and how tiring it had been for me, more often than not, to be the one trying to be consistent about condom use, with inconsistent lovers, and how defeating it felt to acquiesce to the other's request for naked pleasure. At least that's what I tell him, maybe trying to justify my own actions, trying to delimit the borders of my own individual human agency. Perhaps what I am communicating to him, dressed as personal frustration, is actually the forced recognition that I often get tired of safer-sex practices, for fifteen years now, and that, like thousands of others, I tend to "slip" more and more, and simply cannot find better scapegoats for my raw desire than those closest to my queer, desperate self. I promise the counselor that I will return more consistently to this testing site, a mutual, reassuring pact between us to at least keep the questions over queer safety and desire alive. He has no final answers for me either, but the conversation remains. Yet another silence in the open.

My Father and His Son:
Late Summer 2004

Three months later, the roles of patient and counselor in this game of life switch. My then-eighty-seven-year-old father has had two trips to the emergency room in a week, and all the medical exams are not able to determine what is going on with his digestive system. As I translate between him and the young Chinese doctor, I see how disappointed he is to hear that he will need more testing, this time a colonoscopy that will require drinking more nasty fluids to prepare his system. He tells the doctor he simply cannot do it then, that he needs to go home to rest, and that he needs to wait a week. I feel for my father's weariness and admire his successful negotiations with all the medical authorities he's become dependent on. The smiling doctor, understanding my father's discomfort, agrees that it's a wise move. I take out my PalmPilot and coordinate a date when I can drive him back. I want to do this now because once the academic teaching run begins again and students and faculty land on campus, my time with my parents is cut short. As they age, my parents' illnesses give me the urgency simply to care more and just be there. It's a driving routine with multiple doctors, clinics, and hospitals that my oldest sister knows far better than I do. But this time it's my turn. Two weeks later we are in a high-tech clinic near my parents' home. I am taking my father for his colonoscopy. His walk is so much slower now, carefully measuring the distance of each one of the few steps at home, slouching a bit more, his hearing and vision slightly worse, although mentally sharp as ever, all the detailed memories of El Salvador still present. He has been worried all these weeks that it might be something really bad, he tells me, like cancer. I explain to him the many other possibilities, speaking frankly and so self-assured about the eventual negative diagnosis he receives. I am actually reassuring him to reassure myself about my own father's life. Once close to the examination room, I help him undress a little, but leave the bathroom once a friendly white nurse who calls me "hon" smiles and indicates that she will take over. I take with me my father's wallet, his scarf, and his raggedy green faux-leather bag full of medication bottles, all the corroboration of his conditions in the past few years. As I wait for nearly two hours in the lobby, I write in my journal, read a boring academic article, and refuse to think about the future. Once he comes out of sedation I return to the recovery area and realize my father has no idea the procedure has already taken place. I reassure him that all is well, having talked to the doctor for a while. I spare him unnecessary details, and tell him that the doctor has recommended more fiber, prune juice, and another colonoscopy in three years. I especially like this last request from the doctor, as it marks life in time and a date with the future. My father does not laugh but seems a bit amused with being able to make, in his age and at that moment, such a long-term appointment with life. But he is relieved to know it's only a matter of having a better diet. As we prepare to leave, I help him stand up in his white gown, help him remove it, and try not to see too much of his small, aging naked body, more than five decades of psoriasis, and the plastic tubes he now needs to live a relatively normal, though constrained, daily life. Once he is fully dressed, a nurse takes him on a wheelchair close to the curb, where I am ready in my car to take him back to my mother.

I often wonder what my father thinks of me, beyond the academic success and big-mouthed irreverent immigrant clown that I strive to be. I am thinking more of me, his gay son, the end of a particular bloodline (though not the only one for him), and what my queer public life means to him. Months after the colonoscopy, he gets to meet my boyfriend for the first time during a brief visit home I make to talk with my older sister about the progress of the house expansion. My mother, caring as ever, has food ready for her son and his man; she is meeting for the first time a person who's there to comfort and nurture her last child when I am not in my parents' home. The day I told her I had a boyfriend she thanked God.

This could only be a quick first visit for me as I am still trying to put together all the essential pieces in my life, blood and queer kinships. And it's all beginning to feel right. I continue to live between distances: my job site where I teach, do committee work, and try to avoid destructive academic politics; my parents' expanded and now more comfortable place, so loaded and so rich with our histories of immigration, displacement, and struggle; and, for several years, a city of immigrant landings,

Los Angeles, and all its queer Latino present and history of life and death, including the one I am still learning how to negotiate within desire, risk, pleasure, and commitment. Constantly shuffling folders, files, freeways, and feelings is not easy, but I know it is the only way for this queer survival I most desire now. Accepting an award at an academic conference of mostly heterosexual white folks, most decades older than I am, matters; hearing my father appreciate the fact that I can travel sometimes to take him to the latest round of medical exams, matters; and having whatever spaces possible to not simplify Latino and queer worlds, and the survival we all deserve in them, matters too.

La Fiesta de Los Linares

JANET ARELIS QUEZADA

The lanterns on the ground lit the faces of Los Linares as they told jokes and stories. They sat on overturned crates and old cane-bottom chairs. It was hot, and shirtsleeves were rolled back; some feet were bare. They had eaten already, and the relaxation of their mouths slack from chewing the good food allowed the stories to flow freely.

The three wooden structures on the lot were filled with people and candles too, but most of the celebration was taking place outside. The two rooms behind the storefront that faced the road that went by were small and warm. When there weren't any celebrations Doña Tomasa and Teresa, her eldest daughter by her first husband Dagoberto, slept in one back room and Amalia and Yuni slept in the other. The two houses, no more than rooms really, were separated by a patch of land and some grass and tonight had been taken over by two hostile groups. One held the young crowd that wanted to hear music other than that of the merengue trio that had been hired for the night. The other held the strained, earnest voices of a choir singing about the son of God.

The younger cousins went in and out of the store to borrow some sodas for the party, avoiding the entrances to both small houses and trying not to let the store proprietor notice their bottles of malta. Tío Yuni had stopped deducting the amount from his inventory as soon as he had sat down in front of Alberto, Danny, and Chepo for a serious game of dominoes. On the ground around the lanterns sat most of Saturnino and Tomasa's children, the six boys who had grown beards and mustaches in the same places and four of the six girls who were thin and bony, covering their smiles behind their hands as they listened to the picardía of their brothers. Older grandchildren and many friends of the family sat there too. Tato, who had been raised with the Linares boys, was the best and loudest storyteller among them.

Mamá Tomasa sat in her rocking chair, a little bit removed from the group, talking to Teresa and some of the wives of her sons and directing all the action around her. She was gray haired and wrinkled but with a tall spine and a firm way of carrying herself. She searched the faces of her family, looking for anything that she needed to attend to, and then dispatched someone to come bring that person to her so she could advise, admonish, or animar.

Dulce tried to keep out of the elders' sight. She stayed around the circle of people watching the dominoes game, her body reacting appropriately to the drama of the match while her eyes and mind focused on Amalia. She watched Yuni slam down one of the ivory rectangles onto the table. "Así es que se juega, carajo." He was excited and a little bit touched by rum, but not too much, out of respect. Everyone at the party glanced over at Doña Tomasa throughout the night to make sure that nothing that had been said had offended her. In moments of uncertainty and deep tension, when someone had tipped over a bottle, or told a really dirty joke, or two people had begun to argue, she would say calmly to the crowd: "Esta es mi fiesta, y quiero que la disfruten, pero con mucho cuidado. Que no se me alboroten mucho, ¿me entienden?"

Dulce tried to be calm. Eso de no alborotarse mucho was difficult for her. Especially now in the middle of this party at this old house. She had practically grown up here, just like Tato, only much later. She felt comfortable moving about the genial women and men of this family. She felt comfortable pulling the ears of the many children who were running about if they were giving too much lata. But she could not keep her feelings still. They moved con picante like the music that was coming out of the accordion, the tambor, and the guiro. She had a place here among these people: "Esa siempre está allí arrimadita con los hombres, tú sabes, pero no te apures; es bien tranquila." It was okay for her, here, to sit with the men and play poker or to sip a little beer. She wore her big bowler hat that she had bought from one of the New York cousins last year and watched Amalia, hoping, just hoping.

"¿Por qué tiene la cara tan seria, ésa?"

"It's just the game. Look at them; you know how they all get. And Dulce has always been just like the men."

"Amalia!"

"¿Sí, abuela?"

"¿Por qué no bailas? Yo sé que te gusta."

"No tengo mi pareja."

The women gathered around Tomasa looked over at Yuni, Amalia's new husband, and then back at Amalia.

"Este merengue se baila sola," cantó Ramonita.

"Vaya, Amalita, ves; you don't have to dance this with him. Go ahead. I like to see you dance, mija." Tía Teresa laughed.

"Este se baila no importa la hora. ¡Sí, ay! Se baila sola." Ramonita continued singing the popular song and Amalia finally got up.

Amalia closed her eyes and let her hips go into a trance, pulled by the music of the trio. She closed her eyes and shook her shoulders, letting all those New York cousins notice the way a real merenguera danced to the sound of tamboras. She was proud of the eyes she knew were looking her way.

Dulce watched the shadows around the trees that the lanterns made. Some of them flickered with the movement of dancers and others hovered in place. She wondered if she could pick out the shadow that belonged to Amalia. She knew that she could not look at Amalia's face. The music quickened her pulse, almost knocking her down. She watched one of the shadows, now sure that she had found Amalia's form; the rest of the shadows were parejas; this one whirled alone. Mesmerized by the movements, she imagined that slowly the shadow was taking on flesh.

The song was over and the band took a break. Ramonita la Flaca went over to the pile of soda bottles and popped one open. She smiled at Doña Tomasa but was not ready to go over and congratulate her on reaching another year in her life. She was not ready to look into those eyes, yet. But she was more than willing to go back to her spot and play and sing for her.

"Tired of touring?" said Miguel.

"I wish I could keep playing at occasions like this, but . . ."

"But, you are making it big and soon we will have to go to the capital if we want to hear you play."

"I would play for your grandmother anytime."

Ramonita laughed and gulped as much of the soda as she could. She didn't want to talk to anybody else. Her head was full of her plans. Her chords were full of the itch to sing out and her fingers eager to tap the buttons and make the music of this life.

Dulce had been staring at Amalia throughout the whole song. Now that the music was over, though, her eyes seemed to lock into that space where she had been. She could still hear the merengue inside her ears and inside her heart she could still see Amalia dancing like she had that day in the back room of the store by the light of a small lantern. Her hips moving through the air, weaving together the responses to the call of the music, dancing, teaching her to dance:

"Come on Dulce; it's easy and you don't have to be shy. No one is here."

"Amalia, I don't want to do this."

"We both know that's not true."

Silence. Laughter explosions. The music and Amalia's hands pulled at Dulce and they began to shake and turn all over the small square of floor in between the old sacks of rice and the piles of cans and bottles of soda.

The flimsy table almost fell over as Yuni slammed down a domino. Dulce had missed the final moments of the game. Around the table, men laughed and cheered. Danny shook Chepo's hand, and Alberto clapped Yuni's back. The crowd around him launched into debates about the past game, about the obvious mistake and the moment in which the others had all lost to Yuni's luck. Yuni leaned back in his chair, not saying anything for a while, and then began to barajear the dominoes in front of him.

Chepo, who had been the second-highest scorer, moved away from the group and sat down opposite Yuni. He settled into the serious mood of the game again. They needed two new competitors to continue with their tournament. William got up from the circle of laughter where the stories were gathering spit in people's mouths and tears in their eyes. He came over to the table. The only bachelor out of the Linares boys, William lived alone in Santiago and drove a big camión across the country for one of the few market chains. He played tough but was really quiet, unlike the other men in his family. He had been the last to move away from the house, because his mother would not let him go without a wife. She had been afraid that he wouldn't be able to take care of himself. And he did look skinny and worn these last few years. He turned the chair around and sat down with the heaviness of a bigger man. He smiled at Yuni and shook Chepo's hand. One of the neighbors joined them. A new game began.

Dulce looked over at the trio. Ramonita and the two musicians were back in place and the music started again. Amalia danced. Dulce watched Amalia's skirt flouncing from one side to the other. She saw Amalia's shoulders dip and her hair run after her laughing face. Her feet began to tap on the floor at first to the sound of the tambor and then in a beat of their own, trying to send Amalia a message to look over her way.

Some of the people sitting around the circle thought of getting up to dance. The music had been bright and flashy but not tempting at all as they sat there laughing and letting the food course slowly through their bodies. Pero ya se habían bajado los tostones, el arroz, el pollo asado. Legs stretched, knees cracked, and the palms of hands found laps, the backs of chairs, or each other to echo the compas of this fast merengue.

Beatriz, sitting with her brothers and sisters, felt the restlessness of the gathered circle. She had listened to the stories that they told without allowing the words to hook into her mind and take her away from what she always thought about. She looked at the lanterns glow and began to speak in her low voice. Everyone around the circle moved closer and stilled themselves. Beatriz didn't speak often. This story was not going to be one of the verde tales that her brothers loved to laugh about. Beatriz was going to tell them about the family. Doña Tomasa moved her chair into the circle. Even the domino players quieted down. The only ones who did not join the hushed group were Ramonita, her musicians, and Amalia, who were in the middle of a fast groove.

"Iris desde pequeña había trabajado con sus manos. She would build cities made of mud, or as she grew older sew enormous quilts. Hers was a gift that the people recognized around these parts for miles. They would come to ask for shawls and baby clothes for baptisms and communions. Nonin and Paul were congratulated on Iris's gift by their neighbors. Nonin imagined though that everyone was laughing at her fortune, not really envying it."

"Era muda."

"Shh! Muchacha, let Beatriz tell it."

Amalia and Ramonita were in conversation. Ramonita ripped through scales with her accordion and Amalia shook her waist in answer. Amalia opened her eyes and looked into the singer's muddy brown eyes.

Immediately Ramonita flourished a caress. She was excited by this beautiful young woman in front of her who moved, directed by her fingers. She let out a small growl in the middle of the song's phrase, sure

116

that the family was not listening to the music at that moment. Amalia continued to dance but slowly backed away from the intensity of Ramonita's voice. She danced but slowly turned to look in the direction of the domino game. She moved her shoulders but let her eyes stop briefly at Yuni's face, which was concentrating on the patterns made by the black dots on the white frames. She moved her feet from side to side, but sus ojos saltaron to Dulce's face. Dulce's eyes, caught inside of hers, pooled with tenderness.

Dulce took a half step in Amalia's direction but stopped herself. She took off her hat and fanned her face. She sipped a little bit of beer and tried not to run over to where the music was blaring, fighting for the attention of Amalia, the lone dancer. She saw that most of the family was gathered around Beatriz now and that the music held only those strongly enchanted in its circle.

It stopped. Ramonita took another break. Amalia came over to sit by her abuela and listen to her tía.

Dulce went over to see which dominos William held in his hands. She tried to catch Amalia's face again, now almost directly opposite her.

Amalia concentrated on the light, letting her heartbeat become soft and low like the light. She decided that she would not move from her abuela's side for the rest of the night.

"She was a blessed child, but Nonin did not see the blessing. Her daughter could not answer her questions, could not hear her orders. She did things well enough once taught, but you had to stand in front of her to get her attention. And there were times that teje que teje she would not notice anyone standing in front of her for hours. Iris made beautiful shapes, intricate and colorful, but she refused to say a word all throughout her childhood."

Ramonita stopped to listen to Beatriz while she ate some queso frito and mangu. She decided she could take a longer break this time. Amalia did not look like she would get up anytime soon, and the rest of the dancers were tired out. She eyed one of the faded hammocks hanging between two trees at the edge of the circle of lights that the lanterns gave. She nodded over at her boys as they headed toward the game. Piling on a second plate of mangu, she headed over to the trees.

Amalia watched the large shadow of la Flaca disappear into the darkness. She couldn't concentrate on the story. Her blood had slowed but her mind was entranced by the shadows that leapt around her. Everywhere she looked, people's faces grew deep recesses or were hollowed out by the night that was coming for its visit. She looked over at the game. Tío William's bent head made her think of prayer and funerals. His eyes had deep, shadowy rivers under them. She crossed herself. Her eyes attempted the climb upward from his head toward the serious face under the bowler hat; she knew that Dulce was trying to ignore her eyes, that the music had excited her too, that it had made her remember, but she couldn't see Dulce's eyes under the hat's brim.

Dulce flicked her hands, trying not to hear the laughter of that afternoon in the supply room. She pulled her hat lower and thought about what she had just seen. Ramonita and Amalia had turned that public, roaring merengue into something intimate and private. But Amalia had left the area in front of the singer quickly. There was no reason for her to be upset; she looked down at William's hand hesitating over a two/five and looked over at the four ends of the worldly cross that lay on the dented table. Fives and twos on all sides. She thought about what she would do with the domino, where she would place it.

The ropes that held the hammock were frayed and Ramonita groaned as she bent to arrange herself on it while balancing the two plates. Next week she would be in the capital, signing the final contracts with the hotels there to play for the tourists for the New Year's celebration. She settled fully on the low hammock and went over her calculations. It had been a long time since she could think out her future like this. The past few years had been nonstop family celebrations: weddings, confirmations, birthday parties. Once she had found two men who were reliable and understood that she wasn't looking for advances, that she just wanted to play the music, it had been hard for her to have time to herself. All the local families in the province wanted her to come and play for them. It was true that she would have to stop doing this; in fact she only played this one because it was for Doña Linares.

When Virginia had kicked her out of the house in Higuey, she had wandered all over the roads in La Romana, eating hierba and beginning to talk to herself. Because she had come from Virginia's house, no one opened their doors to her. She couldn't even explain to them that she hadn't been a puta. That she lived in the house but did not take part in the trade. Because she couldn't explain Virginia. Not even to herself. Doña Tomasa was tending to the store that day, years back. She was already too old to be working at that kind of job, but she was stubborn. People said that the Linares' mom did not want any of her boys stepping into that store and dying like her husband Saturnino had. When Ramonita asked for una limosna, Doña Tomasa spit by her feet and Ramonita began to turn away. But the old woman had said to wait and then handed her a broom. That was a beginning, and the only reason she had moved away was because Virginia had started coming around again.

Tomasa leaned into her chair, enjoying the sound of Beatriz's voice. She thought of her mother, not able to call her Iris in her mind even now, when she felt that she was so close to seeing her. Ay, Mamá. I worry so much. How can I leave them now when so many of them need me? Divorces, Mamá, and other things that I know you never knew of. And William, he's going to go before I get there, Mamá, I can see it. Eso no es justo. She rubbed her eyes and immediately Bernabe's wife asked if there was something wrong. Teresa handed her a pañuelo with agua florida, and Ermelinda, José and Ana's daughter, asked if she could get her some water. Tomasa took a deep breath and accepted the tin cup. She leaned back and forced herself to look calm. This is all she could do for them.

"Nonin felt that Iris obstinately refused to talk. El Padre Mikael y los vecinos argued that the child could not have such an intention. But Nonin was convinced that Iris could talk if she wanted. She would mutter to her all day while she cleaned the house, trying to shame her into speaking, into giving up this game. When Iris was in her twenties, her mother decided to marry her to Cangrejo. No one had ever taken that man seriously. He had more money than the district judge, it's true, but he was always gruff, ever ready to curse, or spit, rather than talk or smile. He was also sixty and had never been married. Nonin told Iris that if she wasn't going to open her mouth then she would have to satisfy herself with Cangrejo for a husband, because no one else would take her, no matter how beautifully she crocheted."

Amalia sighed heavily and looked back over at Yuni. This time she kept her eyes on his frame. Watched him hunched over the game, that awful vein of his popping at his neck. How many fights they had had since the wedding—quiet, whispered arguments, but pretty soon she felt he would not hold himself back, not even for abuela. He bragged about the store. He gritted his teeth and hissed that "was the only good thing" he had gotten out of the wedding. She listened to the story of her bisabuela, her eyes no longer looking at the shadows or searching for Dulce's smile.

Why do you have to say yes, Amalia?"

"Dulce, por favor, just help me stitch these shirts and don't ask me anything about it."

"You have to explain it to me, or I won't sew a thing."

"Ay, muchacha. Why do you always have to strong-arm to get your way? Sit down. First, I don't have any money."

"That's not an excuse for anything."

"Listen. And you know where my mother is. I can't count on anybody but myself and I don't want them to say that I am taking advantage of abuela. I've lived there for nine years and I don't bring in any income."

"Neither does Teresa."

"Dulce, please. You know it is not the same thing. I can't go to the capital; what would I do there?"

"You don't have to leave; you just don't have to marry him."

"Dulce. Look. It had to come some time or another. And besides, abuela approves; she promised him the store. He is going to make more money from it than she ever could. He's already turned it around since she let him start managing it."

"Tan feo, Amalia."

Amalia stuffed more white lace material into the trunk at the foot of the bed. She tried not to cry. She kept her back to Dulce.

"At least I'm not moving away, Dulce. Can you at least be glad about that?"

The sobs came like wild horses and Dulce was quiet, admonished as she held Amalia in her arms.

The wedding took place without a word of protest from Iris. She nodded when the priest asked her the question, and with that nod, the marriage was done. During the first month the neighbors came by to visit. They saw Iris sweeping the only concrete floor for miles around; they saw her washing clothes in an aluminum tub; they saw her feeding the chickens and pigs in the mornings. She still did not talk.

Cangrejo was never there. The older women tried to talk to her con confianza about the problems that a new wife may have, but Iris showed no signs that she knew what they were hinting at. Nonin came after a few months to quiet the talk of the other women. She had done her duty as a mother, more than that, because she had been able to get her a husband, but the metidos wouldn't be satisfied until she visited her newlywed daughter. The day she came by, her daughter spoke for the first time.

Ramonita coughed to dislodge the lump of platano she felt in her throat. She thought about what it had been like to work and be accepted here with Doña Tomasa after those awful days on the road and after those awful years with Virginia. She hadn't told la señora anything about her past. For a while she had been able to push it far enough away from her consciousness that when Virginia actually showed up at the store, she had a moment of disconnection.

"You're not going to act like you don't know me." But Virginia easily, harshly brought her back to her senses. The broom in her hands had felt like a tree. The small, square room with its shelves of cartons and cans expanded. Her tongue a dead animal, she pointed to the door, but Virginia laughed. "You're not going to get rid of me. Remember, you always invite me in. You need me. You cannot make it on your own."

She heard Doña Tomasa moving around in the room behind the store. She was not supposed to wait on customers—that was still the responsibility of la señora—and Ramonita was afraid that she would hear Virginia's laughter and think she was a customer.

Virginia knocked some of the cartons off the nearest shelf. "You're clumsy, remember. You need some training in grace and manners. I want you to succeed, don't get me wrong. I'm only looking out for your best. No one will want you around if you don't learn these things."

Ramonita rushed to pick up the cartons and put them back on the shelf. She forgot the broom and jumped when she heard the crash.

"You misunderstood what I told you. I didn't want you to leave. I wouldn't allow a defenseless woman like you to fend for herself out there. Let me help you; come with me."

"Ramonita, ¿qué pasa? ¿Me necesitas?"

Ramonita could hear Doña Tomasa washing her hands with the watering can she kept at the door to the supply room. Soon she would tie on the delantar and wipe her hands. Then she would head out to the store front in case customers came by.

"No, señora."

"You won't last here with that old lady. She'll see how you are. You'll do something wrong and offend her."

Ramonita had to tell Virginia that she would come back. Doña Tomasa made it to the storeroom before Virginia left, though. Virginia made a show of buying some items, keeping her eyes on Doña Tomasa and smiling. There had been a couple of visits like that one throughout the months she spent with the Linares.

Ramonita leaned back into the hammock, letting the empty plastic plates slip to the ground. She knew, now, that she didn't need Virginia to teach her how to act. She had been invited to many homes to sing and play. Behind her accordion, no one questioned her past, or the way she behaved. She was allowed many liberties as a merenguera. Sometimes she had to earn her respect the hard way, but she was dependent on no one but herself. Soon her life would be different; she would reach a higher scale and be farther from Virginia and the people who had turned their backs on her. Solita. Así iba a llegar. She knew how to be careful. She could twist her emotions into the purest notes of fast, hard music and share with other people without them even noticing how much they too had given.

Ramonita's snore interrupted the quiet anticipation around Beatriz. Everyone laughed, their bodies loose and open to the delight of release. Tato blurted out the opening lines of his story about the loudest snores he had ever heard, and heads turned toward him, happy to continue this mood. Doña Tomasa intervened, though. Coughing, she asked Beatriz what Iris had said to her mother: "What were that child's first words?"

"He's dead," responded Beatriz. Then she explained how Iris got up from her chair and put away her needles. She walked over to the bedroom and opened the door. Nonin made it to the door through a fog of shock and fear. Lying on the bed was the old man, Cangrejo. Iris continued to speak in a rush of words that sounded foreign to Nonin, who was looking at her daughter with wide-open eyes. Iris continued to speak throughout the preparation for Cangrejo's funeral. She told the women and the men gathered in the house about her wedding night while her mother prayed in silent tears. Iris also talked about the growing baby inside her stomach. The neighbors covered their ears, trying not to let all of those words tangle inside their heads. Iris spoke about the way her tongue had dislodged and unfurled from her mouth in her first words. She explained to everyone that she had sat in the chair and gone about her chores, trying to quiet the restlessness of the freed muscle inside her mouth. She told them that she hadn't known how to control it or if it would make any sense once sounds came out; that's why she hadn't shared her news earlier. Nonin stared through the entierro, not even mumbling the words of prayer that would lay the old man to rest.

Amalia sighed and walked over to the room she slept in. She had to pass the domino game and couldn't help looking over. Yuni was there still. There had been another change of partners during the story, and now William and two other men sat at the table while Chepo looked on

122

behind them. Dulce was standing among that crowd. Amalia looked at Yuni; he was strong and healthy, just a little overweight, but fit for his forty-five years. She didn't bother looking over at Dulce.

Dulce tensed while Amalia glanced over at the game. Then she saw her walk into one of the houses behind the store. She tried to focus on the game again, but the dots came together in front of her without making sense. She left the game.

Amalia's room vibrated with the sound of whispered prayers. Tía Olivera, la única hija de Doña Tomasa presente durante la fiesta que no estaba en el círculo de cuentos, led some of her nieces and friends in a prayer for lost souls. None of them moved as Amalia walked in the room. They did not greet Dulce when she too entered. There were candles all over the room, and the heaviness of the shadows slumped Amalia's shoulders. She looked at the wall. The shadows were all half her size, kneeling in reverent prayer. She noticed Dulce's shadow, tall and still by the door. She knew Dulce wouldn't come in, but she wished that somehow she could. She didn't know how to continue her wish, so she stared at the shadows.

Startled from her sleep, Ramonita jumped up to her feet and signaled to the two men in her band. She shouldn't have let herself get so comfortable. Cochina, she mumbled to herself as she picked up the two greasy plates from the ground. She must have made a sight to the family here with her babas falling all over her chin and probably roncando. Like Virginia said, she wasn't fit for company. This is not what she was hired for.

The music started again. Dulce's shadow began to pulse to the sounds that seemed to come from so far away. Amalia thought of Iris's awful husband dead on their wedding night and shuddered. She watched Dulce's shadow put her arms around her shadow's shoulders. She felt comforted. She watched Dulce and Amalia on the wall sway slowly as if the candlelight were conducting them instead of the music. Ramonita's voice flared out with its fiery force. She watched the shadows speed up their pasos. Ramonita played with anger, but the music sounded joyous and passionate. In the room with the shadows the prayers increased in volume.

"And then she built first one wooden room behind the old concrete house, then another. I was born in the first one. Mamá converted the room into a store. She sold her crocheted quilts, clothes, manteles, sábanas. When I married your father," here Doña Tomasa looked at Teresa, "he insisted on her retiring. He took over and sold the usual supplies of the bodegas. Mamá went to sleep in the second room that he built so she wouldn't be bothered by the noise of people coming in to buy, trade, or gossip. Then Dagoberto died and I married your father." Here she looked around at the grown children in front of her. "Saturnino closed the store and worked the land that we have all around us. It is small, but bountiful. When you were born," she looked at Ana, who was nursing her smallest child, "your abuela died and your papá decided to take the store over. He thought he would be making her spirit happy, but he died. That is why I let none of you open that store again."

"Doña Tomasa, es su fiesta, no es tiempo de llorar por nada."

Ramonita's big voice overturned the chairs and crates; the whole clan was up and dancing to the singers' orders. Doña Tomasa faced her laughing family and tapped one foot to the music in her ears. She looked over at Yuni punishing the tables with small white rectangles and then searched the crowd for Amalia.

"Aunque sea, hice lo que pude por ella," Doña Tomasa said, leaned back in her chair. With her wrinkled fingers she rubbed the shawl her mother had made her that she wore now around her shoulders.

My mother's work is on exhibit here at this gallery."

"What does she do again?"

"Muchacha, how many times do I have to remind you! She is a potter."

"But you said this was called something, something shadow. It was about shadows."

"Capturing the Flesh of Shadows. You like it? I made up the title for her."

"But what is it about?"

"Where my mother is from there are these figures they make that have no faces. They are kind of nice. Dark-skinned women sit with flowers on their laps. Tall women hold buckets on their heads. But none of them have faces. Mom thinks of them as shadows."

"So she is imitating those figures?"

"Right, except there's a twist. She is capturing the shadows that have never been seen by anyone."

"I still don't get what you mean."

"Come in and see."

The figures were similar in size and color to the traditional ones crafted and sold at tourist shops on the island, except all of them came in pairs. Figures supported each other; arms held waists, fingers held shoulders, or elbows. One of the figures wore a ruffled skirt and the other pants, but both had swells under the painted-on blouses.

The centerpiece was a figurine of two shadows dancing. You could hear the fast riff of a merengue in the way the hips were placed. You could see the love in the placement of the hands and the care that the artist had taken to paint them. The title of the piece was "Dulce and Amalia."

Malverde

MYRIAM GURBA

Mom and Dad just got back from a trip to Mexico. They went because Abuelita's not doing too good. It turns out she has dementia. It
also turns out that, drumroll please, my cousin Miguelito works for the
head of a Guadalajara drug cartel. He was so cracked out that he didn't
use a condom when he started getting jiggy with the jefe's youngest
daughter, and that fool got her pregnant. The Jezebel in question is
barely a year past her quinceañera, brunette, and, given what her father
does for a living, tastes like a dewy coca bush.

When he found out about the baby, Miguelito proposed. Mom says
his mom, Tía Ofelia, talks like this was a doomed but noble gesture.
Girl, please, that choice was *so* not motivated by chivalry. Tsk-pssssh, as
if he had a choice. And doomed he is. Very doomed. So many people
want to kill Miguelito, not that that makes him special or anything;
being an assassin's target comes with the territory he snorted his way
into, and this is stressful for Mom. Here's why: Those who execute my
cousin's death warrant are going to strike when a vulnerable window
reveals itself. Let's say this occurs on a warm Saturday night, after Mass,
when Miguelito and his young bride stop by his parents' house so they
can visit with their brand new granddaughter. Like a boa constrictor
lying in wait, picture the fortified SUV that's been idling on the street
all afternoon. Time to pounce, and it comes crashing through the tall

126

gate surrounding the pretty villa, skidding to a halt feet from my aunt and uncle's front door.

Men with guns pour out of the vehicle. The abuelos stop admiring the baby's newest tooth or the baby's curly hair or the baby's tiny fingernails and look up. There's not even time for Tía and Tío's faces to contort with horror and then freeze into ugly masks. Miguelito reaches for his gun, the front door flies off its hinges, and the executioners invade the living room, which is very tastefully decorated. These cowboys don't have silencers, they're that brash, and Pow! A slug in Miguelito's head. Pow! Slugs for anyone with eyeballs and a memory. Tía. Tío. Maybe my prima Marta and her boyfriend or my prima Fiona and her husband. The servants, Paco, Chema. The dog, Yudi. A miniature pinscher. Very yippy.

Collateral damage. Mom worries about her sister winding up dead on the floor. It's not a far-fetched possibility. I've considered it and there's something else, too, something I wouldn't ever tell Mom.

I enjoy being related to a narcotraficante!

Narcotraficante!

Sexy. The word is sexy. Debonair. Gallant. When you say it, it's like saying Pancho Villa! Nothing matches the title in English; all we have is drug dealer, and there's a style, a narco look, that Miguelito's got down pat. Because of its mastery, I had a jump on Mom; mi primo narcotraficante has been in my thoughts for two years now, ever since I saw him on New Year's Eve the last time I visited Guadalajara.

We were sitting at the dining room table having dinner. Tía Ofelia had uncorked the champagne early. She was pouring it with hours to go till the toast and the twelve grapes you eat at the stroke of midnight while you wish for good health and to win the lottery and stuff like that. I kept trying to eat my grapes early because they looked so good, but Mom kept smacking my hand away from the fancy flute glass they were sitting in.

Miguelito smiled as I rubbed my smarting hand. He sat across from me, his expensive cologne bridging the divide between us. He was much quieter than I remembered him. Not playful or silly at all anymore. In fact, about him hung this James Dean aura, a dark, sad prettiness. He politely laughed at Dad's jokes and smoked cigarettes using Tía's exact same nicotine-addicted mannerisms, and after finishing his tequila, he rose and kissed us all goodbye, abandoning me to my parents and drunk aunt and uncle.

They were making so much noise I didn't hear Miguelito leave out the front door. When I looked up from ogling my grapes again, I saw him outside, through one of the big picture windows that looks out onto the stone veranda. Miguelito paused, posing beside a pillar. He lit a fresh cigarette. I watched him inhale and blow smoke out of his nostrils, relaxing. He did a fancy French inhale, a soupy tobacco fog curling out of his mouth, being willed up his nostrils like a snake obeying a charmer. Then, his eyes lost their calm. He quickly patted his waist. I noticed the pistol-shaped bulge under his Versace silk shirt.

¡Dios mío! began my silent Spanglish epiphany as I gnawed at the inside of my cheek, Miguelito looks like a narcotraficante!

I watched him drop his cigarette and crush it with the heel of his motorcycle boot. In tight designer jeans that seemed to be cutting off some circulation, Miguelito hobble-swaggered to his boss's BMW. That sweet car was his Cinderella excuse for bailing so early. Supposedly, he had to have it returned before midnight.

Artists should thank God for people like Miguelito. They're muses and they inspire the heck out of Mexican musicians who romanticize their abbreviated vidas locas in ballads called narcocorridos. These usually tell the story of some Robin Hood type who comes from goat herders, pulls himself up by his bootstraps by cultivating blow, and then gets martyred by the police the day he leaves his AK at home.

Aside from trading in similar commodities, Miguelito's got little in common with these rags to riches farm boys. He's the middle-class son of a factory owner who got in over his head with nose candy and accidentally screwed his way into a crime dynasty. Still, his affiliation with the narco universe gives him panache. And he's got a natural magnetism. Miguelito's unique story could spawn a hit single.

El Corrido del Tucan Tapatío?

Sounds good to me.

Mom hasn't said this, but I know there's something else stressing her out, too. It's Tía's newfound sobriety. She and Miguel recently started attending AA together (yes, Alcoholics Anonymous exists in Mexico), and every time Tía reads in the paper about another slain narco (which is practically every day), the bottle chirps, Drink me! *Drink me!* Mom is trying to be as supportive as possible of her baby sister's struggle to stay clean, but it's hard for her to relate to so many hours spent in meetings, the working of numerous steps, and the distribution of colorful coins.

Mom quit. Tacitly. While I was away at college. She received neither a trophy nor a token for it. Not even a thank you. Because that would mean acknowledgment. And that's dangerous territory for a Mexican.

From Mom, I learned this maxim, indigenous to her homeland, very well: It's best not to mention certain sins aloud. Think the Three Monkeys. See no evil. Hear no evil. Speak no evil. Some things you keep between you and God; the really important things, between you and the Virgin.

I now realize the Three Monkeys have always been with me, but the first time they really came through loud and clear was when I was seventeen. Mom wove them into an object lesson as I was filling out college apps at the breakfast counter. She'd just finished loading the dishwasher and was watching me, remembering.

"You have good grades," she commented, sipping wine from a cheapo goblet. She sat down on a barstool beside me. "What do you think you will study?"

"Art maybe. I dunno."

"My mother was very good," she said, "*is* very good," she corrected herself, "at art." . . . A memory of cramped muscles, me and Ixchel spending the entire summer before seventh grade stiff, posing for Abuelita as she worked on our portraits. . . . She sacrificed a lot to help pay for my university. She sold some of her paintings. Took in sewing. Lots of sewing. . . . Picturing Abuelita at an old-fashioned sewing machine, sweat beading on her forehead and premature canas at her temples, Abuelito watching from the doorway, looking like the El Catrin card, the dandy pulled from a stack of lotería favorites. Always in a three-piece suit, shiny pocket-watch chain glimmering from his vest pocket, a showman like P. T. Barnum, like most cowards a braggart, especially about his job, Guadalajara's leading publicist, its king of bullshit and fantasy. The best lies were the ones he told women. My grandfather, he's the progenitor of many a bastard. I wondered, was Abuelito's shameless squandering of pesos on the ladies the reason Abuelita busted her hump paying for Mom's school?

"Why did Abuelita have to help you so much?" I interrupted. "Abuelito had money. For crying out loud, he has a different pair of wing tips for each day of the week!"

I waited, chewing on my pencil's eraser. Anticipating. Hard. I knew where Abuelito's money went but I wanted to hear Mom say it, to call her dad out for being a player. Since she was drinking, she wouldn't leave out any of the good stuff; she'd leave in all the gory details, like how Abuelito dedicated his first book of poems not to Abuelita but to his mistress, the hideously named Hortencia, and how Mom's big sister,

Carmen, became his secretary after Ofelia and Abuelita brought lunch to his office one time and walked in on him in flagrante with the typist.

After swishing her wine around, making it whirlpool for a couple of seconds, Mom said to me, "Deirdre, when I turned sixteen, I asked my father for money to go to the university. He saw that I was serious about it and he told me to sit at the kitchen table. Once I was seated, he sat across from me and said, 'Alicia, you are a woman. This means you will never be a doctor. It is what you want; I have heard you talking about it, but it's inappropriate. As a woman, and my daughter, you have these three choices. One, you can be a wife. Two, you can be a nun. Three, you can be a secretary. This I will pay for, for you to take classes to learn how to become a typist. I will not, however, waste one cent on a woman's university education. That would be like throwing fistfuls of money into the sewer.'"

I peeled my eyelids back in disbelief. To affirm that what she'd said was true, Mom nodded. She took another sip of wine, savored it, and mused: "My two years of university. My friends. It was me, Rebeca, Beatriz, and Diana. Some of the professors were condescending and belittled us, but there was one, Cuevas, who was kind. He helped me pay for my books my most difficult semester, and his wife would buy me lunch sometimes. Cuevas was important, a very esteemed man. The rector of the School of Chemistry. He made an enormous mistake, though. He failed a group of boys who were members of the Student Federation of Guadalajara. Do you know what the Student Federation of Guadalajara is? The SFG?"

Clueless, I shook my head.

"They make your father's Chicano college clubs," she elaborated, "look like kindergarten games. The PRI backed them. You know what the PRI is? The party that runs the government?"

I remembered, during childhood visits to Mexico, seeing PRI and PAN stenciled to whitewashed brick walls. Abuelito wore a PRI button pinned to his lapel sometimes. I nodded.

"Good," Mom asserted, "Then you can guess that you weren't supposed to tell the kids in the SFG no for anything. The SFG boys, a little army of them—and they looked like an army, and they even wore uniforms to school—ganged up on Cuevas and offered him one chance to modify their F's. He responded to their threat by asking, 'Why don't you take a chance . . . and study?'

"They smiled and thanked him for his suggestion and he didn't hear from them for a week. Then, as he and his wife were leaving their house one afternoon, a Volkswagen van pulled onto his street and drove up to the curb. A machine gun opened fire and t-t-t-t-t-t-t-t-t-t-t, they cut the two of them in half."

Clutching the stem of her wine glass tight, Mom hiccupped and said, "I'm not joking. They really cut them in half. At least Cuevas. He was in two pieces. Bullets got his spinal cord."

"Did they catch the people who shot them?"

Mom laughed. "No. Nobody saw anything!"

"But you said it was afternoon!" I squealed like a silly gringa.

"In Mexico," Mom reminded me bluntly, "nobody sees anything. Nobody hears anything. Nobody says anything. Remember? The December that you were ten? What you saw at the statue of Christopher Columbus?"

I went back to the winter that I was ten. The statue in the middle of the roundabout. Guadalajara at night. Two women. Six men. Mom could see my thoughts as she looked into my eyes.

"You understand me?" she asked.

I nodded.

When Rex became a narco, I went to the botánica by the Masonic Temple and bought an icon of Malverde. Malverde is a guardian angel who hasn't been officially recognized by the Catholic Church yet. He looks suspiciously like Pedro Infante, Mexico's answer to Frank Sinatra, and I've never visited his shrine. It's located near some railroad tracks in Culiacán, Sinaloa, the state where my Tía Carmen lives now.

Who prays to Malverde? Narcos and the people who love them. You could call him our patron saint. It's rumored that in life he was an outlaw, a bandido, and he protects fellow fugitives, answering their prayers. He's not much different from Saint Ambrose, who blesses beekeepers, or Saint Dismas, whose scapulars are worn by undertakers, and if brewers and prostitutes have intercessors to appeal to, it makes perfect sense that those in the drug trade should have their own, too. I think it's just a matter of time before the Vatican recognizes this mustached hero. Malverde merchandising is already a cottage industry in my neck of the woods.

My Malverde icon is small. It's nestled among other trinkets and doodads that fill the altar above my stuffed animal collection. This altar is actually a plain, wood box, painted pistachio green, that's got three shelves in it. It's rather rustic looking and it's filled with stuff that's symbolic to me and probably makes me look, to the untrained eye, like a Santería practitioner. There are handmade dolls sewn by Abuelita.

Miniature foods—tamales, tortas, panes—purchased from stalls at El Mercado de San Juan de Dios. Ephemera from my first communion. Ephemera from funerals: Casimir's (stillborn), Pretty Boy's (murder), Aunt Angelica's and Uncle Steve's (double suicide). Souvenirs, like rosaries, from Catholic articles, stores, and mission gift shops. Some of my childhood teeth. A statue of the Angel Gabriel. Copper milagros shaped like sports cars and Sacred Hearts. Skeletons made of clay and string. Dried roses and carnations. A rattlesnake tail.

I felt like a mafia wife the first night I prayed to Malverde to ask him to watch over Rex. It was a totally over-the-top move, and I confess, Rex isn't really a narco; she's a low-level drug dealer who looks like an adolescent skater boy with boobs. Having sex with the princess of cocaine didn't ensnare her and make her a trafficker, a pink Post-it note did. For some reason, this seems so American to me, that my girlfriend's destiny was ordained by a time-saving device that comes in both pastels and neons.

Rex is in graduate school at Cal State Long Beach; she started this year, and she's studying rhetoric. On a lark, she took a women's studies seminar that came highly recommended and got along well with the handsome butch who taught the course. One day, the woman returned a paper to her without a grade on it. Attached was a sticky memo with this cryptic message: Please see me during my office hours today.

Like any conscientious dork, Rex showed up sweating. Was the woman going to accuse her of plagiarizing? Threaten to fail her because her phone went off during discussion and the ring tone was Flavor Flav professing his own name? Blackmail her for butch-on-butch sexual favors?

"Shut the door," the professor told her. "Don't worry. You got an A." She smiled sheepishly, all crow's feet and straight teeth, maintaining the expression for an awkward couple of seconds. "I know this is rather unorthodox," she continued, "but could you score me some pot?" (Nervous laughter.) "You seem like you know where to get some. It's for my girlfriend. She's new to the area and doesn't have a connection yet."

Rex hadn't smoked out in years, not since the time she got high and acted like she was on sherm. That was scary. She ran around the neighborhood barefoot and braless, doing embarrassing things, frightening children. The experience made her swear off pot forever.

Sensing Rex's hesitation, the butch promised, "I'll pay you a hundred bucks for a dime if you can get it to me by tonight."

Rex reached behind her ear and grabbed the ballpoint pen she keeps tucked there. "What's your address?" she asked, poised to jot it on the back of her grimy hand.

Since that afternoon, Rex has become the Pablo Escobar of the Women's Studies Department, with several middlepeople (this term seems more apropos than middle*men*) comprising her supply chain. Rex delivers the goods, I procure them from Heather, my tattoo artist, and she procures them from a fourth party named Santo. That's all I know about the guy. That his name's Santo. I don't really care to know any more about him. His name scares me.

Around Halloween, I needed to cop from Heather. I also had cash Grandma Luz had surprised me with and given me for my birthday, so I decided to kill two birds with one stone. I scheduled an appointment for weed and work. At high noon, Heather showed up at our building, the goods in her purse and her equipment in her arms. I buzzed her upstairs, let her in, and she followed me to the living room. Heather prepped inks, ointments, and cleansers on a freshly scrubbed TV tray while I watched her from the couch, my exposed wrist waiting on the ratty towel I'd draped over one of its big velvet arms. I looked down at my bluish veins and took a mental picture of them while Heather snapped her gum before spitting it into the trash. Looking up, I saw her kneeling on her twiggy legs beside the coffee table. She'd begun rolling a joint and as she meticulously fashioned it, Heather updated me on her divorce from an Icelandic no-goodnik who'd used her for a green card.

"Wait," I interrupted her diatribe, "does Arnie know Björk?" I giggled.

"Deirdre," began Heather, "that was funny the first three times. It's not anymore."

"Okay," I conceded. "I'll stop."

I enjoy listening to Heather shit-talk Arnie and describe her childhood, which she spent working in her father's funeral home. Heather's stories soothe me and make getting tattooed by her feel like getting my hair done: therapeutic, entertaining. Like most women, I've got a high pain threshold and me and Heather gossip the whole time her needle bites into my skin, marking me with things some people think are silly, things that make assholes ask why. Why would you get *that* on your body?

Because. Because it's fucking fun. And yes, before you ask, it hurts.

Heather gets high on our balcony before working and I've got no apprehension about letting her draw indelibly on me with what others might consider impaired judgment. She's like one of those people who're telling the truth when they claim: I know it sounds weird but I swear I drive better when I'm drunk. Smoking out does not adversely affect her skills. In fact, I think it might enhance them.

133

Once Heather finished tattooing the inside of my wrist, she smeared goo on my new piece and sheathed my forearm in protective Saran Wrap. She collected her stuff, got ready to go, and then we took the elevator downstairs together. As we parted ways, I felt a pang of guilt. I'm employed at a "last chance" school, a place where kids get sent after they've been expelled from every school in town or have just been released from juvie. I got the job when Rex had freshly gotten her AA degree from city college, and in my time teaching there, I've only had three white students, who I've enjoyed watching learn what it feels like to be a minority. Some days, the vibe on campus does get a little *Dangerous Minds*. Like I've got kids who wear electronic ankle bracelets so their probation officers can monitor their movements, and I've confiscated weapons including a knife longer than my foot. Things are fairly harmonious most of the time, though.

I work a split shift at the school, mornings from 8 to 12, afternoons from 3 to 5. I like this schedule because it leaves a huge chunk of daylight to do as I please. I can run to the post office, work out at the gym, or shop for the weekly groceries without any rush hour hassles. I can get tattooed, gossip with friends, and have baggies of marijuana delivered to my front door.

Sigh.

Eddie Chasco. He was one of my pupils. Smart but not that smart. He'd just been remanded to the California Youth Authority for failing a drug test, and there I was, a role model, walking up the street with hands dirtied by drugs that needed smuggling across town.

Oh well. Ni modo, as Mom says. Eddie should've drunk bleach before his exam.

It takes me less than five minutes to get to work. An old bank building two blocks from my apartment houses my school, and the place still looks and feels like what it used to be despite the sign "Oasis: An Alternative Learning Center" mounted out front. Years ago, robbers staged a heist there, leaving two people bullet-riddled, so the nonprofit Oasis acquired the structure hella cheap. Apparently, the urban legend is true; landlords will practically beg you to rent the scene of a violent homicide. Today, the former vault where they executed the two tellers functions as a brain trust, the teacher's lounge/office. The former boardroom, on the third floor, is where I teach history, government, and econ.

Arriving at work, I trudged up the stairs leading to the school's front door. "Virus" was scratched into every glass panel composing the lobby's fish tank face. I shook my head. Virus was Junior Camarena's tag. He doodled it all over the homework he occasionally did and the

134

class work he was pretty good at and on the desk he sat at and he'd be expelled by day's end. His mom would show up tomorrow, screaming about how her son didn't do it, he was framed because he was Mexican with a shaved head, and what's this bill for window replacement about?

I opened the door and saw the principal talking to a guy wearing a suit only a lawyer would wear. They were huddled where the ATM used to be, speaking in hushed tones, commiserating. Things like that'd been happening a lot lately. Auditors arriving unannounced. Frightened board members climbing off the elevator and running to their Mercedes parked in the Jack in the Box lot. All of us peons—teachers, aides, secretaries—could sense unemployment on the horizon.

The principal gave me a stay-away look, so I took the stairs to the third floor. I passed the library, a joke; it'd been created in a day so that the school could qualify for a grant us teachers hadn't seen a penny of. Our principal was driving a new convertible, though. I hurried past the vice principal's closed door and the special programs office and then turned left, entering the refuge of my room. I'd decorated it with posters of revolutionary women. Sojourner Truth knitting, the question "Ain't I A Woman?" scrolling across the top. Patty Hearst wielding her machine gun in front of the Symbionese Liberation Army's blurry hydra. Dolores Huerta, like a brown Norma Rae, at the helm of a strike. Phoolan Devi, the Bandit Queen, her rifle ready to blow balls off of rapists.

The kids started trickling in. I had about fifteen, and that day they were going to read a little about third parties, learn about one in particular, and create a poster about it. After they read, I split them into groups, assigned them their parties, and managed them as they got to work. Amazing depictions of the United States Marijuana Party, the Green Party, the Peace and Freedom Party, and the American Independent Party took shape. I don't think the kids working on the Libertarian Party got it. Instead of images demonstrating the party's commitment to free enterprise, I got a drawing of a Second Amendment–loving hooker riding a moped to the abortion clinic. This was my fault for spending way too much time hanging out at the Green kids' table, going on and on about the mixed feelings I have toward Ralph Nader, explaining the difference between Lebanese (Nader) and lesbian (me).

The groups took the final half hour of class to share their posters with everyone, and then five o'clock rolled around. The kids tidied up and I excused them. I went down to the vault to take care of some odds and ends before leaving, and the janitor locked the lobby doors behind me as I left Oasis, the last one to do so. Slowly, I descended the tiled steps leading to the city sidewalk. I inhaled. The moon was unusually bright, the air was unusually warm, and the night smelled like lilac. I crossed the boulevard, hustling past the small house with the Israeli flag waving on its porch. A busted mattress and guts-spilling-out TV set littered its alley. A little red shack and a big aqua house and then the Lutheran church that's our polling precinct. I turned right, headed down my street, its stoic palm trees making me feel safe. A man was walking his pit bull.

Somewhere, an engine backfired.

All three of us gave a start.

Then I laughed and got my keys out, letting myself in.

As I took the stairwell up to my apartment, I could smell tortillas being fried in vegetable oil. The aroma made me hungry, my mouth watered, and I hurried down the hall, to my door. As I stepped inside, Rex hesitantly called out, "Dee?" and ran to greet me.

She never does that.

She stood under the hall light, adjusting her glasses, and I took note of a very specific look she was wearing, one kids wear when they've already done something they were supposed to get permission to do so ex post facto they ask permission while twisting their legs in a pee-pee dance. As Rex performed this move, she blocked my passage.

"Dee, this afternoon, I went to Cris's to deliver a bag and guess what?"

"What?"

"She found a rabbit!"

"Mhmm."

"She was taking out the trash and she saw something dart under a car out in the alley and she checked behind the rear tire and there it was. A poor, little rabbit."

"Mhmm."

"Cris caught it and she's been keeping it in her garage, but her and Melissa can't keep it for good because they've got dogs that're assholes."

"Mhmm."

"Well, I've wanted to get a dog forever but 'cause of where we've lived I can't have one so I've never said anything, but now I'm thinking a rabbit would be perfect because they're so little and they don't make any noise."

"Rex, is there a rabbit in this house?"

In a small voice, she responded, "Yes."

"Rex!" I stormed past her blockade and into the living room. On our coffee table rested a small cage. A rabbit cowered in the corner. He looked up at me. And glared.

Aquí viene Johnny

RAQUEL GUTIÉRREZ

Ana Roque got her Johnny Rocket, homey."

Ana says this into the mirror, shooting her finger gun toward her chocolate-red reflection as she inspects the small skate-or-die volcanoes erupting hair gel on her scalp. The cool skater guys she envied wore mile-high spikes held up by the gel-hairspray-blow-dryer formula. Depending on the situation, the neighborhood, the disproportionate ratio of truth to reputation, and how much ass she was or wasn't going to pull in that night, Ana would decorate her sideburns with curly-Qs. Other times she would sculpt her own sideburns long and thick like a stray cat. After today's locker-room high school showdown with them nasty cha-chas over a pair of cheap boxers, tonight Ana just wants to meet a girl. Careful not to spill any product on her T-shirt, she parts her hair with a pink jelly glob and a ton of hairspray from that ten-year-old can of Aqua Net stored under the sink, the same pink and silver can her mom used back in the Nelson years.

Ana laughs a gran puta when she remembers this shit. Mamá never goes out anymore, thank God. No more of that cumbia twisting, late-night slurring, freestyle fucking. Mamá and Nelson. Ana and her brother Pancho stayed behind when they went off to church—this was before Nestor came from El Salvador to live with them. Nelson forced them to sit in front of the tele and watch Benny Hinn throw his white-suited televangelist self over the limp legs of some obese black lady in a wheelchair.

137

Who cares, she tells herself, with Johnny Rocket in my pants. With her funky jellied dildo, some luck, and the punch tonight's cheap keg will pack, she just might use it on some fine young light thing from Montebello. *Puta vos, I'm Johnny Rocket.* Ana never Salvi cusses, that is, curses out loud like her Salvadoran uncles would. She wouldn't dare do so at school because she doesn't want any of them to hear how she turns the last syllable up with a sudden lilt in her accent only to get called a chuntara for doing so. That's why she begs Mamá for some money to hit up the allies every week as she and Becky conduct a very successful ten-point anti-chunt program also known as CA—Chuntaros Anonymous. A very painful assimilation process unbeknownst to them as such because it's one thing for your parents to be chuntaros, but you don't have to follow in their faded acid-wash footsteps. Consuming as a way to counter the way of their chuntaro elders. Come Monday morning, she walks in all big and bad in some new Dickies, brown like 31 flavors, snug yet never pronouncing her curves.

Asco! This bathroom fuckin' stinks! Dirty, sweaty huevos and that shitty ring in the toilet forces a quick gag reflex as her skin starts to crawl. She is reminded of the awful junkie shitholes in MacArthur Park. Pancho lives here too, Ana thinks to herself. *It is fucked up how he acts toward Mamá.* Puro gangster pelon but this fuckhead knows dick about slanging or whatever he and his homeboys do, stupid Tupac going to get middle brother killed one of these days. Ana is not going to clean it, seeing that it's not her turn nor is she a little bitch trying to kiss maternal ass. And Pancho can be so stupid on the cusp of cruel with Ana, when he grabs his member menacingly. He taunts Ana with what he thinks she is envious of.

Bex is running on time but too late for Ana's anxious ass. Tonight they cruise east to catch the T-party off the pager number Ana called earlier in the day. She was in charge of finding the party and Bex was going to hook up the ride to get them there. Ana has a friend who knows some girl from Schurr High who throws a Wednesday after-school party with the occasional keg. All these chicks kick it after some support group where they all bitch and moan about liking girls and how their mother's come after them with Bibles and unmarried thirty-year-old men. Montebello girls are notoriously sexy and freaky-liberated, though it is rare to find one who digs butches or Salvadoran dark skin. Still, there is nothing else going on in Pico-Union and Ana is not above femming it up for play.

No one is home, just Ana and fucking Zeppelin. Her rocker horns are superchido and sexy as she stands there practicing looking sensitive although she's just horny and forlorn as fuck. That's how you hook a loca, man. No, not a loca in that mi vida loca kind of way, but a loca all up in that I-never-promised-you-a-rose-garden type of shit. The kind of girl with a serious case of the crazies who pours Elmer's glue all over her hands to let it dry and peel all throughout first period, who puts glittery flower and heart stickers all over her switchblades and Zippo lighters. The kind that cuts deep. The kind that shows off cigarette scars all sweet and alluring like they were dainty hands waiting to be christened with a hundred baby kisses. The kind that Ana always falls in love with. Ana— just a harmless puppy with a hard cock.

The rusty boom box hisses Ana out of her head with the speaker's static vibrating on the toilet seat lid. The music indulges Ana with a feeling of invincibility. She wants to holler in slow motion like a wolf. Ana walks around in a circle, but it's not a circle, it's the mosh pit in her head. She aches to get beat on hard. La Bex hooked up a badass mix— Bikini Kill, L7, Screaming Trees, Iron Maiden, and Metallica.

Bex has her older brother's little records from when he used to go to punk shows at the Anti-Club on Melrose and Fender's in Long Beach, back when there were no Hot Topics in the mall. When it was pure. Thunder bass claps in rapid succession and off-time signatures; it's the rhythm of the beast that beats like a drum, monster beats, a late-night siren scream, a mom too tired to dream. Ghetto birds flapping their wings in between staccato bursts of *Living, loving, she's just a woman.*

Empty room and no one will be home for at least another hour. Johnny Rocket leads Ana, compelling her to pace back and forth throwing reckless punches in the air. She walks in a semicircle in the living room where she sleeps with her two older brothers. No one worried even though they should have about the proximity Ana had to Pancho and Nestor. She certainly looked like a more beautiful, softer version of her brothers, which enabled most people to think that her brothers could never bother in harming such a tough girl when there are so many other fragile little girls in the building for them to victimize. Her big hands, wide hips, flat chest, and strong legs made you believe that she could take care of herself.

Her wiry arms deliver a right hook at the papal plate that sits on the end table; an uppercut for the Jesus Christ of El Salvador, the creepy little-kid version of Jesus on the ugly calendar from the cheap furniture spot around the corner on Sixth Street. She did not consent to share space with these religious surrogate fathers and little brothers. But, Mamá gets the bedroom, and traces of men diminish with each inhale and exhale. Ana never shared the bed with her mother. There was never any room before Mamá gave up all that romantic-tragedy-for-a-man type of shit with Nelson. He constantly spoke of seeing the devil's arm around Ana's shoulders and said she should get baptized in his church. He certainly wasn't her father, but that wasn't Ana's problem. She was used to enduring men like Nelson—men who assaulted her with unwelcome opinions as soon as she ventured outside the apartment. Mamá could only do so much, but to cope with Nelson's limp dick was not an option, especially since all he does is talk about God. Mamá couldn't love God enough for this man or his useless member—todos tenemos vicio.

It was nice to revel in Mamá's absence. Ana was growing cagey the older she got and more so because of Mamá's constant reminders that she preferred the children of strangers over her own brood. Those kids west of La Cienega never got into trouble. None of the sweet blond children Mamá looked after ever grew up to gangbang, run game in the park, be dykes, or sniff glue out of brown paper bags. Mamá's job was her fantasy life away from the home she inadvertently built with her first life's children. It was always difficult to escape one's first life when you are the type of mother who doesn't kill her children by the side of river. All that tragic Llorona mythology is for Mexicans anyway.

Ana successfully conceals her skater spikes and rocker horns from her mother's disapproving tirades. Mamá is never so exhausted that she can't deliver a few devastating critiques on Ana's clothes and masculine mannerisms. Manflora is Mamá's favorite dis, though to Ana's ears it sounds praising. Tough and tender, sweet and salty, penis and vagina—who doesn't want to be a man-flower?

Mamá will come back soon to the one bedroom, corner of 8th and Bonnie Brae, after a marathon shift in Cheviot Hills on the west side. One neighborhood in twenty years, three sons and seven families later—convenient to keep the same bus route, clockwork, except every couple of years she comes home about twenty minutes later than the year before. There's just too many people in L.A. There's just too much of this and not enough of that. Siempre, so that's what this story is about. Excess and lack thereof.

The term they use is "being referred by," though Ana could really only imagine seven families passing her mother around like an orphan. It was *she* who was there to take care of their children, though once they hit ten they didn't need her housebreaking services anymore. How great it will be for Simon and Caitlin to learn Spanish and ass-wiping at such an early age; it will certainly give them an edge in admission at Harvard Westlake hands down. Folks in Cheviot Hills are rich, but not as rich as they are in New York City. In New York they don't hire Salvadoran ladies to watch their kids; they get semipedigreed white college girls to walk their brats. Now that's money.

Ana hears the familiar hum then cough of a car double-parked outside her building.

"Ey! Johnny Rocket!" Bex calls out in a throaty tone. "Let's go, man!"

Ana, who pokes her head out the window and sees Bex behind the wheel with similar spikes busting out of her scalp, tosses her chin up in the salutatory way. She walks back to the bathroom to slurp a quick mouthful of Listerine, winces as it stings her gums, and spits the fiery liquid into the sink. Ana gives her hair another once-over and runs her fingertips along the line of peaks stiffened by her mother's can of hairspray. She straightens her long shorts around her hips and makes sure that the right amount of boxer short is poking above her beltline, careful not to push Johnny Rocket out of the makeshift harness Ana fashioned out of thick rubber bands, an old tube sock, and a small metal belt buckle. She gives her reflection a rascally smirk. *It's on, motherfucker*, she tells herself. Ana hears Bex growing impatient as she blasts the horn, jolting Ana out of her momentary lapse into vanity.

Bex looks at the digital clock on the dashboard, anxious to get through downtown traffic and then all of East L.A. to Montebello. She hates the freeway, making it easier for her brother to loan her his jalopy Civic. Bex exhales deeply and sits back, looking into the rearview mirror as she smoothes down her thickly arched eyebrows. She notices a familiar female body coming into focus, causing her eyes to widen and her mouth to mutter obscenities. The older woman with a salt-and-pepper bob carries two plastic grocery bags in each hand as she walks toward Ana's building from the bus stop. Bex tries to slump down in her seat but knows the woman will suspiciously recognize the car covered in faded punk band and KROQ-FM stickers. Ana is coming down the hall and will be busting through the metal gate shortly. The woman is waddling closer, only footsteps away from the building's decaying entrance. Bex, in an attempt to restrain her nervous energy, unwittingly hits the horn, producing a toot so loud it startles both driver and pedestrian. Ana hears the second honk, smiles huge, and sprints down the hall like a husky boy about to score his first goal. She charges the door and whacks it open. Her grin quickly fades—busted—as she sees her mother whipping her neck away from Bex's honking. As she notices the scandalized expression on Ana's mother's face, Bex peels out, making a sharp right turn up the street.

"Were you going somewhere?" Mamá asks sharply as she scrutinizes Ana's alien uniform. "¿Por qué te miras así?" Mamá hissed her last query and moved toward Ana's torso, feeling the T-shirt. "Ra-mo-nezz." Mamá pronounces each syllable mockingly.

"It's Ramones, Mom," Ana retorts, turning her head to look for Bex.

"Look at your hair. . . . ¿En qué andas, muchachita?" Mamá says as she drops two of the grocery bags and brusquely grabs her daughter's arm. Ana jolts back and her heel gets caught on a pebble, making her lose her balance and narrowly avoid a fall. In trying to regain her composure, Ana's do-it-yourself harness shifts in her pants, creating a noticeable bulge in her crotch. Mamá gasps as Ana tries to smooth the disobedient dildo back down to its dormant state.

"Go upstairs and take that thing off," Mamá says through gritted teeth. Her hand turns into a fist as her body begins to shake. "No sos hombre, ¿qué te pasa?" Ana winced as her mother's hurtful words left their burning mark on her heart, sketching the blueprint for a future deposit of keloid numbness. There was no use in fabricating an elaborate storyline as Mamá emanated such a quiet fury, interminably concerned with retaining her poise in public. Ana stood facing her mother, knowing that she had a better chance delaying physical punishment by remaining in public view then by confronting her mother in their lone apartment. Ana does not budge.

"I don't need to be a man, Mamá," Ana says coolly. "I'm me and other things al mismo tiempo." Ana was tired. The regurgitation of shame was becoming unbearable. Mamá's eyes flashed with rage as she pursed her lips tight, shock and incredulity coursing through vein and artery. Ana crossed her arms and rolled her eyes at her mother's silence, aggravating the woman to respond with an open-handed slap. Before Ana registers the sting on her cheek, a car in the invisible distance is vrooming loudly, a skidding interruption to the showdown on the curb. Ana touches her cheek though her eyes follow the steely blue Honda maneuvering along her street. Fear and relief overwhelm her as she bolts toward Bex and the passenger seat that would transport her to a temporary paradise. Ana lifts the handle, gets inside, and turns to sneer in her mother's direction, defiant and desperate to be seen.

"Wassup, man?" Bex asks. She has seen the wrath of Ana's mother many times in the decade they have been friends. "You know you can crash with me, right?"

"It's all good, man," Ana said, quietly wiping a renegade tear from the corner of her eye. "She's not going to get in my head this time."

The two homegirls drove in silence down Third Street, passing through Little Tokyo and the Toy District with nothing but the pull-out tape deck playing X-Ray Spex through a busted speaker.

"For what it's worth, Johnny," Bex says with her usual optimistic smile, "I'm glad we're going out."

"Yeah, me too," Ana replied, digesting the familiar bittersweet tang between her real and perceived lives. "I just want to meet a girl tonight, ya know."

Haunting José

RIGOBERTO GONZÁLEZ

Don't ask if I believe in ghosts. I refuse to, even as I lie here listening to the strange sounds coming from inside the walls. If this were my old apartment I'd dismiss the noises as the everyday chatter of an old kitchen: the overworked wires in the stove, the pipes beneath the sink, shrinking or expanding in response to the season, the refrigerator creaking with the burden of its own weight. No ghosts there. Only the echoes of the living.

My family, on the other hand, can't get enough of ghosts. They'll sit for hours in the evenings, spinning tales of spectral visitations and paranormal activity—memories of moving objects, hearsay of haunted houses, postpartum possessions, demon dwellings, et cetera. Each time I hear the stories they come with a little more flourish and flair than the earlier versions. That's why it took me so long to lose my fear of the dark, and why, before I became a grown-up and an atheist, I recited every memorized prayer in the catechism—the Ave Maria, the Credo, the Lord's Prayer, et cetera—before I could sleep. Those prayers were like a nice Catholic shield against my grandfather's hoof-footed, chicken-legged, goat-horned, pitchfork-carrying dwarf devils that wandered the shadows after sundown, searching for errant children.

All through my college years I've never taken home a friend or a lover, afraid that my grandfather would come over and commence to entertain his captive audience with his long-winded, implausible, unbelievable stories. I'd be embarrassed to place a friend in a situation like that. Or worse yet, what if my guest witnessed one of my mother's many superstitions—odd, unrecognizable ones like her habit of crossing herself whenever the clock chimes to the hour, or lighting the candle on top of the television whenever the pope appears on the screen? Even other Mexicans don't behave this way.

I would never think to tell my mother about the sounds in my new studio apartment in Seattle. She'd either want to rush over to bless every comer with one of her crazy concoctions of oil and cactus extract or she'd bring it up at the next gathering of ghost telling I happen to stumble upon. "José's new apartment is haunted. Isn't it, José?" she'd say, and then my grandfather would pounce on it, never letting up until I fabricated some acceptable narrative around the whole thing.

There isn't really anything worth talking about anyway. I'm simply unfamiliar with the new place and its noises. All living spaces have them, I've discovered. My old apartment channeled those sounds through the appliances because I spent many an evening preparing an exquisite meal that would earn me an exquisite roll in the hay. That's why I don't date vegetarians. I've also discovered that the best aphrodisiac is meat—steak, preferably, but in moderation. It must trigger something primal in a man when combining the two acts, eating and fucking, so close together. They always come back for seconds.

They also tend to sleep quite soundly when all is said and done. Derek here is snoring like a bull and keeping me up. I could light a firecracker in his ear and he wouldn't budge. It's a miracle I can still hear the sounds inside the walls. Outside, the wind is blowing. But the glass must be bulletproof or something because I can barely detect the rustling of the leaves. I'm not sure yet if this is better, the silence of the outside world. In my old apartment the window was a thin glass and I could hear the passersby stumbling home late at night, arguing all along the sidewalk, or jabbering on their cells to friends in later time zones. This random eavesdropping was like an urban lullaby that eased me into dream. Not that Seattle needs another lullaby: the traffic and the rain are good enough. Maybe that's why I'm having trouble sleeping tonight—I can hear no street noise, and it hasn't rained in a week, and Derek here snores like he dances, without rhythm.

There it is again.

The sounds are coming from inside the walls, not through them. I know the difference. Through plaster and brick the noises that carry are the neighbors'. In the old apartment, I was wedged between Mrs. Hillerman and a Seattle cliché, a musician. Mrs. H always fell asleep with the television at high volume, apparently never forgetting to pop off her hearing aid—the same powerful little amplifier that pressed her to bang on my wall when she could hear my stereo playing. On a bad day, the old lady would be yelling into the phone to one doctor or another, or to the nurse who came over to administer some injection, and the guitar player would be composing insufferable tunes that I've only heard in mediocre musicals played at the local coffee shops. At times like that, I fled my tiny Capital Hill haven and found myself on my mother's couch in that old house across the lake. Why my mother chose Queen Anne I'll never know. There are plenty more inexpensive neighborhoods. Certainly, more inexpensive towns. But no, Mami and Gramps had to follow me here to Seattle and blow the settlement money again on an old fixer-upper that doesn't have a single glimpse of a body of water.

But I digress. My point is that I can tell when it's a human-made sound and when it's something more independent of our obnoxious species. The studio must be made of a thicker material, because I can only hear my neighbors murmuring, even when their voices are loud. No wonder I had such trouble hammering in the nails. I came this close to purchasing a drill. My neighbors here are much quieter—a reflection of their class status, no doubt. But the lack of noise also makes the place feel isolated, empty, and lonely.

Technically I now live in Madrona, where the homes are as big as palaces, but tucked away demurely behind extravagant foliage, as if apologetic about their size. I can still climb on the Number 2 bus to Queen Anne, but it's a much longer trip. It's also a longer drive to the university, where I hope to earn my master's in English in a year or two. However long it takes, my family will be patient, just as they were when I was completing my bachelor's—two years in San Diego and two more years in Tucson. But they follow my tracks from city to city, afraid they'll lose sight of me.

There it is again. It's as if the walls are inhabited. Maybe by those tiny aberrations I've seen in old horror flicks—little green bug-eyed monsters that worm out through the vents to antagonize the new inhabitants of their domain. They're beating on the wall to keep me up, to exhaust me into leaving and giving this place back to them. Or maybe it's muttering I hear, the leadership counsel plotting my overthrow. Maybe they're further along in the plan by now and are giving last-minute instructions to the minions—the miniature henchmen who will have miniature statues erected in honor of the successful coup. Am I listening to myself? I sound just like my grandfather.

"Derek," I say into Derek's ear, not bothering to whisper.

"Huh, what?" Derek utters, half asleep.

"I can't sleep with all this noise," I say. Derek rolls his eyes around as if searching to zero in on the culprit.

"I don't hear anything," he says. He turns around and presses his body against mine. I can feel his penis growing against my leg.

"That's not why I woke you up," I say. "You're snoring too loud."

"Sorry," Derek says. He yawns, showing me his set of perfect white teeth. "Relájate, José. Tenemos clase mañana."

One thing I detest is when non-native speakers address me in Spanish, especially if they're white. And I don't care if Derek is black and as fluent as I am; it still bothers me. I nudge his arm off me and go sit on the chaise. Above it hangs that Alfredo Arreguín poster my mother gave me for my twenty-fourth birthday. She says Arreguín is from Michoacán, just like our family, and that he's exiled out here in Seattle, just as we are. Exile. Is that what this is?

Exile. The dictionary defines it as: 1. Banishment; also: voluntary absence from one's country or home; 2. A person driven from his or her native place.

I toss the dictionary back on the coffee table. Derek has started snoring. And the sounds are here again, coming from inside the walls. Maybe the walls are not inhabited by physical beings at all. I'm not claiming ghosts; I'm claiming something else, something that's not as simplistic, or sensationalistic. Then suddenly there's a crack and I jump. I look behind me, expecting to find a fracture, deep and jagged, running down from the ceiling, but find nothing. I'm scaring myself with my own nonsense. Still, I climb back into bed and into the comfort of Derek's body heat. That and my body blanket of tattoos is all I need to keep me warm. I place my hand along the curve of his hip and eventually, miraculously, I fall asleep.

My eyes open. I believe I've slept a few hours, but when I check the clock across the room I'm dismayed that I've been tricked by a two-minute submersion into the deep unconsciousness. And now I'm wide awake.

Maybe I'll read poetry. That's always boring. But the thought of turning on the light at this hour makes my face hurt, so I opt to leave my old Norton Anthology alone and collecting dust at the base of the bookshelf. Instead I go back to the chaise, to the Arreguín poster of salmon leaping in and out of visibility through the ocean waves.

This time I'm not as jittery when I hear the sounds coming from inside the walls. It's as if I'm getting used to them. When my grandfather talks about his ghosts, he speaks of them so casually, as if they're old friends dropping in to visit. Unlike my mother's visitors, grandfather's ghosts are spirits unknown to him, complete strangers with whom he had no earthly connection. It's as if all those years that he worked in Baja as the entrance attendant at a parking garage, opening and closing the heavy aluminum doors for tourists and locals alike, has earned him the trust of every citizen at the gates of the Otherworld. Random ghosts walk through, and many of them take a pause in their journey to exchange pleasantries with my grandfather.

"Had a fellow here last night," my grandfather will confess without warning. "A poor soul from Oaxaca, who lost his life in a factory. He's going back to his homeland to ask his relatives to ship his body back. Give him a proper burial among his people."

And then just as abruptly my grandfather will scratch his chin and reach across the table for a helping of tortillas.

My mother, on the other hand, claims it's all our dead relatives who get in touch with her, my father included. Old Tía Mariquita came once to reveal where she had hidden her cache of jewelry. My mother sent word to our cousins back in Michoacán and we never heard back from them. My mother says it's because they found the gold and are afraid she'll want to collect her share for relaying the message. I think it's because they dug through half the courtyard by the time it dawned on them what fools they were, following instructions from their crazy aunt up north.

Cousin Braulio came to pay her a visit also. He was our lay-about relative who drowned in a bucket of water. The story is that he came home late one night and was too drunk to bother going into the kitchen to pour a glass out of the cooler. So he knelt down to lap it up from the bucket that had been collecting rain all evening. It was a deep bucket, and a heavy Braulio. He passed out with his head in the water and that was the end of that. We all accepted that explanation, and so did the authorities, who had had their run-ins with this town drunk before. But the version his ghost came to tell my mother made everyone in Braulio's household nervous, enough to have them shut out our branch of the family tree from theirs.

"Josefina," my grandfather asked her. "Are you sure that's what he said?" Even he understood the ramifications of that disclosure.

"Positive," my mother answered. But that wasn't enough for the authorities to reopen the case, and the death of Braulio remained an accidental drowning, not a murder.

These two visits were enough to instill confidence in my mother that she was not out of her mind and that she needed to pay close attention, and even heed those communiqués from the great beyond. So when she claimed that my father had come to tell her that she must let me guide her way through the rest of her life, she made it her mission to move to the same city shortly after I do. We started out in the Caliente Valley, where I was born, then made our way to San Diego, and then Tucson, and now Seattle. What allows her to pick up and leave, dragging my retired grandfather with her, is the money we got after the doctors fucked up my father's kidney surgery and put him in a coma, a state he died in weeks later. All I remember from that time, besides my poor father's frozen body, is my mother sitting at his side, praying, hoping, frightened about staying behind in the country he had brought her to, where I had been born.

Now they follow me, Mami and Gramps—my father's father. As per my father's instructions, they need to be near me, or near enough. I'm the last of the bloodline. I'm precious and the last thread weaving them to this physical world.

If I pursue a PhD, perhaps I'll spare my family another move and simply do it here at the University of Washington. Although it's a peculiar arrangement, this keeping up with my every move, I don't dare defy it. My mother has been through enough. She has certainly given me the space to be who I am. Not only does she overlook the whole gay thing, she's also never objected to my tattoos. I have six, but only two are visible to her—the orchid on my nape and the Guadalupe Posada skeleton on my left forearm. Derek here has made love to the other four: the butterfly on my shoulder blade, the hummingbird on my hipbone, the crown of stars around my pierced nipple, and the swallow on my lower back. So it was with slight trepidation that I informed her I was leaving Capitol Hill.

"You're moving?" my mother said in alarm, her face shriveled up so quickly she was on the verge of tears.

"Just across town," I said. "No further than before." I could see her shaking. I could see her crumbling at the thought of being at the mercy of my capricious, nomadic lifestyle.

"This is a big town," she said, her body deflating with resignation.

Despite myself I reveled in a perverse pleasure. But guilt quickly set in, and I hugged my mother to comfort her, to reassure her that I would never leave her behind. And then I went outside to break the news to my grandfather, and to watch him go through the same state of distress.

Derek stirs in his sleep. He has bent his legs and pushed them up toward his belly. I won't be able to fit my body into his. I suppose I can climb into the other side and spoon him, but that's not why I let a man spend the night. I try to imagine my parents in bed all those years before my father died. I try to imagine how my mother, a widow for almost a decade, has managed the emptiness of her bed without him. Is it any wonder she resorts to these fantasies about the spirit world? It makes her own world that much less vacant.

My mother will always live in fear, I hate to admit. The only change I see in her is in her aging: every year she's grayer and the frown lines on her forehead and around her mouth become deeper with worry. I'm not sure that she was built to survive in any place, but she's doing it somehow, stubbornly sticking to life like a parasite. It's disheartening, but the more time passes, the less I love her. I can feel this loss in my blood. I can feel it thinning out. One day I'll bleed and the fluid will be colorless, transparent as a ghost's.

After this much angst, it'll be disappointing to find out that it's only mice inside the walls, or some infestation of termites—a whole colony of them clustered into one large, pulsing presence. I'm beginning to understand the need for imagination—the need to believe that perhaps it's a restless being trapped behind the wall, like in an Edgar Allan Poe story. He's trying to tell me something, this ghost. They insist on doing that to humans because unlike other ghosts, we the living still have mouths and we can savor a secret or a revelation.

Have I inherited my father's side of the sensitivity to the spirit world, and is it a stranger come to say hello? Or am I more like my mother, attuned to the souls of our departed loved ones, and has my grandmother or even my father come to warn me to knock it off, to stop playing mind games with my poor, living family?

I rise from the chaise and am guided to a spot on the wall where the sounds seem to emanate the loudest. In my weariness I believe I see the wall bubble out like a belly at the moment of exhale. I press my ear and two hands against the cool surface, and then I flatten the rest of my body on it. There's indeed a heartbeat. To get the full effect, I strip off my boxer briefs; my penis sinks into the cushion of my groin. I remain fixed against the wall for a while longer and let my own beating heart communicate with whatever's behind that barrier.

My grandfather contends that there are two types of ghosts: the good ones who will haunt you until you chase them off by asking politely or with obscenities, if the first method doesn't work; and evil ones who come to exercise their last bit of harm before descending into their hell. Those can only be dispelled through a Catholic cleansing.

I believe my guest is a good ghost. But I won't ask him to leave. For a change, I want to be haunted by the dead, and not the living.

"José," Derek calls out to me from the bed. I can see the accent above the e of my name float above his body like a feather from the pillow gone free. "What are you doing?"

I don't answer. I pretend not to hear him, even when he repeats the question. I don't want to explain why I'm standing here in exile with nothing on except my body blanket of tattoos that makes me look like a decoration affixed to the wall.

Imitation of Selena

RAMÓN GARCÍA

The radio transmitted live updates from Corpus Christi, Texas, that warm March day in 1995: Selena, Tex-Mex singing star, had been shot. The Spanish-language TV channels interrupted regular programming to broadcast the standoff between Corpus Christi police and Yolanda Saldívar, Selena's killer, the manager of the official Selena fan club, who was holed up inside her butch four-wheeler with a gun pointed to her crazed, homely face. Hours later Yolanda Saldívar surrendered and Selena was dead, but that was just the beginning.

Selena immediately assumed a new existence, the commercial exploitation of her afterlife: she graced the cover of the Spanish-language edition of *People*; posters of her proliferated at record stores of all sorts; she became the heroine of murals in the barrios and the revered saint of countless altars. Then came the Selena Barbie doll and the cheesy Hollywood movie that transformed Selena into a perfectly nice all-American girl of the Tex-Mex variety. Who could have predicted the unfortunate girl's posthumous powers? Selena sang Americanized Tejano music while dressed in vaquero versions of Versace getups. She seemed destined for oblivion, but the gods, or whatever mysterious powers confer immortality on the mediocre, had another destiny in store. Mexican girls throughout the Southwest, from desolate towns bordering the Rio Grande, to the barrios of East Los Angeles, to every suburb in California and Arizona, shed inexhaustible tears for their murdered idol, their grieving hearts vowing to love her forever.

In Modesto, a semirural suburb in the Central Valley of California, Selena's entrance into the afterlife inspired an unrelenting, contagious carnival of mourning. The Selena myth was so faithfully imitated there that it ended in murder, multiple murders of multiple Selenas.

Here is what happened: The only gay bar in town, the Gold Rush, became the spotlight for a series of killings in the spring of 1996. The Gold Rush is a marginal bar on the outskirts of Modesto; even the gay boys of good standing won't go there because it is a hangout for the town's worst outcasts: the drag queens, the drug dealers and drug addicts, the hustlers, the hardcore cholos, the prostitutes and the prostituted.

The Gold Rush was the kingdom or queendom of Pesticida, a big, fat ex-seventies chola drag queen who was benefactress to a stable of about twenty Modesto drag queens. There were lurid, cruel rumors about the origins of Pesticida's unique name. Some of her young queen entourage claimed that she was deformed by pesticide contamination, but others disagreed. "She has three tits," they joked. "It's because of her Tijuana hormones. They gave her the wrong shots in the wrong places." But only her old guard, the older drag queens, knew that Pesticida had acquired her name when, one monotonous 105-degree summer day in 1979, she single-handedly shot down four pesticide-spraying airplanes with a machine gun she claimed was a gift from a white leftist radical who had smuggled guns to the Sandinistas in Nicaragua. No one was killed, but the ranchers had gotten the message; that year the fields were free of pesticides. "I did it out of a deep revolutionary conviction. Girl's gotta do what a girl's gotta do. Si se puede," the old queens remembered her saying, as she raised her right fist in defiance, Chicano Power style. "But that little number is not going to be repeated. Nothing is worth mascara sweating off your face! Wigs and rifles just don't mix."

For a suburb surrounded by fields, Modesto has an unusually large population of drag queens. And their extravagantly scandalous lives are sanctioned by the Mexicano community, who see in them a grave but necessary aberration of the normal, which they find illustrious in the same way they believe exemplary the abject life of San Martín de Porres, who was not just black, abused, and scorned but also a saint endowed with miracles.

Pesticida was the adoptive mother of young queens who had made the Gold Rush the center of their infamous existence. The town queens, when they reached the age of teenage unreason, ran away from home because their campesino- and cannery-working parents could not understand their untamable greed for female glamour. While other barrio boys played football, got girls pregnant, or joined gangs, the niños reina, as they were called, were primarily preoccupied with the latest Madonna fashions, the most glamorous singers and movie stars, the shades of lipstick, and how to fit into the dresses that they secretly traded with each other. If no one was home, they would gather to simulate beauty contests in which the most realistically pretty one would win. By the time they entered high school and began to have problems at home and at school, they would have established contact with one of Pesticida's drag queens, who mentored them in their transformation from niños reina to young divas.

There would be tears from the mothers of the niños reina (for what they viewed as the ruin of their children), who, consulting the family priest, would be advised to love their strange children despite their shameful behavior; the fathers would turn a blind eye in confusion and repulsion; the grandmothers would say their rosaries and pray to the Virgen that little Joselito be cured of his bad habits, but everyone knew that Joselito would end up at the Gold Rush, a member of Pesticida's distorted familia. That's exactly what happened to a certain José Martínez, who was the first drag queen at the Gold Rush to be killed. He was found in the parking lot of the Gold Rush, five gunshot wounds riddling his purple sequined bell-bottomed pantsuit, an outfit designed by Selena herself, that José Martinez, who went by the name of Ava (after Ava Gardner in *The Barefoot Contessa*), had made in accordance with the pattern illustrated in the book published by Selena's father, *Selena's Dresses: You Too Can Make Your Own*.

Pesticida's girls lived under certain house rules that applied equally to all. The most fundamental law was that one drag queen could not perform the songs of a singing star that another drag queen in the house had previous claims to. If there were disagreements, Pesticida was the absolute arbiter, and her judgment was final. Pesticida held absolute ownership of Selena's stardom. Thus, Ava's imitation of Selena had been a serious subversion of the law.

The second murder claimed the life of Irma, the most beautiful chicken of the house. The youngest queens were called chickens because they were still learning their trade—the personal and public intricacies of being locas, in accordance with their most notorious physical and psychological, God-given attributes. The queens were, in essence, classic actresses. Pesticida ran the Gold Rush like her own personal celebrity studio. She was very fond of Irma because she was creative and, in

Pesticida's words, "artistic and very talented." Irma was born Oscar Salazar, in Turlock in 1970 to farm workers from Michoacán. Oscar Salazar had adopted the name and celebrity traits of Irma Serrano, "La Tigresa," the sexually outrageous Mexican movie star, a notorious exploiter of controversy and scandal. Irma had performed "Si una vez" in full Selena attire—black leather bustier and hot pants. She was shot inside the front seat of her baby-blue Toyota Tercel in the parking lot of the Gold Rush, as she was getting ready to go home at 2:30 in the morning. Her forehead collapsed on the steering wheel, the car horn blaring into the empty Modesto night.

The third murder was of a twenty-year-old transsexual named Bianca, who modeled her 1970s disco queen self-image on Bianca Jagger during her Studio 54 days. His real name was Gabriel Montoya. His parents had emigrated from a small town in Jalisco when he was seven years old. Like the rest of the niños reina, he had dropped out of high school and made a living performing at the Gold Rush. He hooked once in a while and sold a bit of weed or cocaine when money was tight. Pesticida kept a close watch on her subjects' livelihoods, which meant that they had to keep their drinking and drug use to a strict, non-messy minimum. It was understood that love problems or good fortune with men had to be reported to Pesticida, out of respect for her status as supreme mentor, mother, and employer. Pesticida never suspected that individuals with less generous views of her role simply viewed her as a glorified pimp, whose glories were quite cheap. Pesticida, with equal concern for the health of her family and the business she ran, did not allow the girls to have pimps or abusive boyfriends. "I won't have any fucked-up junkie putas in my show," Pesticida said if rumors that certain girls were turning too many tricks reached her ears, or if she saw one of her girls twitching nervously from too much coke. By "show," Pesticida didn't just mean the nightly performances, but the Gold Rush, her own low-budget entertainment kingdom.

One night Bianca was throwing attitude at her fellow drag queens, cutting them down for no apparent reason. She was wired and talking a lot of trash. "I'm tired of that bitch acting up," Pesticida said to one of her drag queens at the bar. The situation was made worse because Pesticida knew Bianca was doing a big trick and not telling her about it. Bianca's man was a dermatologist in Stockton, whom she was finger-fucking for "two hundred dollars a probe," as she put it, when she bragged to her "evil sisters," the other drag queens. The doctor was married and had kids at Stanford, but he had a sexual weakness for Mexican drag queens who could penetrate him in creative ways. He gave Bianca coke as a "bonus" and she would snort it like a fanatic because she thought it was so much better than crank. Bianca pretended to keep from Pesticida what was all too obvious, amounting to a glaring, arrogant affront to Pesticida's intelligence and authority. To make matters worse, one night Bianca decided to perform as Selena, and to sing the song that was Pesticida's most cherished Selena song, "Como la flor." Bianca performed "Como la flor" in the tight-fitting black leather number that Selena wore on the posthumously released album *Selena Forever*.

Bianca's shapely Selena dress was five sizes smaller than Pesticida's; it was, in fact, the same dress size as the real Selena Quintanilla. Bianca's moves and gestures were more Selena-like than Pesticida's, which overall made Bianca a more convincing Selena, and an instant hit, dethroning Pesticida from her Selena throne with a single song. This infuriated Pesticida; she felt humiliated and betrayed. Pesticida barged into the backstage greenroom after Bianca's performance; Bianca was sitting in front of the mirror admiring herself. "Listen, you skanky tranny," Pesticida fumed, grabbing Bianca's skinny wrist. "I want your coked-out ass out of here. You know I am the only Selena in the house and you think you can disrespect me just because you're fucking some old white geezer who fills your ass up with coke. Well, fuck you, Bianca, Gabriel Montoya, whoever the fuck you are. You can go back to picking peaches with your puta mother 'cause you're not setting foot in my house again. Understand?"

Bianca yanked her wrist out of Pesticida's manly grip. There was hate in Pesticida's makeup-plastered face. There was hate and defiance in Bianca's younger, smoother face, beautifully made up to look exactly like Selena.

"Oh, shut up, you old hag. Get over your ugly self," Bianca shouted as she got up to face her. "You're too old and fat to be Selena. Can't you see I'm Selena? Look at me!" Bianca proudly glanced at herself in the mirror and then stared Pesticida down. "Didn't you hear the way they clapped? I was Selena. You never were. You're used up—"

"Get the fuck out of here before I slap your nasty face," Pesticida shouted, pushing Bianca violently to the floor. "If it weren't for me, you'd be a junkie-puta on Ninth Street, which is where you're heading. So get the fuck out of here. Go!"

Bianca insolently picked herself up, grabbed her twenty-two-dollar swap-meet faux Gucci bag from the top of her dresser, and gave Pesticida one last look, very telenovela-like, and walked out of the greenroom. The drag queens getting ready to perform in the second show of the night saw Bianca storm out and knew what it was about. They knew she would not be coming back.

Bianca was found dead in her apartment. Shot through the heart. She was the third drag queen murdered in two months.

A drag queen murdered in a small town is nothing out of the ordinary. A trick at the wrong time and place under inevitably sexually ambiguous circumstances is a recipe for a straight man to commit murder. Drag queens at the Gold Rush got killed once in a while and the Modesto police thought they understood why. Modesto city investigators interpreted the murders as "random acts of hate crimes, possibly linked to prostitution and drugs, possibly in retaliation for victims dressing as women"—that's what the official police reports stated. And it was close to what the *Modesto Bee* reported. Even the Gold Rush regulars, who were not deterred from frequenting the Gold Rush, believed in this commonplace explanation for the unfortunate fate of the unfortunate drag queens. Only Pesticida's girls began to perceive a pattern that had not been considered. The fact was that all of the victims had dared to perform as Selena, violating Pesticida's copyright of Selena's glamour. But that explained nothing. That, in and of itself, was simply a bizarre coincidence until the death of Pesticida herself.

Pesticida was found dead in West Modesto, in the parking lot of the Days Inn Motel, a cheap but respectable motel bordering the barrio. She had checked in by herself in the middle of the day, telling the hotel clerk, an old white lady who was spooked by Pesticida's appearance, that she would be expecting a woman named Yolanda. "Please direct her to my room, if you would be so kind," Pesticida said, very Miss Manners-like, to the frightened matronly clerk, who had never seen a Mexican drag queen in her life.

It quickly became evident that Pesticida's apparent murder was more than just another Selena killing. The gun that killed her was found next to her body on the bloodied concrete. In her purse she carried a collection of strange love letters from a woman named Yolanda to a woman named Selena. The letters were brief, fervent declarations of love and loyalty. One of the eight letters, all dated within a span of two weeks, read:

Corpus Christi, Texas
March 2, 1996

Querida Selena,

I get the sense that you don't trust me anymore. Even after the sacrifices that I've made. They tried to steal your soul, your beautiful essence. But I stopped them. I know you belong to me only, and no

one else. And still, you don't love me. Why, Selena? I worship you
night and day. Why is that not enough? I have waited for you my
whole life. You are my santita, my Selenita. If you say no to me I think
I'll kill myself. I mean it.

Love You Forever,

Yolanda

The letters were variations on a twisted theme, obsessively repetitive.
An analysis of the handwriting revealed that it belonged to the man
whose driver's license was found in a wallet inside the victim's purse:
Rubén Artiega, forty-eight years old, 1346 El Toledo Dr., Apt. 18,
Modesto, California, 95354—Pesticida's address for the last fifteen years.

The authorities would soon discover that the victim was not really a
woman but the man on the driver's license. Pesticida, at the time of her
death, was in Selena drag, dressed in the same jeans and simple white
blouse Selena was wearing when Yolanda Saldívar gunned her down.
The time of Pesticida's suicide coincided, almost exactly, to the time of
day Selena was murdered, on the same day, one year earlier, in the parking
lot of the Days Inn Motel in Corpus Christi, Texas.

Pesticida had staged Selena's murder as her own Tex-Mex crime of
passion. Her descent into madness was a series of self-betrayals in a
privately psychotic but glamorous telenovela tragedy. She was the star of
her own Corpus Christi script, reeling night and day in her delusional
mind, pacing toward its inevitable climax. She had killed her drag
queen daughters who had tried to imitate her. She believed she was the
real Selena, and she became her own crazed love fan. It would all end as
it did for Selena, in tears and blood underneath a confusing sun.

Magnetic Island
Sueño Crónica

SUSANA CHÁVEZ-SILVERMAN

9 julio 2006
Magnetic Island (Queensland), Australia

For K. E. and K. B.

Te tengo que escribir mi sueño. A pesar de los cries—penetrantes, ghostly, badgering o hechizantes—de los pájaros, some of which seem to go on and on, far into the night (y uno de los cuales me despertó por un momento anoche, around 3 a.m.: an electrifying, piercing, mournful, downward-falling wail que me hizo pensar en el último plaintive, beyond-hope cry de Rima, when the Indians were burning down her tree with her *in* it, en la novela *Green Mansions*), I sleep well here.

Duermo profundamente and I wake at first light, or even before, con los primeros llamados de los pájaros del alba: el *too-whee* y *cha-caw, cha-caw,* luego un uncannily pavorreal-mimicking chillido. Todos esos cries pertenecen al enormous currawong. El *wheeeeee-uh* del pop-eyed, nocturnal curlew. Estoy aprendiendo, en persona (well, OK, *in persona*

159

avis), hasta la famosa risa del kookaburra. Can you believe it? Es así: *ooh-ooh-ooh-uh-ah-ah-ah-ah*. Semejante al haunted laugh de un hombre *muuuuy* grande. Like, por ejemplo, el Herman Munster. O mejor, como si riera (as if!) el Lurch, on *The Addams Family*. Remember? Can you hear it?

I had a long dream. Close to morning it all came together, nítidamente y en secuencia. Lo recordé—lo recuerdo—todo. En absoluta, fotográfica precisión. Por eso me he quedado on dry land today. Aunque siempre me ha llamado la atención el coral (OK, OK, more as jewelry, lo admito), tú sabes que me *aterra* el solo pensamiento de un shark. Almost as much as los osos. But I think it was more the human-tiburones I had no desire to consort with today. Por eso I encouraged Pierre y el Paulie to go on that snorkeling trip sin mí. Al Great Barrier Reef. Alegué—and it's true—que el friggin' diurético me hace demasiado sun-sensitive como para pasar ocho horas a la merced del southern hemisphere sun, tan cerca del Tropic of Capricorn y todo, leche solar SPF 45 no obstante. Alegué—bueno, it's actually true—que como me había comenzado la rule (a deshora, just like last August on Robben Island, remember? When that Sangoma in our tour group me hizo comenzar la sangre? What *is* it about my lunar rhythms y el Sur?), I was mortally terrified que la presencia de la sangre would attract an underwater predator. Como por ejemplo un great white. Well it *could*, ¿qué no?

Pero más que nada lo que anhelaba, lo que se me antojaba como un perfect day, era la absoluta soledad. Alone time en un lugar comfy pero extraño a la vez.

For some reason, quería reproducir algo así como el aloneness que había sentido en Cullinan. On the diamond mine. When I first pitched up in South Africa. Pero without the grinding resentimiento. Sin esa horrenda frustración, the dawning sospecha that I'd given my love to someone unavailable, somehow. Someone who didn't have the wherewithal (le faltaba algo fundamental: algo a modo de las herramientas, the skill, the precision y la pasión, OB-vio) to take the full measure of me in that country. En ese su país. Apartheid. South Africa. Someone who didn't even know what (or how *much* of me) he was missing. Or so it seemed to me, entonces.

Todos los días Howard, my true love, went off, con su university degree en mining engineering, con su solid conocimiento telúrico. Y me dejaba en casa. Literally, waving goodbye desde el umbral, me veo en mi pink Norma Kamali skirt, my teensy, grommeted black tank top, standing forlorn and lonely and foreign en la puerta de ese tiny miner's cottage. Sola todo el día. No TV (como si la tele jamás me hubiera gustado . . .), cero amigos. Curling my bare, tanned toes in the pale-red dust outside. Waiting. Waiting for my love. Howard se iba y venía de mí, a diario, y me dejaba, cada vez más, tierra incógnita. O al menos, that was the narrative I constructed for myself—about him, about us—en esos días.

Y dentro de mí el llanto y la rabia y el conocimiento de mi error—de mi largo, irreversible pilgrimage errado—se me subieron a la garganta. Se vertieron, corrosive, en las páginas de mi giraffe-print-covered diary. Hot, bitter, resentful lágrimas vertí en ese diario. Going-away gift de mamá y Daddy.

But why am I remembering this, telling you this *now*? About Howard and me? About my miserable stay in an Afrikaner diamond-mining dorp? Al menos it was pretty brief. Against all odds conseguí chambita— one of just three lecturers in Spanish *en todo el país*—en UNISA. I high-tailed it to Pretoria, not exactly a cosmopolitan mecca—the capital of Afrikanerdom, of apartheid—ay, pero esa es otra.

Anygüey, I think maybe I'm telling you porque ojalá pudiera rebobinar. You know, rewind, to spare my veinte-algo self toda esa angustia ontológica, erótica. Todo eso que viví tan (too much) a flor de piel. Uf! Sha sé, I'm sounding *really* over-the-top, melodramática, downright 'Tine. And besides—sigh—no se puede (spare her). OB-vio.

So, la yo, la que (sobre)vivió hasta aquí, hasta estas páginas, hasta este Sur, este estar aquí rodeada, this time, no por tierra desértica, africana, sino por este intenso green austral, escribiéndote: esta *yo* ha cambiado el script.

Me siento warm, whole, open to the world. Expectant yet relaxed in my skin. "You are the place where something will happen"; recuerdo esas palabras. De la novela *Burger's Daughter* by Nadine Gordimer. Howard me la regaló. Me la regaló en S.F., before he left for home. Cuando la releí el año pasado, antes de volver a Sudáfrica, it struck me as awkward, dated, demasiado Manichaean, its politics demasiado earnest, predictable, in your face. Pero ay, cuánto me conmovió cuando la leí por primera vez, en esos too-long, expectantes meses de 1982, sick with hepatitis (lovesick with yearning), mis padres hoping against hope I'd change my mind and not go.

Pero that *was* me, then. Y OJITO: así también era el mundo—urgente, peligroso. Apartheid wasn't over, not by a long shot. De hecho, estaba, I'd say, en su momento más crispado. Eight long years before Mandela's release. Y eso no era entonces, ni lejos, not even a dream.

Kwa-kwa-kwa, grazna un pájaro, muy cerca de las plantation-style white shutters, abiertas ceiling to floor en esta casa vieja, donde escribo en una gran mesa de caoba, maciza, oscura y pulida. *Ku-wa*, le responde otro, lejos, hacia el lado del mar. *Screee. Too-hoo, too-hoo.*

Sopla una brisa mañanera. No es muy insistente, pero hace frotar las huge, pale gray-green palm fronds, como lijas, but so softly. Their feathery tips intertwine and release. The variegated *massangeana* rustles (oh, ¡cuántas veces te me fracasaste en mi faraway Inland Empire de Califas patio!). A faint, eucalyptus-tinged scent floats toward me; la brisa me hace cosquillas en los tobillos. How odd, the feel of this dry, plant-infused winter breeze against my feet. Heme aquí, sitting by a wall of windows con vista hacia el mar, pero contenida, cocooned por todo este verde.

En mi sueño, I was back on campus. Muchas veces tengo este sueño, como si los parámetros de mi vida fueran los de un recinto universitario. Ugh! *Is* this my life? ¿Cómo en esa novela, *Giles Goat Boy* de John Barth? Anygüey, era un campus de adeveras, as God commands. Huge, sprawling, mucho ladrillo. Bien old world o al menos, Ivy League–ish. Parecía Harvard. En otras palabras: my dream-version of a perfect campus, alegoría de un perfect world.

I had a large, pale, soft leather handbag. Como de gamuza era. New. Pero en todo el revolú del back to school, I had misplaced it. Me sentí totalmente bereft, perdida sin mi bolso. Como si ese bolso contuviera toda mi vida. Todo lo importante. My belongings, mis secretos.

Intuí que había dejado el bolso en el dining hall de una residencia, where I'd gone to look for you. El dorm era enorme. Un beehive de actividad. Students coming and going, medio jostling each other. Como en un *real* campus. Digo, no como en Pomona, where there are so few, el ambiente tan precioso, rarified que casi nunca se ven grandes concentraciones de gente. No me sentía nerviosa ni hostigada. *Nadie me reconocía.* Era ese comforting anonimato I have always loved about a large university. Como Harvard. UCLA. O Berkeley, o Wisconsin.

Bueno, anyway, a pesar de no haberme sentido muy hopeful about its recuperación, my faun-colored handbag was waiting for me en la cafetería. Me la entregó una trabajadora latina, y la abracé, sobbing de puro alivio. And then I went to look for you. Te busqué por toda esa beehive, subiendo y bajando, buscándote entre tanta gente, gente desconocida.

De repente allí estabas. You put your arm out and stopped me, guided me; you pulled me, muy gently pero insistently over the threshhold, into your room. Recuerdo que tu cuarto era grande, y había una luz filtrada, hermosa. You had your own room.

I was standing close to you; nos mirábamos intensamente. No había palabras. Era como si fuera la primera vez que nos veíamos en mucho tiempo. Como si nada, you were rubbing sunscreen all over my face. You were rubbing vigorously, like one does to a child, all over—¡en los ojos, hasta las pestañas! Me reía. *Stop*, te dije. I was afraid you would rub off el Erace concealer que uso, todos los días, on my scar, right by my left eye y sin el cual me siento exposed, unfinished, vulnerable. *Let me*, me dijiste. No importa. You don't need makeup. You're so beautiful.

Al terminar esa (un)cover action, entonces me besaste. Era lento y sublime. I felt the contact, todos los contornos. Sentí tus labios en los míos, gentle pressure. Sentí el frágil contacto con tus dientes, touching the inside of your mouth con la punta de la lengua.

And then, no me acuerdo bien if we were lying down or sitting up, facing one another, en tu cama. It was late afternoon. It was us, *exactly* as we are. Quiero decir: I could feel and ascertain, en el sueño, que era real. Todo parecía heightened. I'd say "slow motion," pero no lo era. It was, rather, that I possessed the attentiveness to time and sensation of a waking dream. I remember your hand was on my lower back. It moved caressingly, hypnotically, firmly. Muy lento. Sólo se desplazaba cosa de one inch. Inch by inch. I was acutely attuned to that very small place, allí, donde me acariciabas.

We had all our clothes on, todavía. They were more or less loose-fitting (como esos olive green pantalones de hombre, from the GAP, pseudo army-navy, que uso; I think I was wearing those). I remember I ran my arm, my hand, up under your shirt. Con la mano derecha te tocaba el flanco, te abrazaba. With my fingertips I could feel your skin, the definiteness of you, warm, present. Con las yemas de los dedos te rocé la piel, sentí el pulso en tu cuello, my fingers skimmed over and paused at your nipple. Taut. Sentí la respiración; it was yours and mine. You drew me toward you, con la mano derecha.

The sun is up now. Frangipani, sun-released, wafts in through these open shutters. Una pequeña mariposa amarilla drifts, pauses near the shockingly purple row of crotons. The fish kite and the hammock stir on the porch, languidly, invitingly.

Esa mano derecha tuya baja. Almost imperceptibly. Slowly, se mueve. Me acaricia la espalda, hace pequeños movimientos circulares hacia las nalgas. You hold my butt, pulling me toward you, onto you. Siento eso, your hand cupping my butt; a la vez mi atención se bifurca, hacia mis dedos, que te acarician el hombro, el antebrazo. Te juro que I *feel* everywhere: where your hand is moving underneath me, holding me, hacia mi sexo; donde mis dedos se mueven en minúsculo vaivén y te acarician el brazo; donde ahora, my lips replace my fingers and contact your upper arm and I taste you. Sutil. Neutral. Un poco salado.

I am poised, just slightly above you. Soft moans escape your half-open mouth. Siento el calor de tu ingle, pressing into me. Our clothes are on, still. No estorba la ropa. Ni nos fijamos. As your hand circles toward, me escucho gemir. I move toward you.

Hay una extraña, oximorónica sensación. Expectant yet satisfied a la vez. There is no idea of reaching, de progreso. Of getting there. Anywhere. We *are* there. Here. Your skin. Cálida, densa. Your hand on me. Humedad. La otra rozándome los labios like you do, drawing my face toward yours. Tus labios reconociéndome los contornos. No hay noción de urgencia. El tiempo es nuestro. Tiemblo de placer, de anticipación, de presencia. I feel you here with me. Somos, es ahora.

I Leave Tomorrow,
I Come Back Yesterday

URIEL QUESADA

A gente preenchia. Menos eu;
isto é-eu resguardava meu talvez

João Guimãraes Rosa
Grande Sertão: Veredas

If you come from Uptown by streetcar you get off at the last stop, just at
Canal Street, near where people who have taken a bus named Desire
transfer and go on to Cemeteries or Elysian Fields. But stay alert,
because this area is full of scoundrels and souvenir shops, and you can
easily get lost. Better if you go directly to the other end of the French
Quarter by Bourbon Street or Decatur, although I recommend Royal to
you, the street with the galleries, cute apartments, and old neglected
houses where the vampire tours stop. You'll pass right by where William
Faulkner lived, and where surely you'll bump into some guy resting
carelessly on a corner, posing as a leisurely artist. He will seek you out
with his eyes, although he doesn't know you, with the hopes that this

165

first contact defines and clarifies, and that you enter easily into a conversation, as if you had been separated only a short time in all your life. He attracts you to his corner with a look that portrays the reflection of all of the water in the world. Despite the fact that at this hour it's impossible to see from a distance the color of eyes, you respond to his command, you try to guess the origin of this vibration that gives you goose bumps until you find its owner leaning on the railing of the cathedral's garden, where a marble Jesus opens his arms to receive everyone, although no one has access to him or to the delicacies of the garden. There's something fragile and false about the young man that doesn't come from his feet, just protected by sandals, or from his extremely white, Indian linen suit embroidered with little red figures, or from his ringlets of carefully disheveled hair. You think of him as an apparition, an ethereal danger that speaks almost in whispers. For you, he will breathe fire, he'll sing his original works, he'll dance with silk veils, he'll try to read your hand to discover that he's in your future, naked with you on a hard old bed of a shotgun house located just a few streets from where your palm began to tremble at the possibility of enjoying the next hours, until the sun returns, rising over the Mississippi, and you both gather your clothes and part in opposite directions. He caresses your life line, inventing hard times that you have survived thanks to your courage and persistence. He predicts travels for you but not riches. Softly he affirms that your rational side is very strong, so much so that it blocks your love line, and makes you doubt and suffer like all those who fear giving themselves over to this simple act of exploring the skin's secrets to the limit.

However, like so many other nights, you close your hand to novel experiences, to the vertigo of uncertainty. You keep your fist clenched, deforming your luck lines. You try to leave the young man without noticing that his hand has followed the movement of yours, trying to envelop it, to create a knot of fingers that moves closer to his lips for him to kiss. You avoid looking him in the eye so as not to be swept away by that torrent that interrogates and disarms you. You prefer to see the confusion of fingers that you can't undo, because each attempt to separate them rouses a new caress, a fresh thread among your desperate life line and that of the young man. But at some point you jump, say something like "I can't do this," and you leave the young man, who takes a couple steps toward you, stops, and shouts to you not to forget that corner where he always feigns to pose carelessly, although really he dedicates himself to waiting to be consumed by the chance imprint on the skin of those unknown.

You walk very quickly, dazed, mingling with the people. You hear when someone says to you, "Hey, mista, listen!" You turn in case the young man has followed you, but it's a very dark black man who calls for your attention, painted like a cemetery's angel, a statue of flesh and bones that has been witness to the conversation between you and the fortune-teller. He's abandoned his pedestal to follow you, carrying unlikely instruments made with old pots and ice-cream containers, making a disturbance as if to announce to the multitudes what has taken place. "I can take you to a place where the most beautiful boys in town . . ."

"I don't want any problems," you repeat, fleeing from life toward the other side of the French Quarter, scared by the constant interference of temptation upon that night of planned and sure goodbyes. The black angel painted white shouts a curse at you and returns to his pedestal, making a commotion. In a few seconds he transforms himself into a statue so that the tourists pose with him and leave him a few dollars in a bucket at his feet. When he returns to the ground, he quits being an angel and is hungry; he'll enter to buy a beer and he'll comment on the latest news with his friends, but we'll never know if you and your story will remain in his memory after this moment. Meanwhile, you move on against the current of people. Your feet wish to disobey you, to go in the same direction as the strangers, to return to the corner before someone else takes the young man. You stop in the middle of the sidewalk, asking yourself which is the right course, if you should pay attention to your heart or to your head. You look for the answer in your hands; you see them so mute, so ineffective when dealing with decisions. Groups of passersby continue running into you, a human statue with neither the makeup nor the act, anchored to that point of the earth as if you had just grown roots. Most of those who pass by grant you a look of curiosity, go around you, and continue on their way. Under his breath, someone encourages you: "Go for it." But you don't want to understand. Even so, you turn your head in search of the corner that has turned into a blurry scene. The cathedral's garden continues casting its shadow upon the street; the railing is reduced to a stroke of Chinese ink. The black-and-white angel stands out underneath the damp glow of the streetlight. Where's the young man? Why doesn't he have a name?

So you continue on your way toward Marigny. You're so agitated that you don't see me, although I wait for you at the place we agreed upon, just under the Pardieu Antiques sign. You dry your hands on the fabric of your shorts; you quicken your step as if you were going to arrive late, and I lovingly think, "You'll try to be on time even in death."

I look at my watch and wash my hands of the matter: 11:34 at night. You're late by just four minutes. I'll take about fifteen more prowling around here, only so as to not leave you waiting at the place where Candide Pardieu will pick us up to go to his goodbye party. You walk so quickly that I detect certain restlessness. You turn toward me, but you can't see me; you look for something else, something beyond these shop windows, the people, what's right in front of you. I also turn around, trying to find what your eyes seek. It's not a gallery or an antique store, I'd bet. Nor is there anyone acting suspiciously, although perhaps a few streets down some delinquent has tried to take advantage of you. I take a few steps, and the air, hot, wraps me up without even the hint of a breeze. There's a stillness that's almost visible despite the noisy, drunken, and falsely uninhibited tourists. I try to see that mysterious object of your interest, but I only find a human statue and a little further away a young man that flirts with some lonely passersby. He flashes them an incredibly white smile, walks a few feet with them, and finally returns to his corner.

I try to find you again, but you're already lost somewhere toward Marigny. We should have met up in Antiques, gone to a certain cafe, and waited for Pardieu, to accompany him on his last night of freedom. But it occurs to me that you prefer to walk with no precise destination in mind. My inner voice tells me it's better that I let you wander, and when they ask for you and you're not there, I will lie, something like: "He never arrived; I was waiting next to the antique store and I didn't see him." Of course it was you that didn't see me, although honestly I let you pass by, fascinated that you had forgotten me and that you were looking for something that didn't include me. But until that moment of explanation arrives, I wait here to contemplate the delicate knickknacks of my friend Candide Pardieu's store. That crazy man has the great ability to turn everything into sugar, including certain tragedies, and, of course, his many mistakes. However, I ask myself how he will feel in prison, where he will be obliged to dress in an orange uniform instead of in his suits made of fresh fabric, delicately tailored and of the highest price, and in his New York shoes and Panama hat. I look at the store windows full of furniture, decorations, lamps, statues, and treasures that run the risk of being neglected if Pardieu's partner doesn't know how to protect them. You can't even imagine how many afternoons I spent sitting in those priceless chairs, shooting the shit with Pardieu, who was a million-aire and a dandy when he was younger, professional trout fisherman in Montana, amateur Spanish mountain-goat hunter, and expert taster of

French wines and young Arabian men. Later, when his family's wealth started to run dry and the need for a conventional job threatened his horizon, Pardieu sat down with pencil and paper to find a way out. He wrote in one column his various abilities, in the other his needs, in the third where he should reside in order to achieve the logical sequence: from ability to work to income to satisfied needs. Like he himself admitted, a decadent dandy can't find money just like that. Nor was he able to part with his family's possessions. Yet, like a good adventurer, he always ended up reporting them, were it in order to write memoirs of his travels, or, more pragmatically, to obtain economic or legal assistance. He recognized that it was very late to start working. So he thought of the bustle of the streets, of the swells of visitors, and he had the idea of opening an antique store on the most prestigious street of the French Quarter. He displayed some personal objects that no longer touched his heart or memory, and he made a lot of money, sitting at the doorway of his business in a velvet armchair that looked more like a throne.

After a few years, Candide had cleaned out all of the Pardieu mansions, without even a few dollars left over as savings. Some internal mechanism awakened a certain obsession with financial security. To us, his friends, he spoke only of that, and when we chatted about him we would say that the solution was easier said than done. Candide would have to work for the first time in his life.

And in some ways he did it because he went to the working-class neighborhoods in search of merchandise, swindling both the ancient owners and the potential clients. Pardieu knew about antiques, and so negotiating with him was like having coffee with one of the local vampires: he would draw you in with his accent slightly affected by his French, he would seduce you patiently, painstakingly, and then when you were at the point of an aesthetic orgasm, he would sink his teeth into your wallet.

Oh, Candide! You've taken good trips down the wrong road. You laugh so much at the world, but you don't realize that someday what goes around comes around. You always wanted to be the same old Candide—generous and extravagant. And you would scold me for my bad-humored, grandfatherly admonitions: "You open the store when you feel like it, you lie to the customers, you owe money to your providers, you continue wasting everything. Candide, think of old age." He did it, but in his own way. A few weeks after my last sermon, they began to loot the cemeteries. I never connected Pardieu Antiques' new offers, discreetly exhibited in a closed-off room in the back, with a reportage in the *Times Picayune*'s Metro section about the desecration of distinguished mausoleums, until one afternoon when I stopped by for a drink. Pardieu was dressed especially elegantly, with a silk tie, very discreet brown suit, and his lucky hat, as if he were traveling. He served me a drink; I sat on a little iron chair and he confirmed that he was expecting visitors. "The police," he explained, smiling. Before allowing me to let a string of questions fly, he said: "Now, for example, you are seated on a beautiful chair attributed to Lafitte, a disciple of Auguste Rodin, who lived in New Orleans from 1885 to 1889. The chair was left in the Debernardi's chapel in 1887, upon the death of Sandra, the great matron. Not too long ago, I rescued the forgotten thing and now it's for sale." I didn't jump from the chair immediately—the truth was I didn't understand—and I obliged Pardieu to be more direct. "You are very naïve, my friend. Realize that more than half of my pieces come from the cemetery."

The arrest was discreet enough. The police, aware that they should protect the prestige of such a distinguished family, took back all the stolen objects at night. The news just took up space in the local news and papers. A few days before his imprisonment, a stranger opened the store. As soon as I knew, I went to visit him and found out that he was one of the many lovers that Pardieu supported with his antique sales. "We should be united in a time of misfortune," he said to me cunningly. I asked him how he was going to continue the business, where he would get the capital. "This is absurd," I said. He explained to me that nothing would be sold. Pardieu wanted to preserve the store as he left it when two policemen arrived, greeted him, and with great pity asked him to accompany them. "The objects are for sale!" I protested, blind as always. "Yes, but no one is going to buy them." And in effect, that's how it was. Every one of the pieces that survived the police record now had a price several times greater than its original. Clients would leave disconcerted, or would demand to negotiate directly with Pardieu, but he, ladies and gentlemen, was getting ready for a long trip to various continents to stock the store with marvelous things never before seen, and in this moment, while you lose yourself in the multitudes, I take another look at the store window and affirm that time has stopped inside there, as if that afternoon Pardieu had left to have a beer with the policemen and was about to return.

Yes, he returned, as justice is served—though slowly—and he had, he has had, he has, some days of freedom. He wanted to convert his store into a museum, to leave it intact for when he completed the inevitable sentence. "It's all I have left after paying the lawyers," he said to us. Two weeks ago, they told him that tomorrow, at eight sharp, he should report to serve his sentence of three years in a minimum security prison. Tonight, we, his friends, will get together to have a huge farewell celebration for Candide. Let him drink the last glasses of champagne, let him smoke his Cuban cigars and his joints, let him have his preferred young men.

"Remember that tomorrow I leave public life," he has confessed to me a few hours ago on the phone, "but I'll return very soon to this sweet moment, to yesterday."

"Yes, Candide," I answered with a lump in my throat. But at this moment I am happy. Surely the limousine has picked him up, after waiting for an hour while Pardieu finishes making up his face. He has put on a white foundation, elongated his eye lines to make them look almond shaped, and accentuated the red of his lips with his favorite liner. With help from some of his lovers, he has put on his dainty shoes and he has gotten into his Mandarin suit. He has his hair pulled back in a little ponytail, and he covers it with some kind of hat that he swears is an original piece.

I calculate that he must be arriving at the meeting spot in a few minutes, to pick up you and me to go together to the Country Club, that old house with discreet salons, billiards, and an enormous pool where the rest of the guests should be bathing in the moonlight. He will make his triumphant entrance a little after midnight to announce again, "I leave tomorrow, I return yesterday," and to cause everyone to think that the water in the pool has been replaced with champagne.

I begin to greet people as I walk along. I look for you without hoping to or worrying about finding you, as you're probably ahead of me; and it's you that waits for me. Yet, I arrive at the cafe where we were to meet and you're not there. Inside, an old man makes his marionette dressed like a harlequin dance in front of a table full of tourists. I can hear the tune from where I'm waiting. While the tourists talk among themselves, the marionette does pirouettes, bows, moves its hips, and smiles without stopping. I believe the tourists are making fun of the old man, but he and his marionette continue to give the show without abandoning their smiles.

When Pardieu's limousine stops, you still haven't arrived. I ask myself if I should wait for you, apologize to Pardieu, or go back to look for you, but it's absurd to go out again into that crowd that wanders from bar to bar, from show to show, and from flirtation to flirtation.

The chauffeur opens the door and invites me in. The Mandarin Pardieu urges me to get in, lifting a glass. Other friends make space. I shoot one last glance toward the street; I get in to the automobile and you, a few streets down, forget about our meeting, and rapidly try to reach the corner where the young man ought to be waiting, although he simply pretends to see the river of people that come and go. You are sure that destiny sweeps you onward; deep down you welcome the surprise, the whim, the humid summer, tonight's circumstances. You arrive at the place where, not too long ago, the young man pretended to lounge, but he's not there either. All that's left is the human angel statue, the thin black man painted totally white, so good at his job that he doesn't seem to breathe, or notice your anxiety. You try to get his attention, bring him back to this world again, but the angel pretends to contemplate what's beyond you. The tourists pose with him, taking photos, tossing money into the box at his feet. You catch on and wave a bill in front of the angel's eyes and say:

"Where did he go?"

The angel changes the position of his arms slowly, like he's learned how a robot would do it. He bends, at the brink of transmitting a divine message. You see that he has eyes marked with reddish lines that make them seem very dark. You see that drops of sweat have cracked the makeup. You feel the angel breathe.

"The guy in a white dress," you insist. "He was around here ten minutes ago."

"Vāikunta?" says the angel in an earthly voice. You have no answer. Nothing else occurs to you but to toss the dollars into the box at the foot of the winged being. "It means Heaven's gates," he affirms with authority.

"Where is he now?" you ask with a hint of desperation. The angel seems like an articulating doll. He lifts his head, but his arms don't commit to a particular direction, and you take out another bill. The spectacle attracts the attention of some people; they begin to make a circle around you. Some ask each other if the angel reads the future, like the fortune-tellers from Jackson Square. He doesn't predict it; he indicates its course, nothing more. You follow where he's pointing, but you only find a sea of people in constant motion. Those interested also try to guess what the secret is that the angel has revealed to you, as if it were possible for a layman's eye to see the aura of such a wondrous feat or to hear the silence that overcomes such commotion.

"Vāikunta," you go demanding through the people. "Vāikunta." You look for his name, although all around you there is only a mass of bodies. They wander around, they glide ghostly about, they dissolve into invisibility. "Vāikunta," you say with the faith of those who repeat the prayer that guides them. "Vāikunta," you require, knowing that no one can answer you except him, the anonymous one, the one who should materialize out of the realm of secrecy.

But I can't see you walking like a crazy man down Saint Peter toward Rampart. I'm arriving at the Country Club, where a man in a frock coat opens the door for us. Pardieu walks ahead, greeting, or better said, blessing the people who converse and drink in the secret salons. With his hands he seems to say: "Here I go, the great clairvoyant, and to all of you I bequeath my graces." A moment before, he had asked me my opinion about his Mandarin suit. "You look like a television astrologer," I answered him between laughs. "Well, as a reward for your sincerity I will honor you with a zodiac title. Tonight you will be Cancer: water, patience, family." I stayed quiet. With Pardieu you never know; it's best to wait for the next absurdity.

We go on toward the back of the old mansion, pass through a doorway made of tall windows, and go out to the pool that's not full of champagne but shines placidly beneath the night. As it should be in such circumstances, there is music though no one dances, long tables with food and bottles, people conversing in low voices. As should occur in Heaven, around the pool many young men bathe in the moonlight. Strewn about on lounge chairs, they're absorbed in contemplating one another, ignoring the rustic reality that exists outside of their world of perfect bodies. "Look at them letting youth pass them by, Cancer," Pardieu says to me, reading my thoughts. "Beauty is excessive and useless, but above all it's the present. No other time matters, nor exists. It is in the present; it vanishes and invents itself all the time in the present."

I can't answer him. A few friends have noticed our arrival and call everyone's attention so as to honorably receive the Mandarin, who will be entering the state prison within a few hours. You weren't persecuted under the sodomy laws still in existence in Louisiana; you didn't defend noble causes, didn't oppose the invisible hands of evil. You have been condemned for selling stolen antiques. Pardieu, how mundane! And so you take your triumphant walk around the pool, dedicating spicy looks and comments to the beautiful men on display in the lounge chairs. The conversation begins: the toasts, the well-wishes that the trip be pleasurable and not too long. "Just two years with good behavior," jokes Pardieu. "I will have learned horticulture, to better the weed crop as soon as I get out." Suddenly Pardieu remembers you. He asks me about

173

you; I shrug my shoulders. How am I going to know that you're going from one side of the street to the other, looking for a face that you have begun to idealize, that you've gone in and out of the bars and tobacco shops several times, any place where Vāikunta could be, the only one, the one who draws you as if he had an identifiable scent, capable of guiding you to a little store where the young man has entered to buy incense? How can I be sure that time hasn't stopped to allow you to rake through the crowd in search of the mythical needle, the one you have found against all odds? In the half-light you see the young man in white, comparing aromas. You slowly move closer, calling him by his name. He registers you as if he knew that you were going to meet there. Outside, time has gone back to normal. Night overcomes the morning once again, and the people continue being the anonymous tumult from before. You find each other; you extend your hand to him, gently order him to read it, and to explain to you what happened in the last few minutes, the manner in which all the coincidences have converged in that instant. "Who brought me to you?" you ask. "An angel," he responds. "Will you continue to be in my future?" you plead. "Your hand is silent. It doesn't want to reveal any more."

I can't explain to Pardieu that the two of you begin to chat, walking slowly toward the quieter parts of the French Quarter. I ignore the fact that you arrive at a red-painted shotgun house, music and murmurs escaping from the celebratory party for the full Eastern moon, as Vāikunta explains to you. To open the door you just have to push. You enter a rather long, candlelit room, with semitransparent curtains hanging from the ceiling and walls. Toward the back there's a bookshelf and a bed. Closer to you, a young man plays a type of drum, while four women circle him, spellbound. Vāikunta asks you to leave your shoes on the little rug next to the door; he greets the rest of the visitors with familiarity and sets about perfuming the house with incense. You sit down with the women, you tell them a false name, and you drink wine with them. The women recite poems to the beat of the drum, get up to dance, caress the hair of the young man and Vāikunta, and drink from tall glasses. After an instant or an eternity, after hearing the mystical experiences that you neither share nor believe, the women beg Vāikunta to sing. The other young man sets his drum aside and gets guitars. The two musicians start up a melody in an unknown language. Although it's impossible to understand them, their faces relay a sentiment that you make your own, and you have a feeling it describes you. Your body starts to feel the music's inflections and you try to repeat a word; you believe parts of that truth. You wish to ask Vāikunta where he learned to play like that. You want to hear some fabulous answer: "In Heaven, at the feet of giant gods, next to the purifying pyre, at the middle of the sacred river . . ." He doesn't answer. One of the women whispers in your ear: "In New Jersey, where he grew up." Better not to know anymore. Suddenly the spell could break, and it could end up that Vāikunta isn't anything more than some James or some David, some good musician from the suburbs dedicated to selling the illusion of a strange language to some naive people. "I don't want to know," you repeat to yourself. "I can't know," I say, drinking another glass and taking a break from the small talk to think of you. Pardieu has lost himself in the interior of the huge house with a few of the moon bathers, and he has now returned to continue toasting and saying goodbye to his acolytes. He has asked me if there's no one that I like, if I haven't decided to stop taking notes on the story to live it, as it's not possible to live and write at the same time: the former goes first and you don't think about it, the latter you make up and doesn't exist except in the confines of the imagination. "You are such a good witness to your own life, Cancer," he has told me confidently. He has had a few drinks, although I know that they never serve enough to make Pardieu lose his lucidity, his elegance, and his proper gait. "When are you going to be that protagonist, eternal spectator?" I accept the challenge with a toast, and I respond to him: "Some day after today, when we are nothing more than history."

Pardieu laughs, gives me a kiss that tastes like champagne, and calls everyone's attention for another speech. He announces that he will go out through the French Quarter in a Carnival-style parade, the second line before tomorrow in preparation for preserving yesterday. The most magnificent clairvoyant decides to make his court up of the zodiac signs. Some young men bring different-colored Venetian costumes. Pardieu points at me and I step forward with my name, Cancer, toward the blue suit. He mentions eleven others and each one is dressed. We take another walk around the pool before leaving. We wait for the limos, with an abundance of alcohol, and Carnival beads and doubloons. Pardieu brings the water signs with him, chooses a few others, and sends the rest of the group to another vehicle. "I leave tomorrow, but I'll arrive yesterday," he whispers obsessively. I'm at the point of commenting, but I stop myself. I'll tell you my feelings later, be it that I remember them or make them up; in the end it's the same.

You will also relay a story to me that's inaccessible, although some day in our springtime walk we may pass the shotgun house and you'll point to the place, saying, "Here four women danced: the gypsy, the spiritualist, the one who saw unicorns instead of men, and the water diviner. They evolved around two barefooted musicians, drawing back the silk curtains, wrapping themselves in them, and then revealing themselves. I was sitting in a cloud of incense when I began to rise higher and higher, until I was floating above everything. The water diviner ordered that the bed in the back be filled with rose petals, and so it was. The other women kept me up with the tips of their fingers, but I wasn't afraid of falling. I wasn't going to fall, not even when the sun rose and the daylight blinded the candles' flames. I would float while there was music, I would come down; I came down slowly, following Vāikunta's song, his voice pure and devoid of all melancholy. I touched, I touch the floor with all of my body when the music dissolved into the incense." The women decide to worship the young drummer, and Vāikunta gives you a kiss that's marked by the expansiveness of the intangible.

The women and the other young man go out silently, leaving behind a few rose petals as a souvenir, and they float, unceremoniously falling every which way. Vāikunta rests his weight on you, and the woman who sees unicorns is amazed because those beings that the Greek Ctesias described for the first time have finally appeared. She leaves you both kissing on the floor of the house, and closes the door, trying to make as little noise as possible. She quickens her pace so as to catch up with her group. The gypsy walks ahead with the young drummer; the spiritualist and the water diviner walk arm in arm, exchanging secrets. Little by little, the street fills with people, until they arrive underneath a balcony where various people in Venetian costumes throw plastic bead necklaces and fake coins to the people. A man dressed as a Mandarin dominates the scene. His suit is the most brilliant of all, as is his manner of speaking. He encourages the young men who pass by on the street to drop their pants and show themselves to the public. Those who dare to do so receive in exchange the most beautiful necklaces and the biggest applause from the public. The women lift their arms and shout for a gift. I look at them from behind my mask, and they seem to look at me, too. They address me with open hands, hoping for a prize. So I throw them necklaces: green for the water diviner, gold for the spiritualist, lavender for the unicorn discoverer, purple for the gypsy. "You're wasting your beads on women, Cancer," Pardieu scolds me. "Yeah, yeah," I respond while I toss a multicolored one to the young man who accompanies the women. "Much better," comments the Mandarin man without neglecting the people. I think it's more likely I'm wasting my life in general, but I keep quiet. I don't confess my secret to you either, like I know that you couldn't sufficiently capture Vaikunta's voice, his body, the way he left a few delicious scratches on your chest and back, the suddenness that put an end to tomorrow and settled into yesterday. And that time in your memory you will constantly return to by way of the word.

For me, secrets are accumulating in my throat until the people of the street leave with their necklaces, exhausted. Several zodiac signs have fallen down drunk on the balcony and in the little living room of the apartment where Pardieu continues saying goodbye without shedding a tear. He has asked me to accompany him to his house, where he'll stop being a Mandarin in order to put on a simple pair of pants and a shirt and to arrive at the prison on time. "I think that the orange prison color looks good on me," he told me a little while ago, and for the first time I notice that his voice quivers. "But I leave today and I return tomorrow, Cancer, I promise you that."

We leave the house and get into the limousine. By the Mandarin's order, it turns onto Royal toward Pardieu Antiques. We get out of the car and look at the showcase in silence. Pardieu can't resist the temptation to pick up the trash that the wind swept toward the door. "I leave tomorrow, I return yesterday," he repeats without fail. He asks me to leave him alone for a minute. I wait for him next to the limousine door, trying not to watch. From here it seems like he's praying. He continues a little longer. If he has been crying he hasn't allowed me to witness it, because he's hidden behind dark sunglasses. When he returns, he takes me by the arm and we get into the car. He anchors himself to me; he demands my strength. I am strong, I answer silently. He who leaves, dies, and my life is full of cadavers.

"I leave tomorrow, I return yesterday," he implores, trying to convince himself. "Are you going to be here, Cancer?"

The secret rises up in my throat. It struggles to leave through my mouth, through my ears, through my hands. I fix my gaze on the surface of the dark glasses that Pardieu wears. My reflection is deformed.

"No," I answer as we leave the French Quarter toward Rampart by way of a street where many lovers are intertwined. "Don't expect of me that which I don't have, Pardieu. Don't ask me to stay in yesterday."

New Orleans

October 2000–March 2001

(Translated from Spanish by Kristen Warfield)

Six Days in St. Paul

STEVEN CORDOVA

When we awoke Saturday morning it had snowed. Snow, in fact, was still falling, and as layer settled upon layer, it seemed another complication, or at least another possible complication, to my six days in St. Paul. Now, in addition to making decisions with Sil and Gerry, a process in which I was the third wheel, each diversion we had planned would have to be reconsidered, each undertaking taken with extra caution. Sil and Gerry would have to take turns driving Sil's four-wheel drive while Gerry's sporty new hatchback—purchased with only front-wheel drive—would have to sit out back, weighed down and snow blind, sleeping its way through my visit.

Sil and Gerry's front yard, despite the fact that it fronts their two-story Victorian home, is not a picturesque lot. It slopes dramatically, and descending the cement steps that bisect the yard, a visitor has to slow himself down—he has to resist gravity—or risk finding himself flat on his face smack in the middle of a two-way road. In the snow, however, that same front yard looked deceivingly peaceful, lovely even. Bruiser, one of Sil and Gerry's two full-grown mastiffs, sauntered up, sniffed at one of my legs, then the other, periodically looking up at me with watery black eyes.

"No need to pack warm provisions," Sil had said to me on the phone the day before.

"Really?" I'd responded.

Sitting at my desk, I was stuffing another edition of the *New York Times* into my already brimming drawer.

"I thought it was always cold in St. Paul at Christmastime."

"Usually it is," Sil said, "but this year it's unusually warm—like it is in New York."

And Sil was right. Or at least the online forecast confirmed his predictions. During my six days in St. Paul, the temperature was to remain mild, mid-thirties, mid-forties. No snow. No snowstorms. No freezing weather.

"It's a conspiracy," I said to Bruiser as I squinted at the glare glancing off the snow. I turned and crossed the ground-floor bedroom, which had been converted into a gymnasium since my last visit. I made my way around the living room couch, around a large leather ottoman, and stood looking out the window. From there, I could see the back yard. Bruiser parked his rump on my foot, and Sil entered from the kitchen, handing me a cup of coffee.

"It's a conspiracy," I continued my thought, "between the airlines, the FAA, and the National Weather Service. They want to keep travelers traveling this holiday season."

"There'll be a layer of ice beneath that snow soon," Gerry said, joining us at the window. "And it'll stay there until March, the way it does every year."

Bruno made his lumbering appearance, panting his way to the window and making it so our little group consisted of three men in sleep-crumpled pajamas framed by two dogs, each dog weighing nearly two hundred pounds. All around us, throughout the house, fish swam in their respective tanks, ornate clocks ticked, and the small, brightly colored birds Sil likes to breed twittered in their cages. Down in the basement, in a hall that connects the guest room to the laundry room, Sil's pet snakes hibernated. But there were no tenants upstairs, not this visit. Sil and Gerry said they'd reached a point where they could forego the extra income, said they liked the house all to themselves—all to themselves and, for the duration of my visit, me.

My previous visits to St. Paul had been made during the spring, that small window of opportunity in which a visitor can enjoy a city that freezes through much of the long winter and is humid and mosquito-ridden through much of the short summer. But not to worry. Sipping at their cups of coffee that first morning, Sil and Gerry reassured me that

179

the inhabitants of St. Paul have to venture out in extreme weather. They underlined that, to avoid cabin fever, we'd go to the Walker again, this time to see the Frida Kahlo exhibition. They insisted we'd still see the new wing of the Minneapolis Museum of Art, that we'd still visit the Russian. The Russian Museum of Art, you see, is housed in a structure designed to replicate a Southwest mission, so Sil and I, who went to high school together in San Antonio, feel at home there. We don't care that, for the citizens of St. Paul, the museum is an architectural anomaly.

What wasn't exactly the same was my relationship with Sil and Gerry. As I said, Sil and I went to high school together in Texas. We were both members of our school's speech and drama team—a small group of friends who've remained in touch through our twenties, thirties, and now our forties. Sil grew into a tall, thin adult but was even thinner as a teenager. He speaks Spanish better than I do, and is considerably darker skinned than I am. And since he looks somewhat Asian around the eyes, he was particularly vulnerable to high school bullies. That vulnerability was no doubt one of the reasons it was easy to want to nurture Sil—that and the fact that Sil's family, never very nuclear to begin with, completely fell apart long before any of us graduated. One day, Sil's long-suffering mother told Sil's father to stick it and she packed up and went off—back to Mexico—essentially abandoning Sil and his sisters. After that, our speech and drama team, our families, took Sil in, now and then passing him off from one family to another.

One of Sil's adopted families saw him through his overdose of pills. Then, after we all graduated, Claudette, one of our best debaters, went east for her poli-sci degree. And it was there, at Harvard, that she saw Sil through his hospitalization for alcohol poisoning. Sil was living with Claudette in her dorm room the night he almost drank himself to death. Actually, he'd been making his rounds of the dorms. He'd stay with Claudette in her room for a while, then with one of Claudette's friends in their rooms, usually for long stints. He had nowhere else to live, nowhere else to be, really. But despite his desperate circumstances, despite his fragile appearance, he would make it to adulthood pretty much the way he'd made it through puberty—by being pushy, by being willful and unabashedly clear in his likes and dislikes of people and places and things to do. His ability to master the practical—to cook, to furnish and decorate a comfortable home, to plan and guide trips to just about any place on the globe—made him a good addition to any crowd, even if his own abilities made him perpetually impatient with those whose talents lay elsewhere. His tough skin was a necessity, I suppose.

How could he let anyone in—anyone really in—when letting people in meant they might abandon him?

On my previous visits to St. Paul nothing untoward had taken place, never a scene, never an early departure, but Sil's pushiness had rubbed me wrong, chaffed me, forced me to keep my mouth shut. Those trips were made during my own partially disclosed, half-hearted attempts to get clean of my own addictions, which had kicked in full force later than Sil's, after I'd moved away from San Antonio to live in New York City. Giving myself over to those habits had meant losing touch with my family and hometown friends. Kicking those habits had meant kicking the docility that had been my response to a family life as chaotic, in its own way, as Sil's. Antidepressants helped, talk therapy helped, and one result of it all seems to be that the New York assertiveness my many years in the City had already begun to develop have only been fortified.

To make for more possible complications, during my visits I sometimes judged Sil to have grown into a pretentious and insufferably materialistic man. He had to have the best of everything, all the trappings of stability: the elephantine large-screen TV, the frequent vacations—to Amsterdam, to Japan, to Argentina—the most expensive meals at the nicest restaurants in whatever city he happened to be passing through. It's true; he liked to pick up the bill whenever the three of us ate out. He liked to be generous and extravagant when giving orders to waiters. And all that was well and good. And certainly I, with my modest means and money-draining New York City life, benefited from his newfound prosperity. I smoked the expensive pot he and Gerry always had ready and waiting to smoke. I ate the expensive meals Sil had learned to make when he attended culinary school. I would take advantage of the gym he'd set up on the ground floor now that he'd switched careers and was making his living as a personal trainer.

But his generosity, like his materialism, seemed to have dubious aims, one being the need to show that he'd more than gotten his life together, another being the need for control he had always felt entitled to. He's fond of saying, "It's my way or the highway."

I've asked myself if, perhaps, I'm envious of Sil, of his possessions: his large, surround sound TV speakers, his fine art collection, and his long series of pet dogs—loveable, all of them, but, like Bruno and Bruiser, large and expensive to keep. I've asked myself, too, if I'm just jealous of Sil's long line of boyfriends, many of whom he'd attracted at his most dysfunctional.

But once, between my visits to St. Paul, a third party confirmed my feelings about Sil. I was spending a week in San Antonio. Sil needed to make a trip to San Antonio himself—to check up on a house he still owns in Alamo Heights. So we met up often. Sil would spend days with my family and me and then we all said good night to him each evening as he departed to his expensive hotel room. One night Sil took me and one of our high school friends, Daniel, out for dinner. I kept quiet most of the meal, amused by the effeminate Hispanic waiter who waited on us. He was visibly happy to be serving two gay men who could speak Spanish, and Daniel, a handsome white boy with dark hair and green long-lashed eyes. When I wasn't watching the waiter, I watched the tourists on the River Walk and was happy that I could only half-hear their drunken conversations through the restaurant windows. While Sil did most of the talking, I watched the waiter. I watched the tourists. I forked tuna steak into my half-smiling face. A few days later, back in New York, I received an e-mail from Daniel. It read: "Sil's a little bourgeois, isn't he? A little . . . full of himself, isn't he?" Sitting at my desk, I smiled, and I felt confirmed, felt wickedly glad that Daniel heard how much Sil talks about himself, how any question Sil asks about anyone else's life is only peremptorily listened to before he returns to the subject of himself and his own life.

This trip, however, my first winter trip to St. Paul, I found Sil had mellowed some. I heard him, at least once, apologize for an outburst of condescension and irritability toward Gerry. "I'm sorry," he said. "I'm sorry, you're right. I'm wrong." His materialism seemed to have abated a bit, too—if only because he was running out of room to store everything—and the usually immaculate house was even somewhat less kept. I stayed in a basement where Sil and Gerry had set up a guest bedroom with a small refrigerator and a small, adjoining toilet and shower stall. Getting in the shower one morning, I dropped a tube of foot scrub Sil had stuffed into my Christmas stocking. Lifting my hand out of a corner behind a water pipe where the tube had lodged itself, I found I was holding a handful of cobwebs. This would never have happened in the past.

Sil even seemed to be developing an ability to talk about more things than himself. All three of us habitually went to bed before ten o'clock. But my first night there, Sil and I stayed up late talking and smoking pot long after Gerry had gone upstairs, allegedly to go to bed. Sil inquired about my health, my medications, and my time off hard drugs. We had a long talk about my brother, a ne'er-do-well Sil is fond of, then turned to my mother and her health problems. Sil updated me on his sisters, their children, and even turned, for some reason, to the topic of transgender people. I was surprised by the sympathy Sil could show for people whose lives are very different from his own. When I cocked my head at the sounds of Gerry moving around upstairs, Sil said, "Guess he hasn't gone to bed yet. Gerry spends lots of time burning porn DVDs and talking to his online buddies." I was sitting on a stool at one end of their large wooden table. Beneath the surface of the table there are two layers of storage shelves stuffed with kitchen supplies. With my elbows on the surface of that table, more than a bit stoned, I was allowing myself to be hypnotized by the paths the fish made as they swam one way then the other and back again in the tank against the window. "It's his only vice," Sil added. "So I let him get away with it."

I liked to comfort myself, during my trips to St. Paul, that Sil and Gerry at least have not given in to that ever-growing desire among middle-class gay men and women—the desire for children—a desire that I, at my snidest—perhaps at my most selfish—think of as little more than a penchant for status symbols. *Look at what I can afford*, I imagine those children's parents secretly gloating, *see what I have the power to obtain.* Visiting Sil, I at least don't have to compete with a child to find a bit of time with an old friend. I do, however, have to compete with Gerry.

In fact, it was Gerry who would grate on my nerves during my six snow-filled days in St. Paul. His attention span, never very grown-up to begin with, had grown even shorter. We could only watch or go out to the most action-packed, special-effect-filled movies. Even *The Fearless Vampire Killers* was too slow, too yesterday, and far too uninteresting for Gerry. I had to monitor the length and subject of any anecdote I related—nothing too long, please, nothing too serious—assuming of course that I could get a word in over Gerry's loud, booming voice, his erratic drumming of the table with the thumbs of his thick hands. "Let's go bowling," he'd say one minute. "No," he'd say the next, "let's stay in—play a game."

Hadn't I found Gerry's childishness endearing in the past? Maybe. Yes, definitely. I can be childish myself, playful, downright immature, and Gerry was always good for joining in on a little tomfoolery. It's also likely that Gerry had gained my sympathy more than my ire on previous trips. The extent to which he had to live under Sil's thumb easily induced sympathy. One spring trip, for instance, we drove to a lighthouse on the shore of Lake Superior. Sil drove for the last leg of the trip while I pulled the lever under my chair and reclined. Gerry stretched out in the back. I think I napped. The drive was long and we were all relaxed. Sil nevertheless got impatient once we'd all arrived.

"What's taking you two so long?"

"Jesus, Sil, give us a minute, would you? We're putting on our sneakers," I snapped back. "And is it really necessary to speak to us that way?"

I must have shot a look at Gerry for not backing me up as I hopped out of the four-wheel drive, because as we stood outside the doors on the passenger side, he looked at me in his childlike way and said, "I know, I'm so pussy whipped. I know, I'm sorry."

So, the behaviors Gerry had to put up with from Sil in their life together might have always made Gerry the object of my sympathy, but Gerry was in his fifties now. And Sil, as I've said, had, in his way, matured. And my coming more and more into myself made me perhaps less and less patient with Gerry. In that impatience, I was like Sil, I suppose, wanting everyone else to be competent at whatever it is I'm competent at. Maybe that's one reason Sil and I are and probably always will be friends, or something like friends anyway. What made the situation more intolerable for me was the fact that Gerry wasn't stupid, not really. I think that he'd just grown accustomed to playing the part of the dumb husband. Occasionally, I'd seen Gerry show resistance to that role, like the time he was leafing through one of my book-review magazines in the backyard. He put the magazine down on the backdoor steps where I was sitting and said, "I wish I read." I offered to make a few suggestions, to take him shopping at B&N or, better yet, a secondhand bookstore, but Sil chimed in from the barbecue cooker, saying, "He won't read."

I shot him a perturbed look.

"He *won't* read," he repeated, flipping over the ground turkey.

"See how mean he is," Gerry said as he winked at me. But that was it. That was the extent of Gerry's resistance, and, in that particular instance, at least, his resistance had the advantage of not taking itself too seriously. But now it seemed exhausted, depleted, all gone and not nearly as resistant as the snow and ice that lay outside the house and, indeed, all around us.

It was during another spring trip to St. Paul that Gerry said, "That is St. Paul." And then, pointing in the other direction, past Sil in the driver's seat, he said, "And *that*, that is Minneapolis."

"St. Paul—Minneapolis—St. Paul—Minneapolis," I said from the back seat, swiveling my head, rapid fire, back and forth, left and right, until Gerry joined in. "St. Paul—Minneapolis—St. Paul—Minneapolis . . ." And *that* was the Gerry I loved—the childish, tom-foolish Gerry.

And since it might not be fair to say that Sil or Gerry, one more than the other, got on my nerves—they are a couple, after all—the two cities, side by side, may serve as the best way to describe my feelings toward them. Visiting Sil and Gerry was like visiting two places at once. One place was the scene of a happy coupling, though I must say it was Sil who, for the most part, gave that impression, Sil being the one who would reach out a hand from whatever seat he was in, the driver's seat or the passenger's seat, and lay it on Gerry's knee. Sil would say warm things to Gerry over dinner conversations, things like "Well, I've found the one, I found the man I want to spend the rest of my life with." Gerry would either ignore what Sil had just said, or say, "Yeah, right." "What Gerry means to say," Sil would come back, "is that *he's* just not sure he'll be around much longer." Those awkward moments were the other Sil and Gerry, the unhappy couple in a parallel city, a troubled locale in which the bridge between two places might collapse, just as the I-35W bridge collapsed in 2007, plunging a good number of the Twin Cities' citizenry into the Mississippi. Sometimes, while we were waiting for our dessert to be brought out, perhaps during a lull in the conversation, Sil would suddenly snap at Gerry, "Who are you gawking at over there?" (Like me, Sil was given to eyeing other men he found attractive, but he never did so in front of Gerry. And he never gawked. Gerry did.)

After dinner out one night, back at the house, Gerry was showing me their new dining room set. It was made up of six tall-backed wooden chairs and a long stately table with fold-out leaves. "You guys are going to have a lot to move if you ever do move back down to the Southwest," I said. "Or Sil will," Gerry responded. "Well, that was an unexpected remark," I thought to myself. But it made me realize, Sil was the one who always talked about their plans to move back to the Southwest. Gerry never mentioned any such desire.

What exactly Sil and Gerry's problems were, I can only make an informed guess at. My guess, though, would be as informed as anyone else's, because one of Sil and Gerry's problems is that they don't have many friends. Their relationship is their primary and practically their only relationship. Sil has professional friendships with some of the men and women he trains. They fly him to their residences across the country to set up their home gyms. Sometimes they have him cater their soirees. He has entree into their homes. They pay him extravagantly. But those relationships remain limited by status. For his part, Gerry supervises maintenance workers—working-class stiffs, ex-cons, and immigrants—at an expensive high-rise residence. And those employees sometime endear themselves upon Gerry, and vice versa, but, again, socioeconomics prevent any real relationships from ever forming. In bed by ten every night, Sil and Gerry don't go to bars. Nor do they have much sense of community. On the contrary, they are weary of anyone who wears his or her sexuality like a badge, including me. Out at restaurants or wandering the aisles of stores, my loudness, my penchant for letting out a campy, risqué remark, or the way I can't resist rubbernecking a handsome man—all these behaviors are sure to draw Sil and Gerry's ire. "This *isn't* New York," they say in unison. One night, James Dean's bisexuality somehow came up in conversation. Sil was incredulous. So, once I got back to New York, I e-mailed him an entry on Dean from GLBTQ.com. Sil e-mailed back, "Oh, yeah, like I'm going to believe that Dean was bisexual because some gay website says he is."

To boot, sex seems to have become an ongoing issue between Sil and Gerry, just as the ebbs and flows of sex—ebbs, in particular—become an issue in just about any relationship. While Gerry was upstairs watching porn one night, Sil related an anecdote to me. In the anecdote, Sil had been stricken by mono. After giving Sil his diagnosis, his doctor playfully asked him who he'd been kissing. Sil answered, "I don't kiss. I don't get kissed, not even at home." Gerry, for his part, burned more and more porn from the web and sometimes flirted with me. Don't get me wrong, I'm attention-starved enough not to mind. This trip, however, it crossed a line for me. I think we were talking about an actor one afternoon—Daniel Craig, I think—about how Gerry and I had the hots for him. I told Gerry I'd seen a photograph of Craig meeting the Queen of England. "Even the Queen looked like she wanted to wrap her legs around him," I said. "Hell," Gerry came back, "*I'd* wrap my legs around him, and usually I prefer to have men wrap their legs around me." Then, getting up from the couch, he looked back and down at me. "If things were different, you know you and I would be doing something like that right now, don't you?" It wasn't that I was morally shocked. I'd fooled around with John, one of Sil's exes, during a period in which Sil and John were particularly busy making each other particularly miserable.

What made me uncomfortable about Gerry's raising the image of me with my legs wrapped around him probably has more to do with sexual snobbery. Gerry remains as muscular as ever, but he shuns cardio and any kind of yoga, refusing to stretch or jump up and down because he thinks it's too girly. So his midsection has long been going soft. And, as I've said, this trip I'd been finding him childish and annoying. That childishness manifested itself, not just in his booming voice, now louder than ever, but in his full, wide mouth, the bottom lip of which had taken to hanging open. In the past, those lips didn't detract too much from his Cuban handsomeness or his square ex-boxer's shoulders, his salt-and-pepper hair, or the tattoos beneath all that hair on his arms. Now, however, with the lower lip hanging loose and ever looser, he seems like a stupid schoolboy daydreaming in class. He drinks a lot of coffee, too, and not through a straw (as I do). So, to add to the loose-lip effect, his teeth long ago began to yellow.

If I didn't want to have sex with Gerry, though, it seemed there was someone else who did. That someone was Brendan. Brendan and his "boyfriend" Clayton were new friends of Sil and Gerry's. Sil and Gerry had been mentioning the couple since the night I'd arrived. I think they were excited to finally have friends to introduce me to. Sil even brought them up on the phone and in a few e-mails as we were planning my trip. So by the time Gerry picked them up at the airport on the day after Christmas, after they'd arrived from visiting Clayton's family somewhere in nowhere U.S.A., I already had a pretty good idea of the role they played in Sil and Gerry's life. Brendan, it seemed, was not only younger than any of us but also attractive, at least to Sil and Gerry. Any tip Brendan provided on fashion or grooming was therefore received by Sil and Gerry as the kind of attention that's hard to come by from a callow youth. That advice was heeded too. When I got off the plane, I complimented Sil on his haircut. Sil responded, "Yeah, Brendan told me I should keep it long 'cause it looks good, and I figure when you get a compliment from a cute, bitchy gay boy, you're doing something right."

The other role Brendan and Clayton played in Sil and Gerry's life had more to do with what was lacking in the latter couple's relationship. That is, whatever problems Sil and Gerry had in their own relationship, it seemed, at least to Sil and Gerry, that Brendan and Clayton had more. Clayton, it seemed, had told Brendan that Brendan wasn't really "his type," which is why they never had sex. Brendan related this tidbit to Sil and Gerry, who, of course, related it to me. I say "of course" because I sensed it gave Sil and Gerry pleasure to gossip about their friends' dirty laundry. Gossiping about Brendan and Clayton's problems made it possible for Sil and Gerry not to have to discuss their own. Given all that, the impression that Brendan and Clayton made on me, once they arrived from the airport and stripped themselves of winter gear to meet me, was blasé. Brendan was tired and sat on a stool at the kitchen table not saying much. Clayton, a pudgy man with round wire-frame glasses who seemed to be in his late forties, but was actually younger, was politeness itself. They complained about the members of Clayton's family who they'd been visiting. They complained about the weather and travel conditions, but I didn't sense any of the tension between them that Sil and Gerry had made infamous. In fact, that was one of the things Gerry and Sil liked to harp on: that for all their problems, Brendan and Clayton could be pleasant company. They sometimes went as far as fawning on each other.

Brendan did come out of his stupor for a moment that night. He leaned over and said to me, "We know you're a whore." I laughed and bumper-carred his shoulder with my own. I was glad to have someone reflecting the image I create for myself back to me—even if it was someone as seemingly dull-witted as Brendan. I had to repress my campy side when I was alone with Sil and Gerry. Brendan, for the moment, came as a breath of fresh air. So I didn't even try explaining to him that my whoredom was mostly an empty boast, an easy way to be funny, to get a laugh, that I never had nearly as much sex as I'd like to. And I definitely didn't tell I'm largely, unwillingly celibate. Brendan didn't seem interested in hearing it. Instead I thanked Sil and Gerry for enhancing my reputation, and, sitting around the large kitchen table with the storage shelves beneath it, we all laughed.

I should admit, at this point in the story, that the next morning Gerry conveyed to me what Brendan thought of me. "Brendan thinks you're cute," Gerry said, punching away at his computer keyboard, then adding, as he took his hand off the keyboard and met my eyes, "Don't you think that's nice? I think that's nice." I did, of course, think it was nice. But both Brendan and Clayton were scheduled to come over for dinner and a movie that night, and the last thing I wanted to do was to stop having a relaxing time away from New York. Though I thought it might be fun to watch, I didn't want to complicate all the marital tensions between Sil and Gerry and, to boot, Brendan and Clayton. Besides, too many years in New York City ogling too many men far too good looking for their own or anyone else's good has left me awfully picky, jaded, and not a little bitter. Brendan, by those eastern seaboard standards, was slim pickings. Yes, he had nicely set hazel eyes, arms that were smooth and substantial, but beyond that everything else fell away when compared to the health and ultra-fashion-conscious men of New York City. Gerry's reputed impetuousness didn't help matters any. So I must have said something noncommittal, something like "I guess it's nice. Yes, I guess it's nice he thinks I'm attractive."

What finding out that Brendan thought I was attractive did do for me, however, was set up false expectations of a pleasant evening. I'd been looking forward to the elaborate meal Sil had been preparing for since my arrival. Now Brendan seemed to have a reason, in me, to want to be among us, not to get bored or whiny. And soft pudgy Clayton—well, Clayton seemed to be the type who would be docile and easygoing, no matter the circumstances. Sil and Gerry said he would be happy to work on the model Christmas house he had been building out of Graham crackers, marshmallows, and other edible items while the rest of us watched a movie after dinner. Sil and Gerry, together with Brendan and Clayton, had begun the little arts and crafts project before I arrived. Sil and Gerry and Brendan's model homes were proudly displayed around the house. But Clayton, a disciplined, ex-military man, was intent on making his extra neat and extra sound, completely presentable and patriotically ready for inspection.

Clayton in fact went right to work that second night, arranging, gluing, wiping, and rearranging as he stood up straight and leaned over, squinting all the while, to examine his handiwork. Sil was bending over the stove as he cooked, stirring pots, chopping and spicing, and waving away anyone who tried to help. If the dogs weren't begging to be let out, or to be let back in, they had to be shooed off the couch where there wasn't enough room for them, for Gerry, Brendan, and myself. Gerry was channel surfing but eventually put down the remote and left *The Yule Log* on. *The Yule Log* is a program I had never seen before. It's a film loop of a Yule log burning in a fireplace, with Christmas carols and music playing in the background.

The Yule Log, as it turned out, gave the only warmth any of us could enjoy that evening, even if it was only the warmth of the TV screen. The company certainly provided no warmth at all, unless you count the heat between Gerry and Brendan. Watching *The Yule Log*, Brendan and Gerry and I were still on the couch. Brendan was leaning his head on Gerry's shoulder, and Gerry had his hand on Brendan's leg. I sat on the other end of the sofa, trying to convince myself their little display of affection was simply part of the holiday spirit we were all doing our best to feign, but quickly developing circumstances didn't allow me to convince myself of that for very long. Brendan began complaining that his shoulder ached. He asked Gerry to rub it. Then he took to whispering to Gerry.

When Gerry was through massaging Brendan, Brendan asked, in a somewhat forced matter-of-fact tone, if Gerry wouldn't mind giving him a spinal adjustment. Gerry promptly said that no, he wouldn't mind at all and they both went upstairs.

Bruiser immediately took advantage of the couch space. The dog was by this time used to my disciplining him and ordering him about, so I did my best to get him off the couch, but instead he mounted me, his outstretched one hundred and eighty pounds of dog to my one hundred and forty pounds of outstretched, small man. He began to lick me, ounces of his accumulated slobber pouring its way onto my face. Sil entered the room to grab a cookbook off a shelf. He didn't ask where Gerry and Brendan were but he did ask if I was French-kissing the dog as he walked back to the kitchen with his long, slightly hunched torso its usual one step or two behind his long legs. Despite my canine dilemma on the couch, I noted Sil always had an awkward gait. No matter how much dignity he carried himself with, no matter how much he worked out, he'd always be awkward. But who was I to be thinking of dignity and grace? The sight of my struggling beneath Bruiser, breathlessly exclaiming, "Bruiser—oh, Bruiser," must have looked and sounded like that awkward thing called passion.

Other than my being mounted by a dog, the evening proceeded so mundanely, so repetitiously, I can't even say exactly what happened next. I managed to free myself, probably only because Bruiser wanted to be let out. I alternated between channel surfing and dragging my slippered feet into the kitchen to check on Sil and Clayton's progress, and checking my e-mail in the computer room. At some point, Sil sat down at the kitchen table to let the dishes he was preparing cook and then cool, and he began playing with the various buttons and dials of the digital camera Gerry had given him for Christmas; Clayton continued to construct his gingerbread house. Lost in their individual enterprises, they barely spoke a word to each other or me. Bruiser, when he wanted to be let back in, could be heard letting out his customary single bark from the backyard.

Things took a turn for the worse when Gerry and Brendan reappeared and asked if we all wanted to go bowling after dinner. "No," Sil said, closing the refrigerator door shut. Gerry and Brendan persisted, proposing that Gerry and Brendan could go by Clayton and Brendan's place and pick up Brendan's ball. "No," Sil said, snapping open the lid on a can of Coke. Gerry and Brendan turned to Clayton, and to me, for support. I looked noncommittally back and forth between the two couples.

Conferences followed—one couple upstairs, the other off in a room downstairs. "It's my way or the highway," I heard Sil say. "Damn it, Sil," I heard Gerry reply. I heard an upstairs door abruptly slammed shut. Sitting at the kitchen table, I felt foolish and in the way. I took a hit off the pipe and shooed Bruiser away. His thick, weighty tail was slapping my leg. I watched the fish in the tank and smoked another hit. Then Gerry was in the room with me, standing just inside the kitchen doorway. "Listen," he said, "I really want to know. Do *you* want to go bowling?" A cloud of smoke filled the room as I exhaled. I simply stared at Gerry, neither nodding nor shaking my head, but moving it in a combination of nodding and shaking. "Gerry," Sil shouted, "leave him out of this and get back over here."

Gerry lingered a moment. At a loss of what to say, and not knowing what else to do, I stretched out my arm, offering him the pipe and a small, purple lighter. He took a hit, staring at Clayton's gingerbread house. "I can't believe," he exhaled, "*how nice* Clayton's house looks."

"Gerry!" Sil called, his footsteps approaching the kitchen.

"God, I sound so stupid," Gerry said and left the room, swinging his arms and moving fast.

"All right, all right, Bruiser," I rolled my eyes. "I'll take you out again." His tail was slapping at my leg, harder this time.

In the backyard, I let Bruiser in the wire-fenced area where the dogs were kept in good weather, and he trotted to the far end of the enclosure, disappearing beneath the shadow of a stand of trees where he planned, I supposed, to relieve himself. When he reappeared, he trotted back to my side of the playground and hopped up, resting his forelegs on the top of the fence. We stared at each other, keeping time to the sound of his breathing. I told him he better not kiss me again. He tried to lick my face, missing only because I pulled away. I decided that even if Sil and Gerry and Brandon and Clayton hadn't settled things, it was time to go back in. It was cold. I only had on a T-shirt, pajama-bottoms, and boots.

The only problem was I hadn't unlocked the door from the inside and I had shut it completely closed behind me. I was locked out. I knocked and called to Sil and Gerry. No response. I trudged through a stretch of snow to a window where I could see in. I didn't see anyone, not Sil or Gerry or Brendan or Clayton, so I trudged back and knocked some more. Then I started knocking harder, banging at the door. "Damn it, guys," I shouted. "I'm locked out. It's cold!" No response.

I went down the three wooden steps to the door again and back to the window. With still no success in spotting anyone inside, I was heading back to the door when I saw the fence gate swinging open in the wind. I panicked. I thought I'd only added to the bad situation indoors by losing Bruiser outdoors. Then I heard it, the heavy breathing behind me.

"Fuck, fuck, fuck," I cried, face down and slapping the ice with my open palm. Bruiser came around from behind me and immediately, apologetically, happily licked my face.

At dinner I ate while simultaneously rubbing and examining my wounds. Sil and Gerry and Clayton made occasional attempts at conversation. Should we play a game after dinner or watch a movie? If so, what game? What movie? Brendan sat, punctuating his silence with requests to pass a bowl or a serving plate. The fish in the aquarium swam from plant to open waters, open waters to oxygen-rich plant just as I, out of my element, had moved from one part of the house to another earlier in the evening, bored and checking my e-mail, bored and smoking more pot.

As it turned out, after dinner, things centered around the TV. Before we watched a movie, Sil stood before Brendan and Clayton and Gerry and I, who were splayed out across the couch, and he videotaped our conversation. At one point, I related an anecdote that apparently went on too long for Gerry because sure enough, when Sil played the footage back, Gerry said, "Oh, God, here comes that long story again. Please, Sil, fast-forward through it." On screen, in the footage, he was sighing, and looking at Brendan throughout my little story. I took it in stride. "Now, Gerry," I joked before I told any other anecdote that evening, "I hope *this* story doesn't *bore* you."

When Sil turned off the playback and joined us all on the couch, I realized, at some point, that I had become the third wheel among not just one but, now, two couples, the only single person on the couch. I felt inferior for a moment, then let go of the feeling of inferiority with a barely whispered, "*Thank God.*"

The next evening, my fourth day in St. Paul, Brendan and Clayton came back to the house after we all met and ate at a trendy Chinese restaurant that catered to gay men. Since I had been left out of the gift-giving between the two couples the evening before, Brendan and Clayton gave me a large, brightly wrapped box. It was a gingerbread house kit. Back at Sil and Gerry's, in return, I gave Brendan a knit hat that Sil and Gerry and I had decided didn't look good on me. I gave Clayton one of the gifts I'd picked up at the Frida Kahlo exhibition. It was the most ill-suited gift for Clayton, but what else could I do? After Brendan and Clayton left, Sil and Gerry and I stayed up late, watching one of their favorite shows. It was one of those sadistic, home-movie shows that highlight people's worst moments. In this case, the subject matter was skateboarders who stupidly tried to glide down a public-stairway banister, only to crash into a pile of broken bones as they bounced out of the camera's view, wannabe Evil Knievels who leap across five of their friends' huddled backs and who end up hurting not only themselves but their friends. Perhaps because of all the underlying tensions of the past two evenings, I laughed along with Sil and Gerry. They sat curled up together at one end of the couch. I had the dogs at the other end, watching the screen through my barely open fingers with my hands held to my face. We were stoned and I didn't feel left out. We were all laughing again.

Despite my relief that the second evening with Brendan and Clayton had been a cinch compared to the injurious first, Sil and Gerry spent a good deal of the next few days diminishing their friends. "You didn't have to give them anything," Gerry said to me, referring to the hat and museum gift I'd given Brendan and Clayton. "God, Brendan is so incapable of saying he's sorry," Sil said. "Instead of apologizing for the bowling thing the night before, he goes out and buys a gingerbread house kit and gives it to you as gift from him and Clayton. It doesn't make up for those bruises on your side, does it?"

It was after listening to a lot of complaining about Brendan and Clayton that I, as I inevitably do, blurted out my opinion. "What I think was rude, what I think was really rude," I intoned, "was when Brendan took to whispering to Gerry on the couch, whispering to him like I wasn't there. And then, to top it off, I thought it was rude when he took Gerry upstairs to give him an—what was it he was going to give him?—an adjustment." Of course, I would later regret having said that, but at that moment, in the silence that followed, I looked up from the couch, looked to Sil, who was standing in the middle of the room, and then to Gerry, who was sitting a few inches away from me on the couch. Sil—Gerry—Sil—Gerry. St. Paul—Minneapolis—St.

Paul—Minneapolis. Would the bridge hold? Or would we all be plunged into the cold and dirty water below? Bruiser lowered himself off the couch. "Fucking screwing around," Sil said, biting his fingernails and glancing a sidelong look off of Gerry, and that was it. The subject changed. The bridge held.

I sometimes wonder what Sil and Gerry said, to themselves or to each other, about what I let loose. I sometimes wonder why I let it loose. I don't quite know myself. Maybe I was taking Sil's side by revealing Gerry and Brendan's little tryst. But it's more likely I let loose what I let loose because I thought Gerry had robbed me of the attention I had coming my way—attention from Brendan, a man-boy, a brat I didn't take seriously and I didn't even like. It's also likely I thought Gerry had lied to me when he told me Brendan thought I was cute, that Gerry felt I needed propping up and set about to do just that. It's also very likely I was angry because Gerry insulted me with his "Oh, God, here comes that long story again. Please, Sil, fast-forward through it." I knew it may only have been Gerry's way of releasing some of his shame and anger over being so "pussy whipped," but I felt injured nevertheless.

My last morning in St. Paul, we all took one more big hit off the pot pipe. The supply was coming to an end. We piled on our winter clothes and walked single file through the fresh path Gerry had scraped from the house to Gerry's SUV and Sil's hatchback. Sil walked ahead of Gerry, his breath rising in puffs behind him. I pulled up the rear, my traveling case on wheels in tow behind me, my gingerbread house kit under my arm. Sil said his hatchback, which we hadn't been using in the snow and ice, needed to be taken out for a spin. We wiped the snow off its windows with our coat sleeves. But when Sil tried to back out, we couldn't get over the snow and ice that had accumulated underneath the wheels. So Gerry and I got out and pushed while Sil kept the car in reverse and put the pedal to the floor. He gunned, the car rolled back and Gerry and I pushed forward, and we had to repeat the process over and over for a good while.

In the back seat of the finally freed car, I said, "You know, for a while there, I thought Gerry and I were going to end up like one of those idiots in that show last night, broken-boned and half-dead."

"Yeah," Gerry said, "but there would have been no camera to catch it all on tape."

"Sil would've gone inside," I picked up the tomfoolery, "taken another hit off the pipe, and waited a while before he dialed 911."

194

"And by that time," Sil concluded, "you both would have been dead."

We all laughed, and I took in one last look at the eaves of the house. Inside, the birds twittered in their cages. On the ground floor, the dogs were probably already asleep, their huge heads resting on their huge paws. The clocks were surely ticking, the aquariums were bubbling, and the fish were doing whatever it is fish do when no one's home. Sil had left a pot of beans on the stove, and they were slowly boiling. Below I'd left my bed unmade, and the snakes were hibernating, waiting for spring. Sil said he would e-mail all the pictures we'd taken and he did. Many of them show all three of us in the house, in various states of dress, with Bruiser and Bruno slobbering, their wagging tails captured in a blur here and a blur there. Still more pictures show us before the Frank Lloyd Wright houses we'd found with the help of the web, or in the middle of a snow-covered park with a frozen body of water behind us, a museum shaped like a mission, all three of us waving and smiling, smiling and waving. Were the three of us waving goodbye to ourselves, to the three of us, for good? A few springs have come and gone since my last six days in St. Paul, but I'm still not sure.

Arturo, Who Likes to Shave His Legs in the Snow

LUCY MARRERO

Arturo at thirty-four years old filled out his bronze body with defined muscles. Despite his strength, he still had a delicate appearance, like one too beautiful to pick strawberries in the California heat—just like his abuela. El jefe, his pink cheeks glowing in the excitement of finding one so beautiful, took her hand as she prepared to jump down from the bed of the truck that had brought her and her husband to the fields that first morning, their brown arms pressed against other brown arms, swaying and jerking with the rocks and potholes in the road. El jefe took his abuela's hand and led her into the office instead, gesturing for her to remove her wide-brimmed straw hat and sit, sit down, please.

Her graceful fingers gripped at the brim as she held the hat over her stomach and pelvis and stood unmoving, praying silently behind pursed lips and tightened jaw: Por favor, no me moleste. Por favor. Por favor, señor, déjame sola.

Arturo looked up from the notebook where he'd been frantically trying to capture the images as they spilled out of his brain, fingers scrambling to keep up. He stood and passed his palm slowly across frosty glass that'd seen winters just as cold as this for more than eighty years. He saw the flakes like tiny down feathers starting to fall.

His flesh immediately puckered with a chill, but still he lingered, palm on the window, for a moment before turning away for the pink-tiled bathroom. It would have made a lovely photograph, the palm against the frosted window, the arm slightly relaxed into an aesthetically pleasing line to the chest, shoulders pulling the body into a relaxed but regal posture, smooth slope of the nose dark against the outside light.

The thick pile of the white rug between Arturo's bare toes contrasted with the hardwood floor, and the radiator blew warm air over his goose bumps, relaxing him as he rummaged in the medicine cabinet. The shaving cream and razor sat lined up on the sink as Arturo let the soft track pants, smoky charcoal gray, drop to the tile and pulled his white T-shirt over his head. He gazed into the mirror, squinting his eyes as if trying to spot something in his reflection. So different without clothes, he thought, turning away from the mirror slightly so that he could see the elegant lines of muscles crossing his back.

Such a delicate balance, trying to find the right clothes to wear. When browsing through burgundy and forest-green sweaters or stark button-downs with muted ties, sometimes his mind wandered, and when he looked down, he found his fingers resting against smooth velvet or cool satin. It startled Arturo to realize he'd somehow moved from the men's section and into the women's. The textures of their clothes were so beautiful, comforting even. His sybarite nature clashed with the standards expected of a successful businessman like himself, and so he would make his way back to the men's section, sighing quietly.

Arturo grabbed a soft towel from the cabinet and inhaled the fresh scent of laundry detergent before gathering up the rest of his supplies and headed out the front door, scanning the yard for the tree stump that kept him company from his desk. It was already covered in a layer of white powder from earlier snows. By four o'clock, about two inches had accumulated, and by then Arturo could no longer resist the teasing little flakes on his skin, the dry cold air that promised to hug his body.

The hairs on his leg popped out as goose bumps covered his entire body, and Arturo shivered. He propped his left leg up on the friendly tree stump. The shaving cream felt warm in contrast to the frigid air as he covered his leg from ankle to knee. The never-changing ritual soothed the cold from his mind as he ran the razor first from knee down to ankle all around until he'd finished the entire lower part of his left leg like a lawnmower, leaving perfect rows of almost-smooth skin. Adding more shaving cream, he then repeated the perfect rows, this time ankle to knee, razor traveling neatly all the way around his leg.

Arturo squinted as a few flakes fell onto his lashes, and more fell from his stylish hair as he switched legs. The snow was falling more insistently now, but still he took his time, savoring the cold as he worked. It was so quiet he could hear the scratch of the razor as it liberated the hair from his skin one row at a time. The expanse of trees outside his front door cordoned him off from the rest of his world, and the neighbors and their poorly concealed curiosity disappeared from his mind as he worked rhythmically.

The small, gloved hands gripping tree trunks were worlds away, the crunch of twigs underfoot unheard.

He ran the soft towel, now damp from the falling snow, down both legs and lifted his heel to inspect the back of each leg. Satisfied, he folded the towel over once lengthwise, once sideways, and placed the shaving cream and razor inside, folding the towel over them once again into a neat little package. Inhaling deeply, he braced himself against the cruel coldness, standing tall for a moment more, lingering just a moment more before heading in, when a juvenile giggle pierced the peaceful silence surrounding him.

His head whipped around to the row of trees barren of leaves, branches bending under their heavy white burden. *There.* Small, gloved hands disappeared from tree trunks and he heard the crunch of snow underfoot, whispers, and small voices in hasty retreat. Arturo gathered himself up quickly, his chin high despite the blood pounding out his heartbeat in his ears. He hadn't dropped the towel, but the package had threatened to lose its contents, and he tucked them safely back into the fluffy, damp towel. Purposefully, he turned back to the front door, his stride proud despite his nakedness. He leaned against the door after closing it, gulping deep breaths, instructing his body to settle down. The towel released its cargo, and faintly Arturo heard the clatter of metal on tile. Puzzled, he ran one hand over his cotton boxers, which had somehow become wet and warm.

Quickly he shed them, grabbed his dropped supplies, and headed for the kitchen, where he deposited everything, including the towel, in the garbage. Eyes fuzzy and unfocused, he stood motionless for a moment, body still, mind whirring with something he couldn't quite grasp. If you had asked him, he would have been unaware of any thought at all. Just a moment of spacing out.

The steam rose in the tiny bathroom, breathing a thin sheen of moisture on the rosy tiles and the mirror on the rusted medicine cabinet. Arturo wet his hair and let the water splash down onto his face, eyes squeezed shut. As he stood that way, his mind wandered without his permission, dragging him back, back into scenes he'd long forgotten.

"Fag!" the chubby brown teenager shouted, cackling and elbowing his skinny friend, the one who hardly ever spoke. They laughed and slapped each other high-five as Arturo hurried past. I don't want to miss warm-up time, he told himself, carefully avoiding mention, even to himself, of the daily menace that interrupted his memorization of class routines.

He walked briskly, arms moving just the slightest bit as he visualized each movement, breathed the steps of the routine in time to the rhythm of his footsteps.

Chas-sé, chas-sé, pique-pique, side.

Hooold—and down, rond de jambe, contract.

He rolled his shoulders back and walked on. He intended to convey nonchalance and confidence, but instead only emphasized his dancer's posture, drawing attention to the way he glided gracefully down the sidewalk, a stark contrast to the slouchy, hunched shoulders of the other teenage boys sitting on stoops and playfully insulting each other at street corners.

Arturo froze, one foot still in front of the other, his weight suspended, not yet committed to the next step. Is someone following me? He drew his feet together and let his backpack drop from his shoulder, eyebrows furrowing dramatically as he enacted the act of looking for something, anything, from its depths. His heart pounded so loudly in his ears he could hardly make out the muffled sound of footsteps. His follower dragged his feet, but he was coming quickly. Arturo realized quickly he needed a plan of action, but before he could think anything at all, he was hit from the side by a wall clothed in baggy jeans and quilted jacket.

They fell, and if it could be replayed in slow motion, it would have been beautiful, the collision of solid body, so compact, into Arturo's lithe and lanky frame. It would have showed the indignation on the solid form's face, sneering, personally affronted, it seemed, by the fragile body he reached out for as if to embrace. Folding his arms around Arturo as he floated to the ground, a swan's drawn-out dying dance, Arturo's knees collapsed, his elbows bent like a hula dancer's, lingering in the air, until the floating, floating, slow embrace was interrupted by the sick thud of flesh hitting pavement.

The water flowed over Arturo's eyes, still clenched shut. He opened his mouth just so, taking in small gulps of air, spitting out the water that snuck in with it, then reached down to shut off the water. As he toweled off, he regarded the shirts hanging in his closet. The shimmer of peach beckoned to him from the hanger furthest to the left of the hanging rod. It always beckoned to him. This time, it was more insistent, and Arturo felt compelled to it, reaching for its soft, smooth skin, wanting it pressed against his own. He slipped into the shirt, slowly, his face showing concentration as he buttoned the iridescent pearl buttons. They glinted with the light as he worked.

He pulled on his favorite black pants, simple and well cut, a contrast to the material above it. Arturo finished dressing, pulling on his jacket that smelled strongly of leather. He inhaled the scent of his father coming home from the third shift to sleep for two hours before disappearing into the predawn morning to catch the truck to the fields. The jacket felt bulky and heavy against the delicate peach underneath.

Contributors

ARTURO ARIAS (b. 1950, Guatemala City, Guatemala) is professor of Latin American literature at the University of Texas at Austin. He is a well-known expert on Central American literature, with a special emphasis on indigenous literature, as well as critical theory, race, gender, and sexuality in postcolonial studies. Prior to joining the University of Texas faculty he was Greenleaf Visiting Professor of Latin American Studies at Tulane University. He is the author of *Taking their Word: Literature and the Signs of Central America* (2007), *La identidad de la palabra* (1998), and *Gestos ceremoniales* (1998), as well as the editor of *The Rigoberta Menchú Controversy* (2000) and a critical edition of Miguel Angel Asturias's *Mulata de tal* (2000). Arias cowrote the film *El Norte* (1984) and has published six novels in Spanish, two of which have been translated into English (*After the Bombs*, 1990, and *Rattlesnake*, 2003). Twice winner of the prestigious Casa de las Americas Award for his fiction, and winner of the Ana Seghers Award for fiction in Germany for his 1989 novel *Jaguar en llamas* (Flaming Jaguar), Arias was given the Miguel Angel Asturias National Award for Lifetime Achievement in Literature in 2008 in his native Guatemala. He also served as the president of the Latin American Studies Association (LASA) from 2001 to 2003.

SUSANA CHÁVEZ-SILVERMAN (b. 1956, Los Angeles, California) is professor of romance languages and literatures at Pomona College in California. Her creative work has been widely anthologized, and her embrace of "Spanglish" as a language of national becoming places her at the vanguard of an emerging "Latino baroque aesthetic." She received her BA from the University of California–Irvine, her MA in Romance Languages from Harvard University, and a PhD in Spanish from the University of California–Davis. She has taught at various institutions including the University of California–Berkeley, the University of California–Irvine, and the University of California–Davis, as well as the University of South Africa. Her academic research and writing center on gender and sexuality studies, memoir and autobiography, Latin American and U.S. Latino literatures, and feminist pedagogies. She is the author of *Scenes from la Cuenca de Los Angeles y otros Natural Disasters* (2010) and *Killer Cronicas: Bilingual Memories* (2004) and coeditor of *Reading and Writing the Ambiente: Queer Sexualities in Latino, Latin American, and Spanish Culture* (2000), and *Tropicalizations: Transcultural Representations of Latinidad* (1997).

STEVEN CORDOVA (b. 1963, San Antonio, Texas) published his first collection of poetry, *Long Distance*, in 2009. His poems have appeared in journals including *Barrow Street, Calalloo, The Journal*, and *Northwest Review*. His work has also been anthologized in *The Wind Shifts: New Latino Poetry* (2007) and *Best Gay Poetry 2008* (2008). Cordova grew up in San Antonio, Texas, and now lives in Brooklyn, New York.

TATIANA DE LA TIERRA (b. 1961, Villavicencio, Colombia) is the author of *Xía y las mil sirenas* (2009), *For the Hard Ones: A Lesbian Phenomenology / Para las duras: Una fenomenología lesbiana* (2002), and various chapbooks, including *Píntame una mujer peligrosa* (2004) and *tierra 2010: poems, songs and a little blood* (2010). In the 1990s de la tierra cofounded and edited the Latina lesbian publications *esto no tiene nombre, conmoción*, and *la telaraña*. She currently resides in southern California and envisions a writers' eco-village in the mountains of Colombia.

RAMÓN GARCÍA (b.1967, Colima City, Mexico) has published poetry in a variety of anthologies, including *Best American Poetry 1996* (1996) and *The Floating Borderlands: Twenty-Five Years of U.S.-Hispanic Literature* (1998), and in the journals *Crab Orchard Review, Ambit, Poetry Salzburg Review, Los Angeles Review*, and *Mandorla: New Writing from the Americas*. He has published fiction in *Story* and *Rosebud Magazine* and is the author of the poetry collection *Other Countries* (2010). A founding member of The Glass Table Collective, an artist collective that formed in 2008, he lives in Los Angeles and is a professor in Chicana/o Studies at California State University–Northridge.

RIGOBERTO GONZÁLEZ (b. 1970, Bakersfield, California) is an associate professor of English at Rutgers University–Newark. He is a prolific writer who has successfully transcended genres and audiences, including as a writer of bilingual children's literature. González is the author of the novels *Crossing Vines* (2004) and *Mariposa Club* (2009).

His poetry collections include *Black Blossoms* (2011), *Other Fugitives and Other Strangers* (2006), and *So Often the Pitcher Goes to Water until It Breaks* (1999). His edited collections include *Camino del Sol: Fifteen Years of Latina and Latino Writing* (2010) and *Alurista: Poems, Selected and New* (2010). His memoir *Butterfly Boy: Memories of a Chicano Mariposa* (2006) won an American Book Award from the Before Columbus Foundation.

MYRIAM GURBA (b. 1977, Santa Maria, California) is the author of *Dahlia Season* (2007), a short story and novella collection that won the Edmund White Award. Her writing has been anthologized in the collections *Life as We Show It* (2009) and *Bottom's Up* (2004). She was chosen to be one of the inaugural members of RADAR Lab, the world's only queer arts residency, which was held in 2009 in Akumal, Mexico. Gurba's favorite crooner is Morrissey and she is working on a new book tentatively titled *The Hunger Crónicas, or Why Some Girls are Bigger Than Others*, a total nod to The Smiths.

RAQUEL GUTIÉRREZ (b. 1976, Los Angeles, California) is a community-based performance writer and cultural activist. She is a cofounding member of the performance art ensemble Butchlalis de Panochtitlan and has written their first play, *The Barber of East L.A.*, currently in production and commissioned by a humanities initiative at the University of Southern California that enabled the troupe to work with Luis Alfaro. Gutiérrez has performed nationally with Butchlalis and has been published in poetry and other journals. She holds degrees in performance studies from New York University and in journalism and Central American studies from California State University–Northridge.

DAISY HERNÁNDEZ (b. 1975, Union City, New Jersey) is the former editor of *ColorLines*, the national newsmagazine on race, and coeditor of *Colonize This! Young Women on Today's Feminism* (2002). She is a former columnist with *Ms.* magazine, and her personal essays have appeared in various anthologies, including *50 Ways to Support Lesbian and Gay Equality* (2005), *Without a Net: The Female Experience of Growing Up Working Class* (2004), *Border-Line Personalities: A New Generation of Latinas Dish on Sex* (2004), and *Sex and Single Girls: Women Write on Sexuality* (2000). Hernández received her BA in English from William Paterson University and an MA in journalism and Latin American and

Caribbean studies from New York University. She is a powerful public speaker and has lectured widely across the country. Her website is www.daisyhernandez.com.

LUCY MARRERO (b. 1978, Dallas, Texas) has published her work in *Hipmama Magazine* (2008), *Sinister Wisdom* (2008), *Young Scholars in Writing* (2009), and *Visible: A Femmethology* (2009). Marrero currently attends Antioch University in Los Angeles and is involved with the Los Angeles chapter of INCITE! Women of Color Against Violence.

ELÍAS MIGUEL MUÑOZ (b. 1954, Ciego de Ávila, Cuba) is one of the premier writers of contemporary Latino literature. He holds a PhD in Spanish from the University of California–Irvine and considers himself a "recovering academic," having left his teaching position in Kansas in 1989 to devote his time and energy to writing. Muñoz's highly acclaimed novels include *Los viajes de Orlando Cachumbambé* (1984), *Crazy Love* (1988), *The Greatest Performance* (1991), *Brand New Memory* (1998), and *Vida mía* (2006). Passionately infused with the theme of exile, his fiction deals with friendships that empower, gender roles, and new definitions of family. Muñoz's stories, memoirs, and essays have appeared in numerous anthologies, including *Herencia: The Anthology of Hispanic Literature of the United States* (2002), *The Encyclopedia of American Literature* (1999), *The Scribner Writers Series: Latino and Latina Writers* (2004), W.W. Norton's *New Worlds of Literature* (1994), and the *Handbook of Hispanic Cultures in the United States* (1993). After leaving his native Cuba as a child, Muñoz lived in Spain, Southern California, Kansas, Washington, DC, and New Mexico. He currently resides in California. The story featured here was adapted from a chapter of his forthcoming novel.

ACHY OBEJAS (b. 1956, Havana, Cuba) is one of the most prolific and well-known writers of her generation. Obejas's major publications include *We Came All the Way from Cuba So You Could Dress Like This* (1994), *Memory Mambo* (1996), *Days of Awe* (2001), and *Ruins* (2009). An award-winning journalist, she worked for more than ten years for the *Chicago Tribune*, writing and reporting about arts and culture. Among literally thousands of stories, she helped cover Pope John Paul II's historic 1998 visit to Cuba, the arrival of Al-Qaeda prisoners in Guantánamo, the Versace murder, and the AIDS epidemic. She is a blogger for vocalo.org and writes regularly about Latin music for the

Washington Post. Obejas has received a Pulitzer Prize for a Tribune team investigation, the Studs Terkel Journalism Prize, two Lambda Literary awards, an NEA fellowship in poetry, and residencies at Yaddo, Ragdale, and the Virginia Center for the Arts. Her work has been translated into Spanish, German, Hungarian, and Farsi. Obejas has lectured and read her work in the United States, Cuba, Mexico, Spain, Argentina, and Australia, and has been a distinguished writer-in-residence at the University of Chicago and at the University of Hawai'i. She is currently the Sor Juana Visiting Writer at DePaul University in Chicago.

URIEL QUESADA (b. 1962, San José, Costa Rica) is a prolific author who writes predominately in Spanish. He is the author of seven books of fiction, including the award-winning novels *El atardecer de los niños* (1990), *Lejos, tan lejos* (2005), and *El gato de sí mismo* (2006), and the short story collection *Viajero que huye* (2008). Quesada holds an MA in Latin American literature from New Mexico State University and a PhD from Tulane University. He lives in New Orleans and is the director of the Center for Latin American and Caribbean Studies at Loyola University. As a scholar, Quesada has done research on a variety of topics that include Latin American detective fiction, popular culture, testimonial literature, and gender and sexualities.

JANET ARELIS QUEZADA (b. 1975, New York City) is a poet whose writing and reviews have appeared in *Curve Magazine* (2009) and *Urban Latino Magazine* (2009). Her work has also been anthologized in the collection *Writing on the Edge: A Borderlands Reader* (2003). She lives in Los Angeles.

CHARLES RICE-GONZÁLEZ (b. 1964, San Juan, Puerto Rico) was born in Puerto Rico and reared in the Bronx. He is a writer, a longtime community and LGBT activist, and executive director of BAAD! The Bronx Academy of Arts and Dance. He received a BA in communications from Adelphi University and an MFA in creative writing from Goddard College. He attended the Bread Loaf Writers' Conference in 2005, 2006, and 2007 and received a residency from the Byrdcliffe Guild in Woodstock, New York. Rice-González also serves on the boards of the Bronx Council on the Arts and the National Association of Latino Arts and Culture (NALAC). His work has been published in many journals and he has written several plays including "What Carlos Feels" (1990), "Pink Jesus" (1997), "Los Nutcrackers: A Christmas Carajo," produced each year at BAAD! since 2004, and "I Just Love Andy Gibb," which was selected for Pregones Theater's 2005 Asunción Play Reading Series and received a workshop production in May 2007. His debut novel, *Chulito*, will be published in spring 2011.

HORACIO N. ROQUE RAMÍREZ (b. 1969, Santa Ana, El Salvador) flew to the United States in 1981 along with two of his older sisters, escaping the brutal US-funded Salvadoran Civil War. He learned English at El Sereno Junior High School in Los Angeles, was a closeted homosexual tennis star at Monrovia High School, and attended the University of California–Los Angeles and the University of California–Berkeley before beginning to teach at the University of California–Santa Barbara in 2003. His oral history- and archival-based work has appeared in the *Journal of the History of Sexuality* (2003), *Queer Migrations: Sexuality, U.S. Citizenship and Border Crossings* (2005), *Archive Stories: Facts, Fictions, and the Writing of History* (2005), *Oral History, Public Memories* (2008), and *Gay Latino Studies: A Critical Reader* (2011). His creative nonfiction writing—part of an emerging "literatura centromaricona" (in the wise words of his colleague Santiago N. Bernal), or queer Central American literature—has appeared in *Mapping Strategies: NACCS and the Challenges of Multiple (Re)Oppressions* (1999), *Virgins, Guerrillas & Locas: Gay Latinos Writing about Love* (1999), and *Queer Codex: Chile Love* (2004). His forthcoming book is *Memories of Desire: An Oral History from Queer Latino San Francisco, 1960s–1990s*.

EMANUEL XAVIER (b. 1971, Brooklyn, New York) is the author of the novel *Christ Like* (2009) and the poetry collection *Americano* (2002), the editor of *Bullets & Butterflies: queer spoken word poetry* (2005) and *Mariposas: A Modern Anthology of Queer Latino Poetry* (2008), and he selected finalists for *Best Gay Erotica 2008*. He has been awarded the Marsha A. Gómez Cultural Heritage Award, a New York City Council Citation, and a 2008 World Pride Award. He has appeared on *Russell Simmons Presents Def Poetry* and continues to perform regularly as a spoken-word artist throughout the world. A compilation CD of his work, *Legendary—The Spoken Word Poetry of Emanuel Xavier*, is available for digital download on iTunes. His website is www.emanuelxavier.com.